Tales From Modern India

TALES

From Modern India

EDITED, WITH AN INTRODUCTION AND NOTES

by K. Natwar-Singh

NEW YORK

THE MACMILLAN COMPANY

Library of Congress Catalog Card Number: 66–23791

FIRST PRINTING

The Macmillan Company, New York

Collier-Macmillan Canada Ltd., Toronto, Ontario

Printed in the United States of America

ACKNOWLEDGMENTS

Acknowledgment is due to the following for permission to reprint.

Rabindranath Tagore, "The Cabuliwallah" and "The Hungry Stones." Reprinted with the permission of The Macmillan Company from *The Hungry Stones and Other Stories* by Rabindranath Tagore. Copyright 1916, The Macmillan Company, renewed 1944 by Rabindranath Tagore and S. L. Polak.

Sarat Chandra Chatterjee, "Drought." From *Indian Short Stories*, The New India Publishing Co., Ltd., London. By permission of Mulk Raj Anand.

C. Rajagopalachari, "Ardhanari." By permission of the author.

Prem Chand, "The Shroud." By permission of Madan Gopal.

———, "Resignation." From *Indian Short Stories*, The New India Publishing Co., Ltd., London. By permission of Mulk Raj Anand.

Mulk Raj Anand, "The Barber's Trade Union" and "The Informer." From *The Barber's Trade Union and Other Stories*, published by Jonathan Cape, Ltd., London. Copyright Mulk Raj Anand. By permission of the author.

R. K. Narayan, "An Astrologer's Day" and "The Blind Dog." Copyright R. K. Narayan. By permission of the author.

Raja Rao, "The Little Gram Shop." Acknowledgment is made to the author and to Oxford University Press, Bombay, India, for permission to reprint "The Little Gram Shop," from *The Cow of the Barricades*, by Raja Rao.

———, "Nimka." Copyright Raja Rao. By permission of the author.

P. B. Bhave, "The Mystery." By permission of the author and of Kutub Popular Private Limited, Bombay.

Krishan Chandar, "The Soldier." By permission of the author. Previously published by the Writer's Workshop, Calcutta.

———, "Kalu Bhangi." By permission of the author and of Sahitya Akademi, New Dehli.

TO THE MEMORY OF MY FATHER

Govind Singhji (1899–1965)

CONTENTS

EDITOR'S NOTE

THIS is the first time that a collection of modern Indian short stories has been made available to readers in the United States. Anthologies of stories translated from single Indian languages like Bengali and Hindi have appeared, but the present work is the first to draw upon most of the major literary languages of India, including English, and I hope it will introduce American readers to the variety and richness of Indian literature.

I am not a scholar. What I say in the Introduction about the evolution of the short story and its place in Indian literature is not a complete scholar's survey of modern Indian literature. What I have done is to submit for the Western reader's pleasure thoughts and preferences of one who has read Indian literature both in Hindi and English. My mother tongue is Hindi and that is the only Indian language I know. The literature of other Indian languages I have approached through English, and my own personal debt to that language is very great.

It gives me particular pleasure to acknowledge the help and encouragement I have received from Mr. Krishna Kripalani, Secretary of the Indian Literary Academy, New Delhi. Without his interest in this anthology it would be difficult, if not impossible, for me to see this project through. I also wish to thank Mr. Faubion Bowers, Mr. Patrick Gregory, and Miss Jane Goldstone for having read through the introduction and made valuable suggestions. I am also very happy to record how helpful I found Mr. S. H.

Vatsyayan's essay on Hindi literature, in *Contemporary Indian Literature, A Symposium* published by the Sahitya Akademi, New Delhi.

Finally, a debt which I should have acknowledged long long ago, I owe to Mr. N. G. Thakar, who taught English at the Scindia School, Gwalior, from 1933 to 1962. He taught me the value of looking *inside* books.

—K. NATWAR-SINGH

Bharatpur; Rajasthan
  India
May 16, 1966

INTRODUCTION

K. NATWAR-SINGH

THE main purpose of this anthology is to give American readers an idea of the richness and variety of Indian literature. The twenty stories included here will, I hope, provide some insight into the workings of the Indian literary genius and the forces and influences that have given it life and sustenance.

The short story has flourished in India. The reasons are many—among them the influence of the great Western short story writers of the nineteenth century and the comparative ease with which short prose pieces in English and Indian languages could be published and distributed. Few Indian writers of importance have neglected this genre: a number of them can be said to have become masters of it. Perhaps in no other branch of creative or literary activity has the feel of the Indian scene been so ably, or so rewardingly, captured.

These stories, I trust, will offer the reader a contemporary expression of Indian literature and life, both rural and urban and in the different regions of India. Almost all the important writers of the past hundred years are represented, and the settings of the stories range from peasant existence (which even today contain echoes of India's remotest past) to the sophisticated and cosmopolitan milieu inhabited by some of India's new but alienated bourgeoisie.

The themes of the stories vary widely—depending in part on the section of India from which the author comes.

The ways of handling these themes show striking diver-
gences. Some of the writers exalt traditional virtues, others
concentrate on the problem of the human predicament in
an ancient country trying to come to terms with the twentieth century. American readers will be reminded here that
American writers are often beset with the problems arising
out of affluence, while Indians and Indian writers face the
problems of poverty. In both countries, the creative artist
has a challenging and difficult—but somewhat different—
role to play. As James T. Farrell has written, "America developed a realistic literature at a time when the Republic
was so secure that criticism and exposure, even in pitilessly
sadistic novels, did not weaken the foundations of the
nation. It is different in the new countries of Asia. These
countries are struggling to become nations. . . . How critical should Indian writers be? Can they write with the
fearless realism and desire for truth of a Zola, or some of
the twentieth century American novelists? If they do, will
they not be weakening their own countries?" * These stories
may provide an answer to some of Mr. Farrell's legitimate
questions.

They are different in style, sensibility, social awareness, in
artistic and creative achievement and élan, but their deep
humanism gives them a unity of spirit that is uniquely
Indian. Nine were written originally in English. They are by
Mulk Raj Anand, R. K. Narayan, Raja Rao, Khushwant
Singh, and Santha Rama Rau. The rest were originally in
Bengali (Tagore and Sarat Chandra), Tamil (C. Rajago-
palachari), Hindi (Prem Chand), Urdu (Krishan Chandar),
Malayalam (T. S. Pillai), Marathi (Bhave), and Telugu
(Padmaraju). Taken as a whole, these stories constitute a
formidable example of the Indian tradition and prove
that the Indian writer, whether his medium is Hindi,
Tamil, Bengali, Malayalam, or English, works within

* James T. Farrell in *The Illustrated Weekly of India*, Bombay,
December 9, 1956.

that tradition. More often than not he does so unconsciously.

In India as elsewhere in Asia the short story is a literary phenomenon of recent origin, the latter half of the nineteenth century. Its development in its present form is largely the result of the impact of Western thought and ideas. Like the civilization of India itself, Indian literature reflects a diversity of races, cultures, and religions, yet within this diversity exists a unified harmony that retains its own very special imprint. It is important to remember that Indian literature is multilingual.

Any adequate comparison with Western literature can be made only by comparing Europe as a whole—a conglomeration of races and communities sharing, to varying degrees, the traditions of a common Indo-Aryan civilization. The Constitution of India recognizes fourteen national languages: ten Indo-Aryan languages consisting of Sanskrit, with its nine progeny, Assamese, Bengali, Gujerati, Hindi, Kashmiri, Marathi, Oriya, Punjabi, Urdu; and the four Dravidian languages of Kannada, Malayalam, Tamil, and Telugu.

The place of English is quite distinct. For all practical purposes it remains the lingua franca of the educated classes throughout the country. Next to their mother tongue, educated Indians (25 percent of the entire population) feel more at home in English than in any other language, Indian or foreign.

The literary and intellectual importance of a language cannot necessarily be measured by the number of individuals using it, but the relative strength of numbers has meaning. Hindi, thus, may be deemed the leading language of India, for it is spoken throughout northern India, by a population of nearly 180 million. The term "Hindi" is used loosely to denote a group of Indo-Aryan dialects which over a period of about five centuries evolved distinct literary forms of their own. Today's Hindi has behind it a vast and varied heritage, embracing as it does the Braj Bhasha, Bhojpuri, Magadhi, and Maithili dialects. The famous poet-saint Kabir (1440–1518) wrote in Bhojpuri although he used Perso-Arabic words which greatly influenced and vitalized Hindi. The predominant position of Hindi has been recognized in the Constitution of India, which confers on it, without prejudice to the remaining thirteen languages scheduled therein, the status of the official language of the Indian Union. Although what is known as Hindi has behind it this varied heritage, in its present standard literary form it is of comparatively recent origin—not earlier than the first decade of the nineteenth century. It was only with the arrival of the writer Prem Chand on the Indian literary horizon, in the early years of the twentieth century, that short stories and novels in Hindi caught the imagination of Indian readers and intelligentsia.

Urdu is in a class by itself. Linguistically, it is Indo-Aryan, born in India and developed like Hindi in the Indo-Gangetic plain. Having affiliated itself with the Persian language—which was the official court language in India for 250 years after the Mughal invasion—it evolved an individuality all its own. Today it is the chief language of some 50 million people of northern India. It is also the official language of the western part of Pakistan. Two of the writers included in this anthology, Prem Chand (1880–1936) and Krishan Chandar (1914–   ), have written some of their best works in Urdu, although in his later years Prem Chand switched to Hindi. A large number of people who know one of these two languages are also well versed in the other, and the intermediate zone where the two meet has been called the zone of the Hindustani-speaking people. Hindustani was the language that Mahatma Gandhi cherished and hoped would one day become the lingua franca of the Indian community as a whole, although Gujerati was his mother tongue. Hindustani was the language that Jawaharlal Nehru used in public for all his countless speeches throughout the length and breadth of the country.

The relative numbers of people speaking other major languages in India were given in the 1961 census: Assamese 6.8 million; Bengali 38 million; Gujerati 18.1 million; Kannada 17.9 million; Kashmiri 1.9 million; Punjabi 9.7 million; Malayalam 17 million; Tamil 30 million; Telugu 33 million; and Marathi 30 million.

To have a proper appreciation of this complex pattern one has to bear in mind the multilingual character of Indian literature. Few Westerners have tried to understand the literary activity that transformed the Indian languages into great and vital vehicles of thought and artistic creation, entitling at least some of them to recognition among the literatures of the modern world. But underlying this diversity was a unity that drew its strength from the conception of India as a nation and its identity with a common Sanskrit culture and civilization.

Traditional Indian literature, whether in the Indo-Aryan or in the Dravidian languages, was mainly devotional and religious on the one hand, and philosophical and mythological on the other. There were important exceptions, the most significant, the plays of Kalidasa and the folk tales and stories like the "Panchatantra"; but for over a thousand years literature was subservient to religious fervor, and was dependent on oral delivery for its propagation. The *Epics*—the *Ramayana* and the *Mahabharata*—were the source from which Indian literature drew most of its material and were, for the most part, passed on from generation to generation by word of mouth. Even Muslim writers writing in Persian and Urdu were influenced by this devotional aspect, as is clear from the work of Kabir.

A major characteristic of traditional Indian literature has always been its didactic tone. Excessive emphasis was laid on moral values—asceticism, renunciaiton, celibacy, sacrifice, and suffering were recommended and respected. This peculiarity in Indian writings still continues today. Its best known exponent is C. Rajagopalachari, who has recently popularized the *Mahabharata* and the *Ramayana* by writing them in simple style for mass audiences.

Indian literature was not truly secularized until the first part of the nineteenth century, when English ideas gained currency. To some extent, however, the multiple character of Indian literature had always existed, and from time to time it received injections from outside. Even in the heyday of early and classical Sanskrit (1000 B.C. to 500 A.D.), which, like medieval Latin, was the language of intellectuals and on whose foundation the unity of India rested for a thousand years, there existed side by side a body of nonconformist literature in other languages such as Pali and Tamil.

As Mr. Krishna Kripalani, the biographer of Tagore, has said, "Indian literature is one of the oldest and one of the youngest literatures of the world. Its ancient record in the *Rig Veda* (1500 B.C.) is admittedly the earliest monument of Indo-European speech." Jawaharlal Nehru has written: "The *Rig Veda*, the first of the *Vedas*, is probably the earliest book that humanity possesses. . . . Yet behind the *Rig Veda* itself lay ages of civilized existence and thought, during which the Indus Valley and the Mesopotamian and other civilizations had grown. It is appropriate, therefore, that there should be this dedication in the *Rig Veda*: 'To the Seers, our Ancestors, the First Path-finders!' "

During its history of over three thousand years, Indian literature has had its high and low points. There have been periods when the creative genius of the Indian mind has given to the world works of great beauty and subtlety, like the plays of Kalidasa, the philosophical writings of Sankara, the poems of Kabir, Tulsidas, and Nanak (1469–1533). On the other hand, there have been periods—the late eighteenth century, for instance—when political chaos combined with intellectual lethargy made it impossible either for the creative arts to flourish or for literature to be appreciated. The English language arrived on the Indian scene at such a time.

From at least the beginning of the Christian era, Indian literature has had two major vehicles: Sanskrit with its many Indo-Aryan offshoots, and the Dravidian languages of South India. It was, however, in the fifteenth and sixteenth centuries that modern Indo-Aryan languages had their richest literary following. The source of inspiration was twofold: a revival of interest in the Sanskrit heritage, particularly as embodied in the great *Epics;* and the upsurge of Vaishnavism, a sect of Hinduism, a widespread cult of devotion to a personal god identified with Rama, the hero of the *Ramayana,* and with Krishna, the hero of the *Mahabharata* and the *Bhagwat Purana.* While the early literature in the Indo-Aryan languages of northern India, was almost entirely in verse, the Dravidian or South Indian languages had some prose writing. The common features of both groups of languages were the classics and the translations and free renderings of the *Epics.* The most famous of these is Tulsidas' *Ram Charitramanas* (fifteenth century) and Kamban's *Ramayana* (ninth century), which appeared in various popular tongues.

Along with adaptations of the *Epics*, there was a considerable output of devotional songs and verse by the poet-saints who flourished during the fourteenth and fifteenth centuries: Sankaradev in Assamese, Chandidas in Bengali, Vidyapati in Maithili, Narasima Mehta in Gujerati, Meera Bai in Rajasthani, Kabir in a mixed form of Bhojpuri and Urdu, Surdas in Baij Bhasha, Ekanath in Marathi, and Guru Nanak in Punjabi. The work of these men warmed the bloodstream of Indian literature down through the centuries.

The arrival of Islam in India (eighth century A.D.) affected the Indian literary scene considerably. Apart from the fact that the development of the Urdu language and literature stemmed from this, several modern Indian languages were enriched by Muslim writers themselves. Through them were transmitted traditions from Arabic and Iranian literatures. Having made India their home, the Muslim writers turned to purely Indian themes for inspiration, for example the heroic tale of the Rajput Queen Padmini of Chittor which inspired Malik Mohammed Jayasi's *Padmavat*, an allegorical narrative in Awadhi written in the sixteenth century. To this may be added the general impact of Muslim thought, particularly in its nonconformist Sufi tradition. This influence is particularly evident in the Kashmiri and Punjabi languages.

India has known many dark ages in her long history, but the latter half of the eighteenth century was an especially dismal period politically and culturally. With the death in 1707 of Aurangzeb, the last of the great Mughals, India experienced administrative chaos, political uncertainty, intellectual apathy, and a general cultural decay. Indian literature became impoverished and ingrown. Only toward the end of the eighteenth century, when the British had became masters of eastern India, did the pattern of literary mores alter. English thus came to India at a time when doors to a progressive and enlightened existence seemed permanently sealed.

The general picture of Indian literature on the eve of the arrival of the British was confused and complex. Its two main sources had been Dravidian and Indo-Aryan religious and literary traditions as embodied in Sanskrit texts and the teachings of Buddha, and the traditional, all-prevailing folklore. Whether the writers were Aryans, Hindus, Buddhists, Dravidians, or Muslims, religious impulse in poetry and prose was ever present. Indian religious literature, in so far as it was not lyrical, philosophical, argumentative, or philological, consisted mainly of manuals of ritual for daily life or for particular occasions—marriages, births, deaths, pilgrimages, vows, and so on.

The foundation of the educational policy of the British government in India was laid down by Macaulay, who had nothing but contempt for Asian literature and once stated, rather recklessly, that he was prepared to sacrifice the entire literature of the East for a single shelf of English books. For him, "the object of British policy should be to promote European literature and science amongst the natives."

It is interesting to note, however, that the demand for Western education had come in the first instance from enlightened Indians themselves. In 1833, Raja Ram Mohan Roy, one of the greatest literary figures of the early nineteenth century, wrote to Lord Amherst, Governor-General of India, protesting the establishment of the Government Sanskrit College in Calcutta. He asked that Western education of a liberal and enlightened kind be made available to Indians. Thus in the early years of British rule in India, the English language was voluntarily and enthusiastically learned by young men in Bengal, and later on by the Indian intelligentsia throughout the country. The political situation in the country was such that while we were denouncing the English in almost every field of life and thought, we were eagerly and enthusiastically learning their language. The service that English rendered to India, particularly in the fields of political science, medicine, and engineering, cannot be minimized. Politically, it developed and strengthened our consciousness of national unity more effectively and dynamically than had ever happened before in Indian history. Although it remained a language of the educated classes, it shook the Indian intelligentsia out of its mental stupor and involvement with the past. It made the revolutionary literature of Europe and America available and these works profoundly influenced the Indian national movement. In addition, it introduced scientific learning and research. Thousands of Indians were able to acquire new techniques and information in these fields.

The English language linked the thinkers and political leaders of the entire Indian subcontinent and this laid the foundation for administrative and political unity. The debt that modern Indian literature owes to English is very great indeed. It would be churlish to minimize it.

The development of modern Indian literature is marked by certain characteristics which it shares with modern literatures in other parts of the world, and by others that relate to the special circumstances of India. One of the latter is a certain dichotomy in the mental attitude of the writer. An intellectual tug-of-war still rages between traditionalism and progressivism. This conflict between orthodox and unorthodox is not unique to India, but there the clash of loyalties is remarkable for its vehemence.

Western thought, represented by an alien government and culture, and with its emphasis on democracy and freedom, stimulated a patriotic and nationalistic reaction which in turn instigated a search for roots. From the beginning of the twentieth century Indian literature was increasingly colored by political aspirations which were passionately voiced in the songs and poems of Tagore, the Tamil poet Bharati, the Bengali poet Kazi Nasrul Islam, and the Urdu poet Iqbal. The writings of Tilak, Gandhi, and Aurobindo also illustrate a dilemma which Indian intellectuals continue to face today.

Jawaharlal Nehru was perhaps the best example of this split; in his own words, he was himself "a peculiar mixture of the East and West." While the intellectual center of the Indian writer, particularly if he writes in the English language, is in London, New York, Paris, or Moscow, his spiritual roots must be in India. His atttraction toward the American Revolution, the French Revolution, the British ideas of the parliamentary democracy and justice, and the Russian Revolution of 1917 is undisputed, and this influences both his mental outlook and his literary output.

At the same time, ancient India has its own indissoluble enchantment and he cannot divorce himself from the teachings of the *Bhagvat Gita* or the spiritual insights of the *Upanishads*. Politically India is a new nation, but as a civilization it is very ancient. The problem of the modern Indian writer is to be Indian first, and at the same time to be modern.

Indian literature was and continues to be influenced by Western writers. To the names of Tolstoy and Gorki, Victor Hugo and Romain Rolland, Dickens and Thackeray are added Pasternak, Sartre, Hardy, even Kipling, and T. S. Eliot and Hemingway. At the same time the reciprocal influence of Indian thought and literature on European and American writers has not been insignificant. A scientific study of Indian literature was begun around 1760 by Warren Hastings, the first Governor-General of Bengal. He knew Sanskrit and Persian, and in a preface to Charles Wilkins' translation of the *Gita,* he wrote that such works "will survive when the British domination in India shall have long ceased to exist, and when the sources which had once yielded all wealth and power are lost to remembrance."

Kalidasa's *Sakuntala* was translated by William Jones in 1789. A German translation appeared in 1823, and Goethe's enthusiastic reception of the book is well known. Schopenhauer too was considerably influenced by the teachings of the *Upanishads* and of the Buddha, and German transcendentalism was in general affected by Indian thought. In England, Edwin Arnold's *Light of Asia* was hailed, as it was in America, where Thoreau, Emerson, Mark Twain, and Walt Whitman all expressed their interest in Indian thought. Thoreau wrote that "the pure Walden water is mingled with the sacred water of Ganges"; and the title of Mr. E. M. Forster's famous novel *A Passage to India* is taken from a poem of Whitman. Other Western writers who were considerably influenced by Indian thought include W. B. Yeats, Romain Rolland, Hermann Hesse, Somerset Maugham, T. S. Eliot, Rudyard Kipling, and Aldous Huxley.

Kipling's influence over his generation's view of India cannot be exaggerated. The outside world looked at India through Kipling's eyes for at least a quarter of a century.

Yet, his acquaintance with India was slender and limited to a small segment of the Anglo-Indian establishment. Apart from the Jungle books, he wrote about officials and military officers and their lives in British cantonments. He was a reactionary in politics, and his jingoism was resented by Indians. That he was a great storyteller has never been questioned, but his Indian characters were generally drawn in the flat. Only after E. M. Forster's *A Passage to India* appeared were Western readers of fiction given a sympathetic and rounded image of Indians.

The greatest impact on modern Indian thought and literature was made by three men—Mahatma Gandhi (1861–1948), Karl Marx (1818–1883), and Sigmund Freud (1856–1939). In the strict meaning of the word, none of these was a man of letters proper.

Marx and Freud introduced the "scientific" spirit, and in the words of Krishna Kripalani, gave "a much-needed jolt to the smugness of the traditional attitude with its age-old tendency to sentimental piety and a glorification of the past."

Each of them unleashed intellectual and political passions which shook Indian intellectuals and men of letters to the very foundations of their polity. Mulk Raj Anand, Raja Rao, Prem Chand, Krishan Chandar, T. S. Pillai, Santha Rama Rau, Khushwant Singh were all influenced by the three modern thinkers—each to a greater or lesser extent. Indian life was exposed to new ideas concerning behavior interpretations from which there could be no turning away. Marx and Freud greatly affected modern Western thought, and it was inevitable that Indians too should feel this impact. But in India the image and personality of Mahatma Gandhi counterbalanced this foreign influence to some extent.

Gandhi's Western mentors were Thoreau, Tolstoy, and Ruskin. He was also much impressed by Carlyle's *On Heroes, Hero-Worship, and the Heroic in History.* The *Gita* and the Bible were, of course, closest to his heart, and another book that impressed him for reasons that are less understandable was Washington Irving's *Mahomet and His Successors*. After spending twenty-one years in South Africa he returned to India in 1914 and provided a powerful ethical stimulus to the literary trend, which had already begun to turn from romanticism toward realism. Gandhi's insistence on non-violence and on the simplicity and purity of personal life touched a responsive chord in the inherent idealism of Indian thought and thus served as an indirect inspiration to creative writing. His own simple and direct style, devoid of all rhetoric, was a healthy corrective to the natural tendency to flamboyance of many Indian writers. Gandhi left his imprint on Hindi and Gujerati literature particularly.

Prem Chand, for instance, influenced by Tolstoy and Gorki, came under Mahatma Gandhi's spell. Prem Chand resigned a minor government job to devote himself to writing about the life of the Indian peasant upon whose uplift Gandhi focused much of his life. Like Mahatma Gandhi, Prem Chand lived in a rural village. His writings attacked caste, Hindu society's treatment of widows, and the custom of child marriage (he himself married a widow against the considerable opposition of the times). He knew rural India intimately and his books give a faithful and moving account of the plight of the Indian peasant, a man subject to foreign government on the one hand, and on the other at the mercy of moneylenders. Prem Chand did not have Tagore's vision nor his sensibility, and when he ventured away from peasant life into other fields and settings, he tended to over-sentimentalize and his characters did not always ring true.

Raja Rao's first novel, *Kanthapura*, was also inspired by Gandhi's teachings of nonviolence. R. K. Narayan wrote a novel in 1956 entitled *Waiting for the Mahatma*, and Mulk Raj Anand's first novel, *The Untouchable*, bears the unmistakable hand of Gandhi.

Marx's influence was widespread in the early 1930s, not only among young Indian politicians but among Indian writers. Mulk Raj Anand and Krishan Chandar, especially, introduced the theme of class conflict into Indian literature for the first time. Krishan Chandar felt that he "has a mission as a short story writer to show the capitalist and the ruling classes in all their brutality and bestiality." To some extent this influence continues in Indian fiction to this day, but it is not so strong a force as it was a generation ago. Political developments in India and abroad since World War II have naturally been responsible for this change.

It is difficult to pinpoint Freud's influence on Indian writers. It exists, obviously, and to an extent it has liberated Indian writing from unscientific superstitions. After the arrival of Islam, sexual inhibitions paralyzed Indian writing. Before that the Hindu attitude to sex had been healthier, perhaps, as illustrated by the classical *Kamasutra* by Vatsayan in the third century A.D. and the plays of Kalidas. Sex had been discussed with frankness and naturalness. However, Islam combined with Victorian morality, and with the narrow Brahmo doctrines reinforced by the asceticism of Mahatma Gandhi, made sex in the first part of the twentieth century a closed subject for literature—except as Gandhi wrote of it in his autobiography, *The Story of My Experiments with Truth.*

Because of Freud, a younger generation of writers and intellectuals could write about sex with more freedom. Thus in the 1950s there was little surprise when Khushwant Singh and Padmaraju wrote their tales of passion and love, "The Rape" and "On the Boat."

Jawaharlal Nehru has a unique place in the world of letters. In his case, it has been said, the gain to politics was a loss to literature. At least two of his books, his *Autobiography* and *The Discovery of India*, belong permanently to the literature of the English language. He wrote elegantly and sensitively. Nehru was for some time president of the Indian PEN Club and enjoyed meeting and talking to writers. He gave them whatever encouragement he could.

Rabindranath Tagore (1861–1941) of Bengal was the first modern writer to give distinct character to the Indian short story, and he was to a large extent responsible for the artistic rediscovery of India by Indians. He absorbed the Western spirit and naturalized it into Indian literature. Tagore was a bilingual writer with the vision to see that if modern Indian literature was to be a living force, it would have to keep pace with the modern age. He infused vitality and flexibility into the Bengali language itself, and introduced an international outlook into Bengali literature in particular and Indian literature in general.

Tagore was well versed in Western literature. The liberal humanism of English writers and poets appealed to him. He particularly read Goethe, Shelley, Keats, W. H. Hudson, Robert Browning, and was a friend and admirer of W. B. Yeats. He neither repudiated the past nor made a fetish of the new. He drew from the Indian classics and folk traditions of his own land, from the *Upanishads*, from the teachings of Buddha, from Kalidasa. Tagore used, adopted, and absorbed European forms and techniques and applied them with great success.

Tagore's main significance lies in the impulse and direction he gave to the course of India's cultural and moral development, and in the example he presented of a genius passionately devoted to his art and no less passionately dedicated to the service of his people and humanity in general. He gave the Indian people faith in their own languages and in their cultural and intellectual heritage, despite the value and influence of English.

The contemporary renaissance of Indian languages is in no small measure indebted to him. Tagore's was a many-sided personality—poet, patriot, playwright, philosopher, painter, composer, educator, universalist, and novelist. His influence on at least two generations of Indian writers was extraordinary and all-pervasive. The novel, the short story, the drama, the essay, literary criticism all have been influenced by him particularly in the various North Indian languages. He was undoubtedly the most vital force in India's modern culture, although his direct inspiration has faded over the past few years. A Tagore revival has taken place recently, both in India and abroad—stimulated by the centenary of his birth which was celebrated in 1961—but it would be true to say that today he is more admired than actually read.

In writing of the Indian literary scene as he saw it in 1945, E. M. Forster sketched the following observations in his collection of essays, *Two Cheers for Democracy:* "Book production: very active, though the authors are miserably paid. Short stories are popular; I read some excellent ones on Bengal. Poetry often echoes T. S. Eliot or Auden. Drama is not prominent. Criticism weak. Indians have a marked capacity for worship or for denunciation, but not much critical sense, as criticism is understood in the West." The situation has changed for the better in the past two decades, but Mr. Forster's comments are partly true even today.

The complex nature of Indian literature naturally multiplies difficulties for the Indian writer, and English continues to be used as a link language and as a matter of social convenience. It is the language that the President of India, Dr. Radhakrishnan, and the Prime Minister of India, Mrs. Indira Gandhi, use to converse with each other.

For those writing in the Indian languages, the barriers of language create major obstacles. This is a problem not unknown elsewhere. For instance, how many Norwegian or Rumanian authors can hope to have their work translated into the more widely used languages? And unless such European writers are translated, their reputations and incomes will remain strictly local and limited. In India, however, unless an author's work is translated into several of its fourteen languages, it can be read only by a small number of his *own* countrymen.

We must also face the fact that the world is not going

to learn Hindi or Tamil, and that our ability to use the English language as an artistic and creative medium should be welcomed rather than disparaged for narrow political reasons. In that respect some of the writers of Africa have faced this problem with a candor which is not always present in India. Mr. Achebe, the Nigerian author, says of English, "I have been given this language, and I intend to use it." Mr. Leopold Senghor, when asked, "Why do you Africans choose to write in French?" replied, "We did not choose it, French chose us." It is often argued by critics of the use of English by Indian writers, that "it is not akin to the genius of India." The answer to this rather shallow approach is that neither are parliamentary democracy, nor the five year plans, nor the protection of individual human rights, which are all an essential and accepted part of Indian polity today.

Perhaps Raja Rao expressed the Indian writer's intention best when he wrote in 1938, "One has to convey in a language that is not one's own, the spirit that is one's own. One has to convey the various shades and emotions of a certain thought, movement that looks maltreated. . . . We cannot write like the English, we should not. We cannot write only as Indians. We have grown to look at the large world as a part of us. Our method of expression has to be a dialect . . . distinctive and colourful as the Irish or the American—time alone will justify it."

Robin White, an American novelist who spent many years in India, says in a thoughtful article in the *Reporter* of February 14, 1963, "Hopeless as the Indian writer's task might seem, the challenge has been met with some success, mainly because the writers themselves tend to be as diverse as the nation."

It is acknowledged that while English and Western literature have acted as catalytic agents, the fundamental inspiration, particularly in the vernaculars, still comes from the *Epics* and Sanskrit. It is true that there is no branch of English literature activity in which Indian writers have not claimed consideration—especially Tagore, Radhakrishnan, Nehru, Sri Aurobindo, Nirad C. Chaudhury (*The Autobiography of an Unknown Indian*), Mulk Raj Anand, R. K. Narayan, Raja Rao, B. Rajan (*The Dark Dancer, Too Long in the West*), G. V. Desani (*All About Mr. Hatter*), Santha Rama Rau, Kamala Markandaya, to mention only a few with international reputations and audiences. Yet the lesser known writers display a tendency to consciously master a foreign language and to indulge in what Kripalani calls "a self-conscious elegance, an undue emphasis on semantic chastity and a tendency to overwrite." Fluency and intensity are not enough; precision and clarity are equally important.

Indian writers face the anomaly that while Indian literature is a unity, writers and readers of a single language hardly know anything being written in a neighboring language. It is necessary to devise further ways and means whereby Indian writers can meet across the barriers of written and spoken languages, and enable their readers to appreciate the immense variety of their own country's literary heritage.

The difficulties of Indian writers today are closely linked with their economic conditions. The Indian writer has to work even harder to survive than his Western or Japanese counterpart. Publishing is not yet a profitable industry. In 1961, 21,000 titles were published—for a population of 430 million this is exasperatingly small. Forty percent of these titles related to literature, while 4.5 percent were scientific and less than 1 percent covered technology and the applied sciences. The social sciences had 30 percent and history, geography, biography, and religion about 15 percent. Of significance too is the fact that out of these 21,000 books, 9,301 were in English, and only 2,805 in Hindi, and 2,043 in Bengali. Big cities like Bombay, Calcutta, Delhi, and Madras, and most of the universities (numbering more than fifty) all have adequate libraries. However, sad to say, book buying and selling do not have the same place in the life of an average educated Indian as they do in the life of his counterpart in America, Russia, England, Japan, or Italy. One reason for this is that any book costing more than Rs.5/- (roughly one dollar) is beyond the reach of 90 percent of the population.

Thus writing in India, with a few exceptions, is not yet a lucrative profession. Those drawn to writing as a profession must come from financially independent homes. Tagore, Khushwant Singh, Santha Rama Rau, and to a lesser extent Raja Rao, T. S. Pillai, and R. K. Narayan either had private means or were supported by the joint family and its system until their books began selling.

A vast majority of Indian writers have to struggle to make ends meet. Prem Chand, who died in poverty, is a striking example. In 1920, he was paid Rs.5/- for a short story, and this was typical for the time. Even today, royalties paid to Indian writers are a pittance in comparison with those of other parts of the world. Rs.100/- ($21.00) is considered a handsome payment for a short story or a magazine article. A best seller is as yet unknown in India, nor are their guilds or book clubs to bolster sales.

Efforts are now being made to correct this state of affairs. A major step was taken in 1954, when the Sahitya Akademi was inaugurated. Its first president was Jawaharlal Nehru himself, and the second was the then Vice-President of India, S. Radhakrishnan. In his inaugural address, Dr. Radhakrishnan defined the objectives of the Akademi as follows: "The phrase 'Sahitya Akademi' combines two words: 'Sahitya' is Sanskrit and 'Academy' is Greek. This name suggests our universal outlook and aspiration. Sahitya is literary composition; academy is an assembly of men who are interested in the subject. So Sahitya Akademi will be an assembly of all those who are interested in creative and critical literature. It is the purpose of this Akademi to recognize men of achievement in letters, to encourage men of promise in letters, to educate public taste and to improve standards of literature and literary criticism."

The future of any literature is, of course, in the hands of its writers. India's literature is no exception, despite the difficulties under which its writers labor. The main creative problem that the Indian writer of fiction faces is to perfect his use of the novel form. Whether in Hindi, Marhati, or English the Indian novel is often static, its characters types rather than individuals.

B. Rajan put it well when he wrote in *The Illustrated Weekly of India* on March 26, 1963, "Both the novel of manners and the novel of the East–West collision tend to be concerned with relatively restricted areas and are not concerned with them at any significant depth. The novel of Indian life is aggressively Indian and the local color seems to all but obliterate the traditional resources of fiction and the ability to use them. The novel of ideas is not always distinguished by intellectual power. The novel of meanings is not merely surrounded but almost stifled by its philosophic envelope. . . . These admissions have to be made, but the truth is that they also have to be made of Indian literature in languages other than English."

Tagore, Prem Chand, Raja Rao, and R. K. Narayan have a sense of form, but a great many others do not seem to possess the standards of literary architecture which are expected of serious writers in the West and Japan.

A similar deficiency exists in the field of critical and descriptive literature. Indian drama too is, as Forster pointed out twenty years ago, weak and provincial, not organic and living. All in all, it is safe to say that the great full-length works of Indian literature, aside from the classics and the holy books, have yet to be written.

But what the Indian has lost to the novel he has won for the short story, where he has successfully handled the interplay of situation and character (see Krishan Chandar's story

"Kalu Bhangi"), and there is no reason why given time he cannot achieve the same results with the novel. After all, America had to wait almost a hundred years after ₃ independence for the arrival of Melville and Mark Twain.

Indian literature today is full of vitality and promise. The literary scene has been watered by many rivers, indigenous and foreign. It draws sustenance and strength from the *Vedas*, the *Puranas*, the *Epics*, the *Panchantantra*, the *Jataka Stories*, Banabhatta, from Sankara Acharya and Kabir, Nanak and Tulsidas, from Kamban and Amir Khusroo, from Bharati and Bankim Chandra Chatterji, from Tagore and Sarat Chandra. It has recived a rich legacy from Western literature in general and English literature in particular—and whatever the fate of English language in India, this legacy will continue to enrich modern Indian literature.

The dilemma of the Indian writer continues to haunt him. B. Rajan wrote in 1965: "The question to be answered is whether the Indian tradition with its capacity for assimilation and its unique power of synthesis can come to terms with the new (and the new is inevitable) without deep erosions in its fundamental character. In creating an image of this challenge there is perhaps a part to be played by the man of mixed sensibility caught between crossfires, whose mind is a microcosm of what he seeks to convey."

This is a noble challenge. Only time can tell whether Indian literature can meet it fully, but it is the editor's belief that this volume offers firm evidence that it can.

RABINDRANATH TAGORE

Rabindranath Tagore was born May 5, 1861, and died August 7, 1941. He was awarded the Nobel Prize for Literature in 1913. Tagore is the best-known figure in the literary and cultural life of modern India. Poet, patriot, novelist, playwright, short story writer, composer, philosopher, educator, painter, he played a major role in the Indian cultural renaissance.

He was born and brought up in an affluent and artistic family. His father and grandfather were eminent men of learning and leaders of thought in Bengal. His brothers and sisters were all talented and gifted individuals. Tagore was a prolific writer who wrote his first poem before he reached his teens and his first novel at nineteen. His best-known work remains the volume of poems called Gitanjali. *Of this book Yeats said, "I have carried the manuscript of these translations about me for days, reading it in railway trains, or on the top of omnibuses and in restaurants, and I have often had to close it lest some stranger would see how much it moved me."*

"The Cabuliwallah" and "The Hungry Stones" were both written in Bengali in the 1890s.

The Cabuliwallah

RABINDRANATH TAGORE

MY five years' old daughter Mini cannot live without chattering. I really believe that in all her life she has not wasted a minute in silence. Her mother is often vexed at this, and would stop her prattle, but I would not. To see Mini quiet is unnatural, and I cannot bear it long. And so my own talk with her is always lively.

One morning, for instance, when I was in the midst of the seventeenth chapter of my new novel, my little Mini stole into the room, and putting her hand into mine, said: "Father! Ramdayal the door-keeper calls a crow a krow! He doesn't know anything, does he?"

Before I could explain to her the differences of language in this world, she was embarked on the full tide of another subject. "What do you think, Father? Bhola says there is an elephant in the clouds, blowing water out of his trunk, and that is why it rains!"

And then, darting off anew, while I sat still making ready some reply to this last, saying: "Father! what relation is Mother to you?"

"My dear little sister in the law!" I murmured involuntarily to myself, but with a grave face contrived to answer: "Go and play with Bhola, Mini! I am busy!"

The window of my room overlooks the road. The child had seated herself at my feet near my table, and was playing softly, drumming on her knees. I was hard at work on my seventeenth chapter, where Protap Singh, the hero, had just caught Kanchanlata, the heroine, in his arms, and was about to escape with her by the third-story window of the castle, when all of a sudden Mini left her play, and ran to the window, crying: "A Cabuliwallah! a Cabuliwallah!" Sure enough in the street below was a Cabuliwallah, passing slowly along. He wore the loose soiled clothing of his people, with a tall turban; there was a bag on his back, and he carried boxes of grapes in his hand.

I cannot tell what were my daughter's feelings at the sight of this man, but she began to call him loudly. "Ah!" I thought, "he will come in, and my seventeenth chapter will never be finished!" At which exact moment the Cabuliwallah turned, and looked up at the child. When she saw this, overcome by terror, she fled to her mother's protection, and disappeared. She had a blind belief that inside the bag, which the big man carried, there were perhaps two or three other children like herself. The peddler meanwhile entered my doorway, and greeted me with a smiling face.

So precarious was the position of my hero and my heroine, that my first impulse was to stop and buy something, since the man had been called. I made some small purchases, and a conversation began about Abdurrahman, the Russians, the English, and the Frontier Policy.

As he was about to leave, he asked: "And where is the little girl, sir?"

And I, thinking that Mini must get rid of her false fear, had her brought out.

She stood by my chair, and looked at the Cabuliwallah and his bag. He offered her nuts and raisins, but she would not be tempted, and only clung the closer to me, with all her doubts increased.

This was their first meeting.

One morning, however, not many days later, as I was leaving the house, I was startled to find Mini, seated on a bench near the door, laughing and talking, with the great Cabuliwallah at her feet. In all her life, it appeared, my small daughter had never found so patient a listener, save her father. And already the corner of her little sari was stuffed with almonds and raisins, the gift of her visitor. "Why did you give her those?" I said, and taking out an eight-anna bit, I handed it to him. The man accepted the money without demur, and slipped it into his pocket.

Alas, on my return an hour later, I found the unfortunate coin had made twice its own worth of trouble! For the Cabuliwallah had given it to Mini, and her mother catching sight of the bright round object, had pounced on the child with: "Where did you get that eight-anna bit?"

"The Cabuliwallah gave it me," said Mini cheerfully.

"The Cabuliwallah gave it you!" cried her mother much shocked. "O Mini! how could you take it from him?"

I, entering at the moment, saved her from impending disaster, and proceeded to make my own inquiries.

It was not the first or second time, I found, that the two had met. The Cabuliwallah had overcome the child's first terror by a judicious bribery of nuts and almonds, and the two were now great friends.

They had many quaint jokes, which afforded them much amusement. Seated in front of him, looking down on his gigantic frame in all her tiny dignity, Mini would ripple her face with laughter, and begin: "O Cabuliwallah! Cabuliwallah! what have you got in your bag?"

And he would reply, in the nasal accents of the mountaineer: "An elephant!" Not much cause for merriment, perhaps; but how they both enjoyed the witticism! And for me, this child's talk with a grown-up man had always in it something strangely fascinating.

Then the Cabuliwallah, not to be behindhand, would take his turn: "Well, little one, and when are you going to the father-in-law's house?"

Now most small Bengali maidens have heard long ago about the father-in-law's house; but we, being a little new-fangled, had kept these things from our child, and Mini at this question must have been a trifle bewildered. But she would not show it, and with ready tact replied: "Are *you* going there?"

Amongst men of the Cabuliwallah's class, however, it is well known that the words *father-in-law's house* have a double meaning. It is a euphemism for *jail*, the place where we are well cared for, at no expense to ourselves. In this sense would the sturdy peddler take my daughter's question. "Ah," he would say, shaking his fist at an invisible police-man, "I will thrash my father-in-law!" Hearing this, and pic-turing the poor discomfited relative, Mini would go off into peals of laughter, in which her formidable friend would join.

These were autumn mornings, the very time of year when kings of old went forth to conquest; and I, never stirring from my little corner in Calcutta, would let my mind wander over the whole world. At the very name of another country, my heart would go out to it, and at the sight of a foreigner in the streets, I would fall to weaving a network of dreams —the mountains, the glens, and the forests of his distant home, with his cottage in its setting, and the free and inde-pendent life of far-away wilds. Perhaps the scenes of travel conjure themselves up before me, and pass and repass in my imagination all the more vividly, because I lead such a vege-table existence that a call to travel would fall upon me like a thunderbolt. In the presence of this Cabuliwallah I was immediately transported to the foot of arid mountain peaks, with narrow little defiles twisting in and out amongst their towering heights. I could see the string of camels bearing the merchandise, and the company of turbanned merchants carrying some of their queer old firearms, and some of their spears, journeying downward towards the plains. I could see— But at some such point Mini's mother would intervene, imploring me to "beware of that man."

Mini's mother is unfortunately a very timid lady. When-ever she hears a noise in the street, or sees people coming towards the house, she always jumps to the conclusion that they are either thieves, or drunkards, or snakes, or tigers, or malaria, or cockroaches, or caterpillars, or an English sailor. Even after all these years of experience, she is not able to overcome her terror. So she was full of doubts about the Cabuliwallah, and used to beg me to keep a watchful eye on him.

I tried to laugh her fear gently away, but then she would turn round on me seriously, and ask me solemn questions.

Were children never kidnapped?

Was it, then, not true that there was slavery in Cabul?

Was it so very absurd that this big man should be able to carry off a tiny child?

I urged that, though not impossible, it was highly improbable. But this was not enough, and her dread persisted. As it was indefinite, however, it did not seem right to forbid the man the house, and the intimacy went on unchecked.

Once a year in the middle of January Rahmun, the Cabuliwallah, was in the habit of returning to his country, and as the time approached he would be very busy, going from house to house collecting his debts. This year, however, he could always find time to come and see Mini. It would have seemed to an outsider that there was some conspiracy between the two, for when he could not come in the morning, he would appear in the evening.

Even to me it was a little startling now and then, in the corner of a dark room, suddenly to surprise this tall, loose-garmented, much bebagged man; but when Mini would run in smiling, with her "O Cabuliwallah! Cabuliwallah!" and the two friends, so far apart in age, would subside into their old laughter and their old jokes, I felt reassured.

One morning, a few days before he had made up his mind to go, I was correcting my proof sheets in my study. It was chilly weather. Through the window the rays of the sun touched my feet, and the slight warmth was very welcome. It was almost eight o'clock, and the early pedestrians were returning home with their heads covered. All at once I heard an uproar in the street, and, looking out, saw Rahmun being led away bound between two policemen, and behind them a crowd of curious boys. There were bloodstains on the clothes of the Cabuliwallah, and one of the policemen carried a knife. Hurrying out, I stopped them, and inquired what it all meant. Partly from one, partly from another, I gathered that a certain neighbour had owed the peddler something for a Rampuri shawl, but had falsely denied having bought it, and that in the course of the quarrel Rahmun had struck him. Now in the heat of his excitement, the prisoner began calling his enemy all sorts of names, when suddenly in a verandah of my house appeared my little Mini, with her usual exclamation: "O Cabuliwallah! Cabuliwallah!" Rahmun's face lighted up as he turned to her. He had no bag under his arm today, so she could not discuss the elephant with him. She at once therefore proceeded to the next question: "Are you going to the father-in-law's house?" Rahmun laughed and said: "Just where I am going, little one!" Then seeing that the reply did not amuse the child, he held up his fettered hands. "Ah," he said, "I would have thrashed that old father-in-law, but my hands are bound!"

On a charge of murderous assault, Rahmun was sentenced to some years' imprisonment.

Time passed away, and he was not remembered. The accustomed work in the accustomed place was ours, and the thought of the once free mountaineer spending his years in prison seldom or never occurred to us. Even my lighthearted Mini, I am ashamed to say, forgot her old friend. New companions filled her life. As she grew older, she spent more of her time with girls. So much time indeed did she spend with them that she came no more, as she used to do, to her father's room. I was scarcely on speaking terms with her.

Years had passed away. It was once more autumn and we had made arrangements for our Mini's marriage. It was to take place during the Puja Holidays. With Durga returning to Kailas, the light of our home also was to depart to her husband's house, and leave her father's in the shadow.

The morning was bright. After the rains, there was a sense of ablution in the air, and the sun rays looked like pure gold. So bright were they that they gave a beautiful radiance even to the sordid brick walls of our Calcutta lanes. Since early dawn today the wedding pipes had been sounding, and at each beat my own heart throbbed. The wail of the tune, Bhairavi, seemed to intensify my pain at the approaching separation. My Mini was to be married tonight.

From early morning noise and bustle had pervaded the house. In the courtyard the canopy had to be slung on its bamboo poles; the chandeliers with their tinkling sound must be hung in each room and verandah. There was no end of hurry and excitement. I was sitting in my study, looking through the accounts, when someone entered, saluting respectfully, and stood before me. It was Rahmun the Cabuliwallah. At first I did not recognize him. He had no bag, nor the long hair, nor the same vigor that he used to have. But he smiled, and I knew him again.

"When did you come, Rahmun?" I asked him.

"Last evening," he said, "I was released from jail."

The words struck harsh upon my ears. I had never before talked with one who had wounded his fellow, and my heart shrank within itself when I realized this, for I felt that the day would have been better-omened had he not turned up.

"There are ceremonies going on," I said, "and I am busy. Could you perhaps come another day?"

At once he turned to go; but as he reached the door he hesitated, and said: "May I not see the little one, sir, for a moment?" It was his belief that Mini was still the same. He had pictured her running to him as she used, calling "O Cabuliwallah! Cabuliwallah!" He had imagined too that they would laugh and talk together, just as of old. In fact, in memory of former days he had brought, carefully wrapped up in paper, a few almonds and raisins and grapes, obtained somehow from a countryman, for his own little fund was dispersed.

I said again: "There is a ceremony in the house, and you will not be able to see anyone today."

The man's face fell. He looked wistfully at me for a moment, said "Good morning," and went out.

I felt a little sorry, and would have called him back, but I found he was returning of his own accord. He came close up to me holding out his offerings, and said: "I brought these few things, sir, for the little one. Will you give them to her?"

I took them and was going to pay him, but he caught my hand and said: "You are very kind, sir! Keep me in your recollection. Do not offer me money!—You have a little girl: I too have one like her in my own home. I think of her, and bring fruits to your child—not to make a profit for myself."

Saying this, he put his hand inside his big loose robe, and brought out a small and dirty piece of paper. With great care he unfolded this, and smoothed it out with both hands on my table. It bore the impression of a little hand. Not a photograph. Not a drawing. The impression of an ink-smeared hand laid flat on the paper. This touch of his own little daughter had been always on his heart, as he had come year after year to Calcutta to sell his wares in the streets.

Tears came to my eyes. I forgot that he was a poor Cabuli fruit seller, while I was— But no, what was I more than he? He also was a father.

That impression of the hand of his little *Parbati* in her distant mountain home reminded me of my own little Mini.

I sent for Mini immediately from the inner apartment. Many difficulties were raised, but I would not listen. Clad in the red silk of her wedding day, with the sandal paste on her forehead, and adorned as a young bride, Mini came, and stood bashfully before me.

The Cabuliwallah looked a little staggered at the apparition. He could not revive their old friendship. At last he smiled and said: "Little one, are you going to your father-in-law's house?"

But Mini now understood the meaning of the word "father-in-law," and she could not reply to him as of old. She flushed up at the question, and stood before him with her bridelike face turned down.

I remembered the day when the Cabuliwallah and my Mini had first met, and I felt sad. When she had gone, Rahmun heaved a deep sigh, and sat down on the floor. The idea had suddenly come to him that his daughter too must have grown in this long time, and that he would have to make friends with her anew. Assuredly he would not find her as he used to know her. And besides, what might not have happened to her in these eight years?

The marriage pipes sounded, and the mild autumn sun streamed round us. But Rahmun sat in the little Calcutta lane, and saw before him the barren mountains of Afghanistan.

I took out a bank note and gave it to him, saying: "Go back to your own daughter, Rahmun, in your own country, and may the happiness of your meeting bring good fortune to my child!"

Having made this present, I had to curtail some of the festivities. I could not have the electric lights I had intended, nor the military band, and the ladies of the house were despondent at it. But to me the wedding feast was all the brighter for the thought that in a distant land a long-lost father met again with his only child.

The Hungry Stones

MY kinsman and myself were returning to Calcutta from our Puja trip when we met the man in a train. From his dress and bearing we took him at first for an up-country Mahomedan, but we were puzzled as we heard him talk. He discoursed upon all subjects so confidently that you might think the Disposer of All Things consulted him at all times in all that He did. Hitherto we had been perfectly happy, as we did not know that secret and unheard-of forces were at work, that the Russians had advanced close to us, that the English had deep and secret policies, that confusion among the native chiefs had come to a head. But our newly acquired friend said with a sly smile: "There happen more things in heaven and earth, Horatio, than are reported in your newspapers." As we had never stirred out of our homes before, the demeanor of the man struck us dumb with wonder. Be the topic ever so trivial, he would quote science, or comment on the *Vedas*, or repeat quatrains from some Persian poet; and as we had no pretense to a knowledge of science or the *Vedas* or Persian, our admiration for him went on increasing, and my kinsman, a theosophist, was firmly convinced that our fellow passenger must have been supernaturally inspired by some strange "magnetism" or "occult power," by an "astral body" or something of that kind. He listened to the tritest saying that fell from the lips of our extraordinary companion with devotional rapture, and secretly took down notes of his conversation. I fancy that the extraordinary man saw this, and was a little pleased with it.

When the train reached the junction, we assembled in the waiting room for the connection. It was then 10 P.M., and as the train, we heard, was likely to be very late, owing to something wrong in the lines, I spread my bed on the table and was about to lie down for a comfortable doze, when the extraordinary person deliberately set about spinning the following yarn. Of course, I could get no sleep that night.

When, owing to a disagreement about some questions of administrative policy, I threw up my post at Junagarh, and entered the service of the Nizam of Hyderabad, they appointed me at once, as a strong young man, collector of cotton duties at Barich.

Barich is a lovely place. The *Susta* "chatters over stony ways and babbles on the pebbles," tripping, like a skillful dancing girl, in through the woods below the lonely hills. A flight of a hundred and fifty steps rises from the river, and above that flight, on the river's brim and at the foot of the hills, there stands a solitary marble palace. Around it there is no habitation of man—the village and the cotton mart of Barich being far off.

About two hundred and fifty years ago the Emperor Mahmud Shah II had built this lonely palace for his pleasure and luxury. In his days jets of rosewater spurted from its fountains, and on the cold marble floors of its spray-cooled rooms young Persian damsels would sit, their hair disheveled before bathing, and, splashing their soft naked feet in the clear water of the reservoirs, would sing, to the tune of the guitar, the *ghazals* of their vineyards.

The fountains play no longer; the songs have ceased; no longer do snow-white feet step gracefully on the snowy marble. It is but the vast and solitary quarters of cess collectors like us, men oppressed with solitude and deprived of the society of women. Now, Karim Khan, the old clerk of my office, warned me repeatedly not to take up my abode there. "Pass the day there, if you like," said he, "but never stay the night." I passed it off with a light laugh. The servants said that they would work till dark, and go away at night. I gave my ready assent. The house had such a bad name that even thieves would not venture near it after dark.

At first the solitude of the deserted palace weighed upon me like a nightmare. I would stay out, and work hard as long as possible, then return home at night jaded and tired, go to bed and fall asleep.

Before a week had passed, the place began to exert a weird fascination upon me. It is difficult to describe or to induce people to believe; but I felt as if the whole house was like a living organism slowly and imperceptibly digesting me by the action of some stupefying gastric juice.

Perhaps the process had begun as soon as I set my foot in the house, but I distinctly remember the day on which I first was conscious of it.

It was the beginning of summer, and the market being dull I had no work to do. A little before sunset I was sitting in an armchair near the water's edge below the steps. The *Susta* had shrunk and sunk low; a broad patch of sand on the other side glowed with the hues of evening; on this side the pebbles at the bottom of the clear shallow waters were glistening. There was not a breath of wind anywhere, and the still air was laden with an oppressive scent from the spicy shrubs growing on the hills close by.

As the sun sank behind the hilltops a long dark curtain fell upon the stage of day, and the intervening hills cut short the time in which light and shade mingle at sunset. I thought of going out for a ride, and was about to get up when I heard a footfall on the steps behind. I looked back, but there was no one.

As I sat down again, thinking it to be an illusion, I heard many footfalls, as if a large number of persons were rushing down the steps. A strange thrill of delight slightly tinged with fear, passed through my frame, and though there was not a figure before my eyes, methought I saw a bevy of joyous maidens coming down the steps to bathe in the *Susta* in that summer evening. Not a sound was in the valley, in the river, or in the palace, to break the silence, but I distinctly heard the maidens' gay and mirthful laugh, like the gurgle of a spring gushing forth in a hundred cascades, as they ran past me, in quick playful pursuit of each other, towards the river, without noticing me at all. As they were invisible to me, so I was, as it were, invisible to them. The river was perfectly calm, but I felt that its still, shallow, and clear waters were stirred suddenly by the splash of many an arm jingling with bracelets, that the girls laughed and dashed and spattered water at one another, that the feet of the fair swimmers tossed the tiny waves up in showers of pearl.

I felt a thrill at my heart—I cannot say whether the excitement was due to fear or delight or curiosity. I had a strong desire to see them more clearly, but naught was visible before me. I thought I could catch all that they said if I only strained my ears; but however hard I strained them, I heard nothing but the chirping of the cicadas in the woods. It seemed as if a dark curtain of two hundred and fifty years was hanging before me, and I would fain lift a corner of it tremblingly and peer through, though the assembly on the other side was completely enveloped in darkness.

The oppressive closeness of the evening was broken by a sudden gust of wind, and the still surface of the *Susta* rippled and curled like the hair of a nymph, and from the woods wrapt in the evening gloom there came forth a simultaneous murmur, as though they were awakening from a black dream. Call it reality or dream, the momentary glimpse of that invisible mirage reflected from a far-off world, two hundred and fifty years old, vanished in a flash. The mystic forms that brushed past me with their quick unbodied steps, and loud, voiceless laughter, and threw themselves into the river, did not go back wringing their dripping robes as they went. Like fragrance wafted away by the wind they were dispersed by a single breath of the spring.

Then I was filled with a lively fear that it was the Muse

that had taken advantage of my solitude and possessed me —the witch had evidently come to ruin a poor devil like myself making a living by collecting cotton duties. I decided to have a good dinner—it is the empty stomach that all sorts of incurable diseases find an easy prey. I sent for my cook and gave orders for a rich, sumptuous *moghlai* dinner, redolent of spices and *ghi.*

Next morning the whole affair appeared a queer fantasy. With a light heart I put on a *sola* hat like the *sahebs*, and drove out to my work. I was to have written my quarterly report that day, and expected to return late; but before it was dark I was strangely drawn to my house—by what I could not say—I felt they were all waiting, and that I should delay no longer. Leaving my report unfinished I rose, put on my *sola* hat, and startling the dark, shady, desolate path with the rattle of my carriage, I reached the vast silent palace standing on the gloomy skirts of the hills.

On the first floor the stairs led to a very spacious hall, its roof stretching wide over ornamental arches resting on three rows of massive pillars, and groaning day and night under the weight of its own intense solitude. The day had just closed, and the lamps had not yet been lighted. As I pushed the door open a great bustle seemed to follow within, as if a throng of people had broken up in confusion, and rushed out through the doors and windows and corridors and verandas and rooms, to make its hurried escape.

As I saw no one I stood bewildered, my hair on end in a kind of ecstatic delight, and a faint scent of *attar* and unguents almost effaced by age lingered in my nostrils. Standing in the darkness of that vast desolate hall between the rows of those ancient pillars, I could hear the gurgle of fountains plashing on the marble floor, a strange tune on the guitar, the jingle of ornaments and the tinkle of anklets, the clang of bells tolling the hours, the distant note of *nahabat*, the din of the crystal pendants of chandeliers shaken by the breeze, the song of *bulbuls* from the cages in the corridors, the cackle of storks in the gardens, all creating round me a strange unearthly music.

Then I came under such a spell that this intangible, inaccessible, unearthly vision appeared to be the only reality in the world—and all else a mere dream. That I, that is to say, Srijut So-and-so, the eldest son of So-and-so of blessed memory, should be drawing a monthly salary of Rs.450/- by the discharge of my duties as collector of cotton duties, and driving in my dogcart to my office every day in a short coat and *sola* hat, appeared to me to be such an astonishingly ludicrous illusion that I burst into a horselaugh, as I stood in the gloom of that vast silent hall.

At that moment my servant entered with a lighted kerosene lamp in his hand. I do not know whether he thought me mad, but it came back to me at once that I was in very deed Srijut So-and-so, son of So-and-so of blessed memory, and that, while our poets, great and small, alone could say whether inside or outside the earth there was a region where unseen fountains perpetually played and fairy guitars, struck by invisible fingers, sent forth an eternal harmony, this at any rate was certain, that I collected duties at the cotton market at Barich, and earned thereby Rs.450/- per mensem as my salary. I laughed in great glee at my curious illusion, as I sat over the newspaper at my camp table, lighted by the kerosene lamp.

After I had finished my paper and eaten my *moghlai* dinner, I put out the lamp, and lay down on my bed in a small side room. Through the open window a radiant star, high above the Avalli hills skirted by the darkness of their woods, was gazing intently from millions and millions of miles away in the sky at Mr. Collector lying on a humble camp bedstead. I wondered and felt amused at the idea, and do not know when I fell asleep or how long I slept; but I suddenly awoke with a start, though I heard no sound and saw no intruder—only the steady bright star on the hilltop had set, and the dim light of the new moon was stealthily entering the room through the open window, as if ashamed of its intrusion.

I saw nobody, but felt as if someone was gently pushing me. As I awoke she said not a word, but beckoned me with her five fingers bedecked with rings to follow her cautiously. I got up noiselessly, and, though not a soul save myself was there in the countless apartments of that deserted palace with its slumbering sounds and waking echoes, I feared at every step lest anyone should wake up. Most of the rooms of the palace were always kept closed, and I had never entered them.

I followed breathless and with silent steps my invisible guide—I cannot now say where. What endless dark and narrow passages, what long corridors, what silent and solemn audience chambers and close secret cells I crossed!

Though I could not see my fair guide, her form was not invisible to my mind's eye—an Arab girl, her arms, hard and smooth as marble, visible through her loose sleeves, a thin veil falling on her face from the fringe of her cap, and a curved dagger at her waist! Methought that one of the thousand and one Arabian Nights had been wafted to me from the world of romance, and that at the dead of night I was wending my way through the dark narrow alleys of slumbering Bagdad to a trysting place fraught with peril.

At last my fair guide stopped abruptly before a deep blue screen, and seemed to point to something below. There was nothing there, but a sudden dread froze the blood in my heart—methought I saw there on the floor at the foot of the screen a terrible negro eunuch dressed in rich brocade, sitting and dozing with outstretched legs, with a naked sword on his lap. My fair guide lightly tripped over his legs and held up a fringe of the screen. I could catch a glimpse of a part of the room spread with a Persian carpet—someone was sitting inside on a bed—I could not see her, but only caught a glimpse of two exquisite feet in gold-embroidered slippers, hanging out from loose saffron-colored *paijamas* and placed idly on the orange-colored velvet carpet. On one side there was a bluish crystal tray on which a few apples, pears, oranges, and bunches of grapes in plenty, two small cups, and a gold-tinted decanter were evidently awaiting the guest. A fragrant intoxicating vapor, issuing from a strange sort of incense that burned within, almost overpowered my senses.

As with trembling heart I made an attempt to step across the outstretched legs of the eunuch, he woke up suddenly with a start, and the sword fell from his lap with a sharp clang on the marble floor.

A terrific scream made me jump, and I saw I was sitting on that camp bedstead of mine sweating heavily; and the crescent moon looked pale in the morning light like a weary sleepless patient at dawn; and our crazy Meher Ali was crying out, as is his daily custom, "Stand back! Stand back!!" while he went along the lonely road.

Such was the abrupt close of one of my Arabian Nights; but there were yet a thousand nights left.

Then followed a great discord between my days and nights. During the day I would go to my work worn and tired, cursing the bewitching night and her empty dreams, but as night came my daily life with its bonds and shackles of work would appear a petty, false, ludicrous vanity.

After nightfall I was caught and overwhelmed in the snare of a strange intoxication. I would then be transformed into some unknown personage of a bygone age, playing my part in unwritten history; and my short English coat and tight breeches did not suit me in the least. With a red velvet cap on my head, loose *paijamas,* an embroidered vest, a long flowing silk gown, and colored handkerchiefs scented with *attar*, I would complete my elaborate toilet, sit on a high-cushioned chair, and replace my cigarette with a many-coiled *narghileh* filled with rosewater, as if in eager expectation of a strange meeting with the beloved one.

I have no power to describe the marvelous incidents that unfolded themselves as the gloom of the night deepened. I felt as if in the curious apartments of that vast edifice the fragments of a beautiful story, which I could follow for some distance, but of which I could never see the end, flew about in a sudden gust of the vernal breeze. And all the same I would wander from room to room in pursuit of them the whole night long.

Amid the eddy of these dream fragments, amid the smell of *henna* and the twanging of the guitar, amid the waves of air charged with fragrant spray, I would catch like a flash of lightning the momentary glimpse of a fair damsel. She it was who had saffron-colored *paijamas*, white ruddy soft feet in gold-embroidered slippers with curved toes, a close-fitting bodice wrought with gold, a red cap, from which a golden frill fell on her snowy brow and cheeks.

She had maddened me. In pursuit of her I wandered from room to room, from path to path among the bewildering maze of alleys in the enchanted dreamland of the nether world of sleep.

Sometimes in the evening, while arraying myself carefully as a prince of the blood-royal before a large mirror, with a candle burning on either side, I would see a sudden reflection of the Persian beauty by the side of my own. A swift turn of her neck, a quick eager glance of intense passion and pain glowing in her large dark eyes, just a suspicion of speech on her dainty red lips, her figure, fair and slim, crowned with youth like a blossoming creeper, quickly uplifted in her graceful tilting gait, a dazzling flash of pain and craving and ecstasy, a smile and a glance and a blaze of jewels and silk, and she melted away. A wild gust of wind, laden with all the fragrance of hills and woods, would put out my light, and I would fling aside my dress and lie down on my bed, my eyes closed and my body thrilling with delight, and there around me in the breeze, amid all the perfume of the woods and hills, floated through the silent gloom many a caress and many a kiss and many a tender touch of hands, and gentle murmurs in my ears, and fragrant breaths on my brow; or a sweetly perfumed kerchief was wafted again and again on my cheeks. Then slowly a mysterious serpent would twist her stupefying coils about me; and heaving a heavy sigh, I would lapse into insensibility, and then into a profound slumber.

One evening I decided to go out on my horse—I do not know who implored me to stay—but I would listen to no entreaties that day. My English hat and coat were resting on a rack, and I was about to take them down when a sudden whirlwind, crested with the sands of the *Susta* and the dead leaves of the Avalli hills, caught them up, and whirled them round and round, while a loud peal of merry laughter rose higher and higher, striking all the chords of mirth till it died away in the land of sunset.

I could not go out for my ride, and the next day I gave up my queer English coat and hat for good.

That day again at dead of night I heard the stifled heart-breaking sobs of someone—as if below the bed, below the floor, below the stony foundation of that gigantic palace, from the depths of a dark damp grave, a voice piteously cried and implored me: "Oh, rescue me! Break through these doors of hard illusion, deathlike slumber and fruitless dreams, place me by your side on the saddle, press me to your heart, and, riding through hills and woods and across the river, take me to the warm radiance of your sunny rooms above!"

Who am I? Oh, how can I rescue thee? What drowning beauty, what incarnate passion shall I drag to the shore from this wild eddy of dreams? O lovely ethereal apparition! Where didst thou flourish and when? By what cool spring, under the shade of what date groves, wast thou born—in the lap of what homeless wanderer in the desert? What Bedouin snatched thee from thy mother's arms, an opening bud plucked from a wild creeper, placed thee on a horse swift as lightning, crossed the burning sands, and took thee to the slave market of what royal city? And there, what offi- cer of the Badshah, seeing the glory of thy bashful blossom- ing youth, paid for thee in gold, placed thee in a golden palanquin, and offered thee as a present for the seraglio of his master? And O, the history of that place! The music of the *sareng*,* the jingle of anklets, the occasional flash of daggers and the glowing wine of Shiraz poison, and the piercing flashing glance! What infinite grandeur, what end- less servitude! The slave girls to thy right and left waved the *chamar*, † as diamonds flashed from their bracelets; the Badshah, the king of kings, fell on his knees at thy snowy feet in bejeweled shoes, and outside, the terrible Abyssinian eunuch, looking like a messenger of death, but clothed like an angel, stood with a naked sword in his hand! Then, O, thou flower of the desert, swept away by the bloodstained dazzling ocean of grandeur, with its foam of jealousy, its rocks and shoals of intrigue, on what shore of cruel death wast thou cast, or in what other land more splendid and more cruel?

Suddenly at this moment that crazy Meher Ali screamed out: "Stand back! Stand back!! All is false! All is false!!" I opened my eyes and saw that it was already light. My *chaprasi* came and handed me my letters, and the cook waited with a *salam* for my orders.

I said: "No, I can stay here no longer." That very day I packed up, and moved to my office. Old Karim Khan smiled a little as he saw me. I felt nettled, but said nothing, and fell to my work.

As evening approached I grew absentminded; I felt as if I had an appointment to keep; and the work of examining the cotton accounts seemed wholly useless; even the *Niza- mat* ‡ of the Nizam did not appear to be of much worth.

* A sort of violin.
† Chowrie, yak-tail.
‡ Royalty.

Whatever belonged to the present, whatever was moving and acting and working for bread seemed trivial, meaningless, and contemptible.

I threw my pen down, closed my ledgers, got into my dogcart, and drove away. I noticed that it stopped of itself at the gate of the marble palace just at the hour of twilight. With quick steps I climbed the stairs, and entered the room.

A heavy silence was reigning within. The dark rooms were looking sullen as if they had taken offence. My heart was full of contrition, but there was no one to whom I could lay it bare, or of whom I could ask forgiveness. I wandered about the dark rooms with a vacant mind. I wished I had a guitar to which I could sing to the unknown: "O fire, the poor moth that made a vain effort to fly away has come back to thee! Forgive it but this once, burn its wings and consume it in thy flame!"

Suddenly two teardrops fell from overhead on my brow. Dark masses of clouds overcast the top of the Avalli hills that day. The gloomy woods and the sooty waters of the *Susta* were waiting in terrible suspense and in an ominous calm. Suddenly land, water, and sky shivered, and a wild tempest blast rushed howling through the distant pathless woods, showing its lightning teeth like a raving maniac who had broken his chains. The desolate halls of the palace banged their doors, and moaned in the bitterness of anguish.

The servants were all in the office, and there was no one to light the lamps. The night was cloudy and moonless. In the dense gloom within I could distinctly feel that a woman was lying on her face on the carpet below the bed—clasping and tearing her long disheveled hair with desperate fingers. Blood was trickling down her fair brow, and she was now laughing a hard, harsh, mirthless laugh, now bursting into violent wringing sobs, now rending her bodice and striking at her bare bosom, as the wind roared in through the open window, and the rain poured in torrents and soaked her through and through.

All night there was no cessation of the storm or of the passionate cry. I wandered from room to room in the dark, with unavailing sorrow. Whom could I console when no one was by? Whose was this intense agony of sorrow? Whence arose this inconsolable grief?

And the madman cried out: "Stand back! Stand back!! All is false! All is false!!"

I saw that the day had dawned, and Meher Ali was going round and round the palace with his usual cry in that dreadful weather. Suddenly it came to me that perhaps he also had once lived in that house, and that, though he had gone mad, he came there every day, and went round and round, fascinated by the weird spell cast by the marble demon.

Despite the storm and rain I ran to him and asked: "Ho, Meher Ali, what is false?"

The man answered nothing, but pushing me aside went round and round with his frantic cry, like a bird flying fascinated about the jaws of a snake, and made a desperate effort to warn himself by repeating: "Stand back! Stand back!! All is false! All is false!!"

I ran like a madman through the pelting rain to my office, and asked Karim Khan: "Tell me the meaning of all this!"

What I gathered from that old man was this: That at one time countless unrequited passions and unsatisfied longings and lurid flames of wild blazing pleasure raged within that palace, and that the curse of all the heartaches and blasted hopes had made its every stone thirsty and hungry, eager to swallow up like a famished ogress any living man who might chance to approach. Not one of those who lived there for three consecutive nights could escape these cruel jaws, save Meher Ali, who had escaped at the cost of his reason.

I asked: "Is there no means whatever of my release?" The old man said: "There is only one means, and that is very difficult. I will tell you what it is, but first you must hear the history of a young Persian girl who once lived in that pleasure dome. A stranger or a more bitterly heartrending tragedy was never enacted on this earth."

Just at this moment the coolies announced that the train was coming. So soon? We hurriedly packed up our luggage, as the train steamed in. An English gentleman, apparently just aroused from slumber, was looking out of a first-class carriage endeavoring to read the name of the station. As soon as he caught sight of our fellow passenger, he cried, "Hallo," and took him into his own compartment. As we got into a second-class carriage, we had no chance of finding out who the man was nor what was the end of his story.

I said: "The man evidently took us for fools and imposed upon us out of fun. The story is pure fabrication from start to finish." The discussion that followed ended in a lifelong rupture between my theosophist kinsman and myself.

SARAT CHANDRA CHATTERJEE

Sarat Chandra Chatterjee (1876–1938) was a Bengali novelist and short story writer. Born in a poor home near Calcutta, he had no formal education and began to write only when he was nearing thirty. His first story, "Mandir" ("Temple"), was published in 1907. Thereafter he took the literary world of Bengal by storm. His reading public extended over the entire subcontinent and his books were translated into all the major Indian languages. Although he came into conflict with conservative and orthodox critics and fiercely attacked sham morality, his style is direct and simple and he preached no sermons. Sarat Chandra wrote a dozen novels and many short stories in which he created a picture of rural Bengal at once colorful and tragic. His popularity in the 1920s and 1930s rivaled Tagore's. Several of his novels have been made into successful Indian films.

Drought

SARAT CHANDRA CHATTERJEE

THE village was called Kashipur. It was a small village, but its *Zamindar* was smaller still. Yet his tenants dared not stand up to him. He was so ruthless.

It was the birthday of his youngest son. It was noon. Tarkaratna, the priest, was on his way home from the land-lord's house, where he had been offering prayers. It was nearing the end of May, but not a patch of cloud could be seen in the sky. The rainless firmament poured fire.

At the end of the field, beside the road, there stood the house of Gafur, the weaver. Now that the mud walls were in ruins, the courtyard touched the public highway, and the inner privacy was thrown on the mercy of the passers-by.

"Hey! Gafur! Is anybody in?" called out Tarkaratna, standing in the shade of a tree by the roadside.

"What do you want? Father is down with fever," answered Gafur's little daughter, aged ten, appearing at the door.

"Fever! Call the scoundrel!"

The noise brought Gafur out, shivering with fever. A bull was tied to the old acacia that leaned against the broken wall.

"What do I see there?" demanded Tarkaratna, indicating the bull. "Do you realise that this is a Hindu village and the landlord himself a Brahmin?" His face was crimson with indignation and the heat of the sun. It was to be expected that his words should be hot and harsh. But Gafur simply looked at him, unable to follow the import of his words.

"Well," said Tarkaratna, "I saw it tied there in the morning and it's still there. If the bull dies, your master will flay you alive! He is no ordinary Brahmin!"

"What shall I do, Father? I'm helpless. I have had fever for the last few days. I can't take him out to graze. I feel so ill."

"Can't you let him graze by himself?"

"Where shall I let him go, Father? People haven't threshed all their paddy yet. It's still lying in the fields. The straw hasn't been gathered. Everything is burnt to cinders—there isn't a blade of grass anywhere. How can I let him loose, Father? He might start poking his nose into somebody's paddy or eating somebody's straw."

Tarkaratna softened a little. "But you can at least tie him in the shade somewhere and give him a bundle of straw or two to munch. Hasn't your daughter cooked rice? Why not give him a tub of boiled rice water? Let him drink it."

Gafur made no reply. He looked helplessly at Tarkaratna, and a deep sigh escaped him.

"I see; you haven't even got that much? What have you done with your share of straw? I suppose you have gone and sold it to satisfy your belly? Not saved even one bundle for the bull! How callous you are!"

At this cruel accusation Gafur seemed to lose the power of speech. "This year I was to have received my share of straw," said Gafur slowly after a moment's hesitation, "but the master kept it all on account of my last year's rent. 'Sir, you are our lord and master,' I implored, falling at his feet. 'Where am I to go if I leave your domain? Let me have at least a little straw. There's no straw on my roof, and we have only one hut in which we two—father and daughter—live. We'll patch the roof with palm leaves and manage this rainy weather, somehow, but what will happen to our Mahesh without food?'"

"Indeed! So you're fond enough of the bull to call him Mahesh! This is a joke."

But his sarcasm did not reach Gafur. "But the master took no pity on me," he went on. "He gave me paddy to last only two months. My share of straw was added to his own stock —Mahesh didn't have even a wisp of it."

"Well, don't you owe him money?" said Tarkaratna, unmoved. "Why shouldn't you have to pay? Do you expect the landlord to support you?"

"But what am I to pay him with? We till four *bighas* of land for him, but the paddy has dried up in the fields during the droughts in the last two years. My daughter and I have not even enough to eat. Look at the hut! When it rains, I spend the night with my daughter huddled in one corner— we can't even stretch our legs. Look at Mahesh! You can count his ribs. Do lend me a bit of hay for him so that he can have something to eat for a day or two." And Gafur sank down on the ground at the Brahmin's feet.

"No, no! Move aside! Let me go home, it's getting late." Tarkaratna made a movement as though to depart, smiling. "Good God! He seems to brandish his horns at me! Will he hurt?" he cried out with fright and anger, stepping hurriedly back from the bull.

Gafur staggered to his feet. "He wants to eat a handful," he said, indicating the wet bundle of rice and fruit in Tarkaratna's hand.

"Wants to eat? Indeed! Like master, like animal. Hasn't even a bit of straw to eat and must have rice and fruit. Take him away and tie him somewhere else! What horns! He will gore somebody to death one of these days." Edging a little, the priest made a quick exit.

Looking away from him, Gafur silently watched Mahesh, whose two deep, brown eyes were full of pain and hunger. "Didn't even give a handful," he muttered, patting the bull's neck and back. "You are my son, Mahesh," he whispered to him. "You have grown old and served us for eight years. I can't even give you enough to eat—but you know how much I love you, don't you?"

Mahesh only stretched out his neck and closed his eyes with pleasure.

"Tell me," went on Gafur, "how can I keep you alive in this dreadful year? If I let you loose, you will start eating other people's paddy or munching their banana leaves. What can I do with you? You have no strength left in your body—nobody wants you. They ask me to sell you at the cattle market. . . ." At the very idea his eyes filled with tears again. Wiping his tears on the back of his hand and looking this way and that, he fetched a tiny bunch of discolored old straw from behind the hut. "Eat it quickly, my child, other-wise . . ." he said, softly, placing it before Mahesh.

"Father . . ."

"What is it?"

"Come and eat," answered Gafur's daughter, looking out of the door. "Why, have you again given Mahesh straw from the roof?"

He had feared as much. "It's old straw—it was rotting away," he answered, ashamed.

"I heard you pulling it, father."

"No, darling, it wasn't exactly . . ."

"But you know, father, the wall will crumble . . ."

Gafur was silent. He had nothing left but this hut. Who knew better than he that unless he was careful it would not last another rainy season. And yet what good was it really?

"Wash your hands and come and eat. I have served your food," said the little girl.

"Give me the rice water; let me feed him."

"There is none, father—it has dried up in the pot."

Nearly a week had passed. Gafur was sitting in the yard, sick of body and anxious. Mahesh had not returned since the day before.

He himself was helpless. Amina had been looking for the bull everywhere from early morning. The evening shadows were already falling when she came home. "Have you heard, father? Manik Ghose has sent Mahesh to the police pen," she said.

"Nonsense!"

"Yes, father, it's true. His servant said to me, 'Tell your father to look for the bull at Dariapur . . . .' "

"What did he do?"

"He entered their garden, father."

Gafur made no answer.

"At the end of three days, they say, the police will sell him at the cattle market."

"Let them," answered Gafur.

Amina did not know what the "cattle market" meant. She had often noticed her father grow restless whenever it was mentioned in connection with Mahesh, but today he went out without saying another word.

Under the cover of night, Gafur secretly came round to Banshi's shop.

"Uncle, you'll have to lend me a rupee," said he, putting down a brass plate under the seat. Banshi was well acquainted with this object. In the last two years he had lent a rupee at least five times on this security. He made no objection today either.

The next morning Mahesh was seen at his usual place again. An elderly Mohammedan was examining him with very sharp eyes. Not far away, on one side, Gafur sat on the ground, all hunched up. The examination over, the old man untied a ten-rupee note from a corner of his shawl, and, smoothing it again and again, said: "Here, take this. I shan't take anything off. I'm paying the full price."

Stretching his hand, Gafur took the money, but remained silent. As the two men who came with the old man were about to take the rope round the animal's neck, he suddenly stood bolt upright. "Don't touch that rope, I tell you. Be careful, I warn you!" he cried out hoarsely.

They were taken aback. "Why?" asked the old man in surprise.

"There's no why to it. He's my property—I shall not sell him; it's my pleasure," he answered in the same tone, and threw the note away.

"But you accepted the deposit yesterday," all three said in a chorus.

"Take this back," he answered, flinging the two rupees across to them.

Gafur begged for rice water from the neighbors and fed Mahesh. Patting him on the head and horns, he whispered vague sounds of endearment to him.

It was about the middle of June. Nobody who has not looked at an Indian summer sky would realize how terrible, how unrelenting, the heat can be. Not a trace of mercy anywhere! Today even the thought that some day this aspect of the sky will change, that it will become overcast with soft, vapor-laden clouds is impossible. It seemed as though the whole blazing sky would go on burning day after day endlessly, to the end of time.

Gafur returned home at noon. He was not used to working as a hired laborer, and it was only four or five days since his temperature had gone down. His body was still weak and tired. He had gone out to seek work, but in vain. He had had no success. Hungry, thirsty, tired, everything was dark before his eyes. "Is the food ready, Amina dear?" he called out from the courtyard.

Without answering, his daughter quietly came out and stood leaning against the wall.

"Is the food ready?" Gafur repeated without receiving an answer.

"What do you say? No? Why?"

"There's no rice, father."

"No rice? Why didn't you tell me in the morning?"

"Why, I told you last night."

" 'I told you last night,' " mimicked Gafur. "How am I to remember what you told me last night?" His anger grew more and more violent at the sound of his own voice. "Of course, there's no rice!" he growled, with his face more distorted than ever. "What does it matter to you whether your father eats or not? But the young lady must have her three meals! In the future I shall lock up the rice when I go out. Give me some water to drink—I'm dying of thirst. . . . So you haven't any water, either!"

Amina remained standing with bowed head as before. Realizing that there was not even a drop of water in the house, he lost all self-control. Rushing at her, he slapped her face noisily. "Wretched girl! What do you do all day? So many people die—why don't you?"

The girl did not utter a word. She took the empty earthen pitcher and went out into the afternoon sun, quietly wiping her silent tears.

The moment she was out of sight, her father was overwhelmed with remorse. He alone knew how he had brought up that motherless girl. He knew that this affectionate, dutiful quiet daughter of his was not to blame. They had never had enough to eat even while their little store of rice lasted. It was impossible to eat three times a day. Nor was he unaware of the reason for the absence of water. The two or three tanks in the village had all dried up. The little water that there was still in the private tank of Shibu Babu was not for the public. A few holes had been dug at the bottom of the other tanks, but there was such crowding and jostling for a little water that this chit of a girl could not even approach them. She stood for hours on end and, after much begging, if somebody took pity on her, she returned home with a little water. He knew all this. Perhaps there was no water today or nobody had found time to take pity on her. Something of the sort must have happened, he thought, and his own eyes, too, filled with tears.

"Gafur! Are you in?" somebody cried out from the yard. The landlord's messenger had arrived.

"Yes, I'm in. Why?" answered Gafur bitterly.

"Master has sent for you. Come."

"I haven't had any food yet. I will come later," said Gafur.

Such impudence seemed intolerable to the messenger. "It's master's order to drag you to him and give you a good thrashing," he roared, calling the man ugly names.

Gafur lost self-control for the second time. "We are nobody's slave," he replied, returning similar compliments. "We pay rent to live here. I will not go."

But in this world it is not only futile for the small to appeal to authority, it is dangerous as well. Fortunately the tiny voice seldom reaches big ears or who knows what might happen? When Gafur returned home from the landlord's and quietly lay down, his face and eyes were swollen. The chief cause of so much suffering was Mahesh. When Gafur left home that morning, Mahesh broke loose from his tether, and, entering the grounds of the landlord, had eaten up flowers and upset the corn drying in the sun. When finally they tried to catch him, he had hurt the landlord's youngest daughter and had escaped. This was not the first time this had happened, but Gafur was forgiven because he was poor. If he had come round, and, as on other occasions, begged for the landlord's forgiveness, he would probably have been forgiven, but instead he had claimed that he paid rent, and that he was nobody's slave. This was too much for Shibu Babu, the *Zamindar*, to swallow. Gafur had borne the beatings and tortures without protest. At home, too, he lay in a corner without a word. Hunger and thirst he had forgotten, but his heart was burning within him like the sun outside. He had kept no count of how time passed.

He was suddenly shaken out of his listlessness by a shriek of a girl. She was prostrate on the ground. The pitcher which she had been carrying tumbled over, and Mahesh was sucking up the water as it flowed onto the earth. Gafur was completely out of his mind. Without waiting another moment he seized his plowhead he had left yesterday for repair, and with both hands struck it violently on the bent head of Mahesh. Once only Mahesh attempted to raise his head, but immediately his starving, lean body sagged to the ground. A few drops of blood from his ears rolled down. His whole body shook once or twice and then, stretching the fore and hind legs as far as they would reach, Mahesh fell dead. "What have you done, father? Our Mahesh is dead!" Amina burst out weeping.

Gafur did not move nor answer her. He remained staring without blinking at a pair of motionless, beady, black eyes.

Before two hours were out the tanners living at the end of the village came crowding in and carried off Mahesh on a bamboo pole. Shuddering at the sight of the shining knives in their hands, Gafur closed his eyes but did not speak.

The neighbors informed him that the landlord had sent for Tarkaratna to ask for his advice. How would Gafur pay for the penance which the killing of a sacred animal demanded?

Gafur made no reply to these remarks, but remained squatting with his chin resting on his knees.

"Amina, dear, come, let's go," said Gafur, rousing his daughter at the dead of night.

She had fallen asleep in the yard. "Where, father?" she asked, rubbing her eyes.

"To work at the jute mill at Fulbere," said the father.

The girl looked at him incredulously. Through all his misery he had declined to go to Fulbere. "No religion, no respect, no privacy for womenfolk there," she had often heard him say.

"Hurry up, my child; we have a long way to go," said Gafur.

Amina was going to collect the drinking bowl and her father's brass plate. "Leave them alone, darling. They'll pay for the penance for Mahesh," said Gafur.

In the dead of night Gafur set out, holding his daughter by the hand. He had nobody to call his own in the village. He had nothing to say to anybody. Crossing the yard, when he

reached the acacia, he stopped stock-still and burst out crying loudly. "Allah," he said, raising his face towards the star-
spangled black sky, "punish me as much as you like—
Mahesh died with thirst on his lips. Nobody left even the
tiniest bit of land for him to feed on. Please never forgive the
landlord his sin, who never let him eat the grass nor drink
the water you have given." They set out for the jute mill.

Translated by S. Sinha.

C. RAJAGOPALACHARI

C. Rajagopalachari was born in 1878 in the southern district of Salem, a thousand miles south of Delhi. His family were high-caste Brahmins but very poor. His school and college education was completed at Bangalore and he took his L.L.B. at Madras. "I did not go abroad for any education. I practiced law from 1900 to 1919. I never became a 'writer.' I was interested in social reform and the freedom of India. I wrote as and when I felt inclined, naturally only to further these causes and not as a professional or dedicated author."

Mr. Rajagopalachari joined Mahatma Gandhi's Non-Co-operation Movement in 1919 and was imprisoned several times between 1921 and 1942. In 1937, he was elected Prime Minister of the state of Madras under the scheme of provincial autonomy introduced by the British before World War II. After independence he served as Governor of Bengal, and from June, 1948, to January, 1950, he was Governor-General of India. He was Home Minister of India, 1950–1951, and Chief Minister from Madras, 1952–1954. At present he is the leader of the Swatantra (Freedom) party. In 1962, he came to the United States as a member of the Gandhi Peace Delegation to discuss the nuclear test ban with President Kennedy.

His publications include: The Fatal Cart and Other Stories; Way Out; Marcus Aurelius; *and* The Ramayana *and* The Mahabharata (*in English and Tamil*). *He lives in Madras and edits an English weekly called* Swarajaya.

Ardhanari

C. RAJAGOPALACHARI

ARDHANARI was a Harijan boy from the village of Kokkalai in Salem district. He went to Delhi with Sri Malkani, Secretary of the Society for the Service of the Untouchables. When Sri Malkani was in South India, he was very pleased with this boy, whom he met at Salem, and immediately decided to take him to Delhi with him. There he put him in a school and looked after him. He spoke to a well-known firm of traders in Delhi and got him a job in their office at Rs.60/- a month. As Ardhanari was honest, diligent, and had personality, he got on well. He was getting Rs.150/- a month before he was twenty-four; and when, sometime later, a place in a big mill belonging to the same firm fell vacant in Bangalore, they sent Ardhanari there on a salary of Rs.200/- a month.

He spent two happy years in Bangalore. His immediate senior, Govinda Rao, had had training in Manchester for two years. He and Ardhanari were of about the same age, and, as he liked Ardhanari's disposition and manners, they became close friends.

Govinda Rao had a sister called Pankaja. Brother and sister loved each other very much. Their parents had died when the girl was just ten years old, and she was now twenty and unmarried. She and Ardhanari often met as she accompanied her brother when he visited Ardhanari and when the latter came to see her brother. When Govinda Rao found that his sister and Ardhanari seemed to like each other, he was glad. He often asked himself: "Why should not these two marry and settle down here?"

One day Govinda Rao asked his sister, "Pankaja, have you ever thought about your marriage?"

"I have no strong feelings on the matter," she replied.

"Then, what about marrying our Ardhanari?"

Pankaja showed no objection to being thus questioned, but she evaded the question by talking about something else. Some weeks later, the same matter was broached again, casually.

"Why, Gopy, are you tired of me already? Am I a burden to you?" she said at first, and laughed. Then she began to cry. Girls, especially those who have lost their mothers, are very sensitive.

"Stupid, don't talk of being a burden or of my getting tired of you. Just tell me if you care for the idea of marriage. If you say no, that will please me, because then I can always have you with me," he said, and wiped her eyes. Then he said again, "Mother is dead. Who else is there to ask you what you feel about it?"

"If it comes about, I shall go through it. But what is the point in discussing it now?" asked Pankaja.

"You two seem to like each other. And as we have left off caring about caste or family, why should you not marry him?" he asked.

"What, indeed, have we to do with caste? But we do not yet know what he feels about it," said Pankaja.

"Don't worry about that. He must think himself very lucky if he gets someone like you for his wife," said Govinda Rao. He was sure there was no one to compare with his sister in the whole world.

When Ardhanari was told about this, his joy knew no bounds. But a minute later his face fell. "But how can that be, Govinda Rao?" he asked.

"Why? What is the trouble?" asked Govinda Rao.

"What is my caste and what is yours?" said Ardhanari.

"Oh! The question of caste! Nonsense!" Govinda Rao exclaimed and laughed. "What is a Brahmin? What is a non-

Brahmin? We stopped thinking about such things long ago. If you like each other and finally decide to marry, we need not worry about caste."

"I belong to the Coimbatore district. I am a Saiva Mudaliar." That was what Ardhanari had told them. A Saiva Mudaliar is a vegetarian high-caste non-Brahmin. Having said this on some occasion out of snobbish fear, he was unable to withdraw it afterwards. He was ashamed to confess the truth about his caste. In Delhi a few knew his antecedents, but none in Bangalore.

"What is Pankaja's wish?" asked Ardhanari.

"Pankaja seems to like you. Her replies to my questions show that she is willing."

"Is it not proper that I should ask her and find out for myself?" said Ardhanari.

"Yes," said Govinda Rao.

Thus the affair was put off. He resolved that he would tell Pankaja the truth, whatever might happen. But later his resolution failed.

"Why should I go out of my way to tell her this? If I do, Govinda Rao and Pankaja will both hate me. They say that they do not care for caste distinctions. But yet if they come to know that I am a pariah, they will never give their consent. Besides, I shall be considered a liar," he thought within himself.

Next day he thought the matter over again and went to Govinda Rao's house, intending to disclose the truth. But, again, on the way he debated within himself, "When we two love each other, what reason is there to consider this caste question? Why should we give any quarter to this injustice? Who created caste? Is it not all a lie? Why should I make so much of it and speak to her about it? Why should I speak to her about it and spoil the whole business? They have told me distinctly that they do not care about caste. Why, then, should I refer to it at all?" He made up his mind to suppress the truth.

"Pankaja, do you really like me? Shall we get married and live together?" he asked.

"But do you want to?" said Pankaja.

Ardhanari's father Muniappan, his brother Ranga, and mother Kuppayee all lived in the *cheri*, or pariah quarters, of the village Kokkolai. Both while in Delhi and in Bangalore, Ardhanari used to send them twenty rupees regularly every month. It was a princely allowance to them, and they lived on it very happily. They did not know what their son was earning, but twenty rupees a month seemed a great fortune to them. Unfortunately, Muniappan had the drink habit. When he began to get money regularly every month, his drinking became worse. Ranga did not like this, but could not prevent it. He was a teacher in a village school and was unmarried. When his mother pressed him to find a wife, he would say, "Not now, wait for some time more," and always put off the matter.

Ardhanari, after his transfer to Bangalore, used to visit his people twice a year. When he found his father addicted to drink, he felt ashamed beyond measure. He could not bear the dirt and untidiness of the house. He would stay there for only a day or two and then return as soon as possible.

"We will go with you, Ardhanari," his father would say whenever Ardhanari got ready to return to Bangalore.

"No, indeed. If they see you with me, they will dismiss me," Ardhanari would reply.

"Yes, Father, we people should not go there," Ranga would say.

Because he sent them money regularly, they would not argue much more about it. Thus it went on for some time.

Ardhanari thought it would be best for him to go somewhere far in the north again, once he was married.

"Though they are very kind to me, if they know that I am a pariah, things would certainly go wrong. Even supposing they do not mind, yet when they see the life and habits of my father and my people, Pankaja would certainly be disgusted. She would not even look at me afterwards." Ardhanari would talk to himself in this strain again and again, and further strengthen his resolve to hide the truth. He decided to marry as soon as possible and go away to some place in the north. He wrote letters to the directors of the company he served and asked for a transfer to some other mill in North India.

One day Pankaja quite unexpectedly said, "Ardhanari, I want very much to see your mother. We have both decided that you should take leave for a week and we all three should go and visit Coimbatore, Ootacamund, and other places. What do you say?"

Govinda Rao also said, "There is not much work in the office now. The first week of next month will suit us all very well."

Ardhanari's heart beat fast. "Oh, yes, we can do that. But I have a letter today that there is a severe epidemic of cholera in our village," he said.

Pankaja was all anxiety on hearing this. "Cholera! Have you asked your people to move elsewhere? Why not ask them to come over here?" she said.

"I was just thinking of doing so," said Ardhanari.

After three days Ardhanari got a letter from Ranga:

Blessings to small brother Ardhanari.

There is severe cholera here. There have been many deaths. We are afraid. Father continues as before. He does not listen to our advice. The money that you sent this month is all spent. If you can send us thirty rupees, we think of locking up the house and going to Salem to stay there till this fear of cholera is over.

Yours affectionately,

Ranga.

Ardhanari was surprised and shocked. "What is the meaning of this? What I said in deceit has turned out to be true. God is trying me, perhaps," he said to himself, and was undecided as to what he should do. He then thought he would send the money next day.

Ardhanari got no sleep that night.

Bad thoughts, shameful thoughts, kept stirring in his mind. Whenever he thought of his father, he felt disgust. The wish often arose in his mind that his father would die of cholera and relieve him of all this misery. Next moment, he would censure himself for this thought. He tossed restlessly on his bed all night and in the morning he took a cold bath. The postman brought letters. As he had expected, there was another letter from his village. With trembling hands, he opened it and read:

Father is suffering from cholera. We are greatly afraid. *Mariayee* must save us. We have not a *pie* with us. . . . Ranga.

When he read the letter, Ardhanari's face grew dark. He remained seated in his chair for quite a long time. He did not send any money that day.

Nor did he send any money the next day.

"How is cholera in your village?" asked Pankaja.

"Still very bad, I'm afraid," said Ardhanari.

"Is there enough sugar in the coffee?" asked Govinda Rao.

"Oh, yes! It is very good," said Ardhanari.

When he returned home, there was a letter waiting for him.

Mother too has cholera symptoms. You have not sent us any money. We are helpless. Come at once. . . . Ranga.

Ardhanari sent no money that day either. He had turned his heart into stone. "This disgraceful feature of my life will now disappear forever. This release looks like God's kindness to me. There is no *Dharma* or justice higher than His will. Why should I try to circumvent it? If father and mother die, there will then be nothing left to prevent my marriage with Pankaja."

Suddenly, "Tut! Tut! What a sinful thought, you wicked

man," someone appeared to reprimand him. When he turned his head round, he saw Pankaja standing behind him. He was alarmed that his secret was out. Then his mind grew clear again. No one had spoken. It was just an illusion of his mind.

"How did you come in without making any sound?" he asked.

Pankaja laughed, "I knocked at the door three times and then entered. You are worried about something, so you did not hear me come in," she said.

"I must go to my village. It appears the cholera is worse there now. My father and mother are there and I must make some arrangements for them," he said.

"Yes, that should have been done long ago. If you go there now, you must be very careful. You must neither eat nor drink while you are there," she said.

Ardhanari left for Salem the same night. But instead of going straight to Kokkalai, he delayed on the way, and only reached it after four days. His mother was already dead and poor Ranga had followed her. Only his drunkard father had escaped and was alive and well.

"Please take me to Bangalore. What shall I do here after this?" he begged Ardhanari. Ardhanari would not hear of it. He was adamant. "I will send you enough money. You must remain here. Do not ask to come with me, for I cannot take you," he said. Father entreated son like a helpless child.

"I can't stay here," he sobbed. Ardhanari refused to be moved by his weeping. "How can I give up Pankaja?" he said to himself, and would not listen to his father's lamentations. Next day he placed a ten-rupee note in his father's hand and left for Salem.

"Alas! What have I done! I have killed my mother and brother. Why did I do this? Is there another villain like me in this world? How can I forsake my father like this? What shall I tell Pankaja?"

Immersed in such thoughts, he could not sleep in the

train. When he arrived at Bangalore, he walked, in a dazed manner, the whole way to his house. There, he bolted the door and lay down. He did not send word to Govinda Rao or Pankaja about his return, nor did he go to the office.

The same night he took his luggage and again went to the railway station and bought a ticket for Salem.

At Salem, he heard that an *Adidravida* (Untouchable) had drowned himself in a well in Kokkalai. When he got to Kokkalai, he learned that the man was his own father.

Someone said that they were holding an inquest at the police station over Muniappan, the drunkard. He did not go there, but, unnoticed by anyone, returned to Salem and took a train to Bangalore.

"Pankaja, you must try to forget me," said Ardhanari.

"I shall do that afterwards. Tell me the news from Salem," said Pankaja.

"They are all dead. They are dead because I did not do what I should have done. I have lost all interest in life now. I am going to resign my job and go to my village. Please forget me," he said.

She looked at him two or three times. Then she got alarmed and ran to tell her brother.

Ardhanari had fever. At first the doctor said it was typhoid, then he said it was brain fever. He had to stay in bed for over a month. Govinda Rao and Pankaja remained at his bedside without rest till, after the fourth week, the fever came down.

"There is no more cause for anxiety," said the doctor. Very soon he was well enough to sit up in bed.

"I am a pariah, a sinner. I am really an untouchable, a liar. I renounce marriage. For God's sake, forget me," said Ardhanari.

Pankaja laughed. "What do I care of what caste you are? Why should we part from each other?" she said, trying to soothe him.

Ardhanari did not agree. "You do not mind my caste, I

know. But I am a murderer. I have killed my father and mother," he said, and told them the whole tale.

When he was quite well, he resigned his job and returned to Kokkolai. He is now the *Samiar,* or ascetic, who conducts the school in the Mariamman temple.

Translated by C. R. Ramaswami

PREM CHAND

Prem Chand (1880–1936) is generally acknowledged as the greatest novelist and short story writer in Hindi. He was born in a lower-middle-class family in North India. Dhanpat Rai Srivastava (for that was his real name) was a product of the Indo-Persian culture and he grew up in an atmosphere where both Hindi and Urdu were used and spoken. During his fifty-six years he wrote ten novels and about two hundred and fifty short stories. His earlier works were written in Urdu but in 1914 he switched to Hindi.

His childhood and youth were distinguished by extreme poverty and domestic tragedy. Both his parents died before he was out of his teens and so did his young wife. He held minor government jobs and after Soze-watan, his first collection of short stories, was banned in 1907 because of its nationalistic overtones, he wrote under the pseudonym of Prem Chand. His two literary and spiritual mentors were Tolstoy and Gandhi. He was also influenced by Victor Hugo and Romain Rolland. Marx and Freud were making their impact on Indian intellectuals at that time and Prem Chand was not untouched by this, but he had no faith in revolutionary methods and hence was more attracted to Gandhi's teachings. In 1920, when Gandhi launched the Non-Co-operation Movement against the British, Prem Chand resigned his government job and devoted his whole time to writing.

Prem Chand knew rural India at firsthand and he depicted the life of the peasantry with aston-

ishing faithfulness, insight, understanding, and sympthy.
He was a first-rate creative artist, immensely industrious
and painstaking. He was deeply moved by the lot of his
countrymen under foreign rule and he made his protest in
unequaled prose and without bitterness.

Prem Chand died in 1936. Chronic bankruptcy and ill
health were his lot throughout life. For him, fame and recognition followed death. A few months before he died his
best-known and most ambitious novel, Godan, was published. He had also translated into Hindi Shaw's Back to
Methuselah, Tolstoy's short stories, and Anatole France's
Thaïs.

"The Shroud," reprinted here, is brilliantly constructed.
To read it is to explore some of the neglected corners of our
mind and to be confronted with a dimension of life for
which there are no answers this side of the grave. Somerset
Maugham once said, "Money is the sixth sense which en-
ables you to enjoy the other five." Lack of it can make one
behave like a beast. The naked realism of "The Shroud" is
terrifying, and yet there is an economy of words and absence
of sentimentality that places Prem Chand among the greatest masters of the Indian short story.

The Shroud

PREM CHAND

At the door of the hut, before a fire which had already gone out, sat father and son; inside lay Budhia, the son's young wife, in the throes of childbirth. Now and then she would give out wails heartrending enough to upset them.

It was a winter night. Nature seemed dumb, and the village was all but darkness.

"Looks as if she won't last," said Ghisu. "It's been a hectic day. Why not peep in and see?"

"If she must die why doesn't she hurry?" said Madhav, irritated. "What can I do about it?"

"You're a heartless lout," rejoined Ghisu. "She made you happy for one whole year, and now this callousness!"

"Maybe, but I can't stand her writhing and wriggling."

Theirs was a family of cobblers notorious in the village. If Ghisu worked for one day, he would rest for three. Madhav was such a shirker that for every half an hour of work he would smoke for one hour. With the result that they hardly ever secured work. Neither would they dream of work if they had a handful of corn at home. When they starved for two or three days, Ghisu would climb a tree and fell some firewood and Madhav would take it to the market and sell it. While the money lasted, the two would loaf about. Then starvation would compel them to gather twigs or search for some job.

There was no dearth of work in the village. It was a peasant community where labor was always in demand. These two, however, were sent for only when the employer was obliged to get one man's work done by two.

Had Ghisu and Madhav turned sadhus they would have been happy indeed, for they were contented by nature and had great patience.

Theirs was a strange existence. A few earthen pots in the hut were all they owned. Tattered rags covered their naked-ness. Thus they floated through life, indifferent to every-thing. Heavily in debt, they suffered indignities, were even beaten up. But did they care?

So miserable was their life that people gave them petty loans even when there was little chance of their being re-paid. When the harvest time came, they would pilfer pota-toes and peas which they baked and ate or they dug up sugarcane which they munched at night.

Ghisu had spent his sixty years in such precarious exist-ence. And, like a worthy son, Madhav had followed in his footsteps. In fact, the son was outdoing his veteran father. And now too they sat before the dying embers and baked the potatoes which they had pilfered from someone's field.

Ghisu's wife had died long ago, but Madhav was married only last year. Ever since Budhia had come she had tried to bring some sort of order in the household. She would grind corn or cut grass to buy a seer of wheat flour for these shameless creatures to devour. This had only made these parasites idler. They even gave themselves airs. When offered employment they would shamefacedly demand double the wages. And now this woman was dying of labor pains and these two were waiting for her to die, so that they could sleep in peace!

Picking a potato from the ashes and peeling it, Ghisu said, "Do peep in and see what's happening. Must be the doing of some evil spirit. Even a witch doctor here will charge a rupee."

Madhav feared that if he went inside, Ghisu would gobble

up most of the potatoes. He replied, "I'm afraid to go in there."

"What's there to be afraid of when I am here?" asked Ghisu.

"Why don't you go in yourself?" rejoined Madhav.

"When my wife died," went on Ghisu, "I did not budge from her side for full three days. But yours, won't she feel shy before me? I who have never seen her face all these days, must I now look on her naked shame? What a state she must be in! Seeing me she won't even be able to writhe and toss freely!"

"What's worrying me is, what shall we do if a baby is born? We've no molass, no oil, no dry ginger in the house."

"Everything will come—let God give the baby first! The very people who now grudge us a copper will send for us and offer us silver. I had nine sons and never a thing in the house. But God somehow helped me ashore."

In a society where the lot of the hardworking peasant was not much better than theirs, and where only those who exploited the poor enjoyed the plums, such an attitude was nothing surprising. We might even say that Ghisu was much wiser than the peasants. Instead of following the herd of unthinking peasants, he had joined the unsavory ranks of the idlers, though he lacked the means to follow the ways and principles of the tribe. And so while others of the tribe had become leaders and headmen of the village, he was looked down upon. But he had the consolation that despite his destitution, he did not have to work half as hard as the peasants, and that no one could take undue advantage of his simplicity and his misery.

The two went on picking up the potatoes and eating them burning hot. They had not eaten anything since yesterday and could not wait to let them cool. Their tongues were repeatedly scorched. Once peeled the potatoes didn't seem too hot on the surface, but as soon as they were bitten into, the inside burnt their tongue, palate, and throat. There was more hazard in keeping the burning balls in the mouth than to swallow them, for inside the stomach there was ample machinery to cool them down. And so they went on swallowing fast, although the effort brought tears to their eyes.

Ghisu thought of the Thakur's wedding feast he had attended twenty years ago. The satisfaction which that feast had given him had made it memorable. He remembered it to this day.

"Can't forget that feast," said Ghisu. "Never since then had I such a bellyful of such food. The bride's people had fed all and sundry, young and old, with *puris* fried in pure ghee. Chutney, *raita*, three vegetables cooked dry and one in curry, curds and sweets. How can I now describe how delicious the feast was! No rationing, mind you. You had everything you wanted and as much. The people ate and ate until there was no room for a sip of water. But still the attendants go on pouring hot, round, fragrant *kachauris* on the leaf-plates. We protest, spreading our hands over the plates but they keep on pouring. And after we had washed, they gave us betel leaf and cardamom. But how could I look at betel leaf when I could hardly stand on my legs! I rushed straight to my bed and stretched myself out. The Thakur was indeed a large-hearted fellow."

Relishing all these delicacies in his mind, Madhav said, "Nobody gives us such feasts these days."

"How can they?" replied Ghisu. "Those days were different. Nowadays everyone thinks of economy. Don't spend on weddings! Don't spend on the last rites! What, I ask them, will they do with all this money grabbed from the poor? The grabbing goes on all the same—the economy is only in spending."

"You must have had about twenty *puris*?" asked Madhav.

"More than twenty."

"I would have eaten fifty."

"I couldn't have taken less than fifty. I was a hefty fellow. You're not even half of me."

They finished the potatoes, drank some water and lay down near the fire, covering the bodies with their dhotis, their legs curled up beneath their bellies. Like two large pythons coiled up.

And Budhia went on moaning.

II

In the morning Madhav went inside the hut. His wife lay cold, dead. Flies hovered round her face. The stony eyes stared fixedly upwards. The body was covered with dust. The child had died within the womb.

Madhav came running to Ghisu, and the two started wailing loudly and beating their chests.

The neighbors heard their wails and hastened to offer the customary condolences to the unfortunates.

But there was little time for much weeping. A shroud had to be procured and the firewood to cremate her; money was as scarce in the house as meat in a kite's nest.

Father and son hurried to the *Zamindar* weeping. The *Zamindar* hated the very sight of them. Time and again, he had thrashed them with his own hands, now for stealing and now for not turning up in time for work.

"What's the matter, Ghisu? Why this weeping?" asked the *Zamindar* contemptuously. "You're hardly to be seen these days. Looks as though you don't want to live in this village."

Touching the ground with his head Ghisu said with tears in his eyes, "I'm in great trouble, Master. Madhav's woman passed away last night. She was in great pain the whole night, Sire. We sat by her and got her what medicines we could, but she has deserted us. And now there is no one to give us a bread. We're undone, the home shattered. I am your slave, Master. Who but you will now make the last rites possible? We've spent everything we had on her illness. The body can be cremated only if the Master is kind. Where else can I go but your door?"

The *Zamindar* had a kind heart, but to do a good turn to Ghisu was like dyeing a black blanket. His first impulse was to tell him bluntly, "Get out of here. You never come when sent for, and today you are fawning on me because you are in dire need. You good-for-nothing *badmash!*"

But it was no occasion for anger or punishment. Fuming silently the *Zamindar* threw two rupees at them, without a look or word of consolation, as though casting off a burden.

Now that the *Zamindar* had parted with two rupees, how could the village moneylenders and shopkeepers dare refuse! Ghisu knew well enough how to trumpet the *Zamindar's* favor. Some gave him a two-anna piece, some a four-anna bit. Within an hour he had collected full five rupees in cash. Besides, he got some foodgrain here, some firewood there.

At noon Ghisu and Madhav set out for the market to buy a shroud. Other helping hands began cutting bamboo and other wood. The kind-hearted women of the village came to have a last look of the dead body and went back shedding tears over Budhia's fate.

III

On reaching the market Ghisu said, "We've enough fire-wood, Madhav, to cremate her. Haven't we?"

"Yes, we have enough," replied Madhav. "What we need now is a shroud."

"Let's buy a cheap one then."

"Yes, of course. It'll be dark by the time the body is taken out. Who sees the shroud at night?"

"What a silly custom that she who didn't have a rag to cover her living body should need a new shroud at death!"

"Just to be burnt with the body!"

"What else! Had we these five rupees earlier, we could have got some medicines for her."

Each had an inkling of what was in the other's mind. They went about the market from one cloth shop to another. They saw various kinds of cloth, silk and cotton, but could select nothing—until it became dark. Then, led by some mysterious power, they found themselves in front of a tavern and, as if the visit was predetermined, entered it.

For a while they stood undecided. Then Ghisu approached the counter and said, "Sahuji, a bottle for us too!"

This was followed by snacks and fried fish. The two of them sat in the veranda and went on drinking in peace. After several rounds in quick succession, they were in a state of exhilaration.

Ghisu spoke, "What use would have been a shroud? It would have been burnt after all. It couldn't possibly have accompanied her!"

Looking upwards at the sky—as if invoking the gods as witness to his innocence—Madhav said, "Such is the way of the world. Why otherwise would people give thousands of rupees to Brahmins? Who knows whether it is repaid in the other world?"

"The rich have money, let them waste it! What have we to waste?"

"But what will you tell the people? Won't they ask, where is the shroud?"

Ghisu laughed. "We'll tell them the rupees slipped down the waistband and got lost on the way. We searched hard but couldn't find them. People won't believe it, but will give us again all the same."

Madhav too laughed at this unexpected luck. He said, "She was a good soul, poor girl! Even in death she is feeding us."

More than half the bottle was now gone. Ghisu ordered two seers of *puris*, chutney, pickles, and meat. The shop was just across the road. Madhav hurried there and brought back the delicacies on two leaf-plates. A whole rupee and a half was spent. They had only a few coppers left.

They sat and ate the *puris* in great style, like a lion feasting on its prey in a forest. No one to answer to, no dread of public censure. They had got over such scruples long ago.

Ghisu philosophized, "Having brought us such joy, will she not be blest for it in the next world?"

Madhav reverently bowed his head in agreement. "Certainly she will be. O God, you know the hearts of all! Please take her to heaven. We bless her from the depth of our hearts. Such food we never had before!"

A moment later, Madhav had a doubt. He said, "We too shall go there one day, isn't it so, Dada?"

Ghisu made no reply to this naïve query. He did not want his present enjoyment to be disturbed by thoughts of the other world.

Madhav went on. "Suppose she asks us there, 'Why didn't you give me a shroud?'—what will you say?"

"Nonsense!"

"But ask she must!"

"How d'you know she won't have a shroud? D'you take me for such a fool? Have I been woolgathering all these sixty years? She shall have a shroud and a much better one at that!"

Madhav was unconvinced. "Who will give her?" he asked. "You've swallowed up the money. It's me she will take to task, for it's I who put the vermilion on her head!"

Ghisu flared up. "I tell you she shall have a shroud! Why don't you take my word?"

"Why not say who will give it?"

"The very people who gave it now. Maybe, they won't put cash in our hands."

As it grew darker and the stars shone brighter, the tavern became livelier. One sang, one bragged, some hugged one another, or thrust glasses to their companions' lips. The atmosphere was exhilarating, the air intoxicated. Some there were who got tipsy with the first round. More than the liquor it was the air that did it. Harassed by life they were drawn hither to forget for a while whether they were alive or dead or whether they existed at all.

And these two, father and son, continued to sip and be merry. All eyes were riveted on them. How lucky to have a whole bottle to themselves!

Having had their fill, Madhav gave away the leftover *puris* in the leaf-plate to a beggar who was standing and staring at them with hungry eyes. And for the first time in his life he felt the pride, glory, and the thrill of "giving."

"Take it, have your fill and bless her," said Ghisu. "She is dead to whom this is due. But your blessings will surely reach her. Let each hair of your body bless her. This is very hard-earned money."

Madhav again looked at the sky and said, "She will go to heaven, Dada. She will be queen in heaven."

Ghisu got up and as if floating on the waves of joy said, "Yes, my boy, she will go to heaven. She never harassed or bullied anyone here. And dying she has met the biggest craving of our life. If she doesn't go to heaven, will these pot-bellied ones go there—they who loot the poor right and left and bathe in the Ganges to wash away their sins and pour oblations in the temple?"

The mood of reverence underwent a swift change. Instability is a characteristic of intoxication. A fit of grief and despair overcame them.

Madhav said, "But the poor thing suffered a lot in her life, Dada. How painful was her death!"

Covering his eyes with his hands he started weeping and wailing aloud.

Ghisu consoled him. "Why do you weep, my boy? Rather rejoice that she is freed from this web of illusion. Escaped from this tangle of misery. She is lucky to have broken loose so soon from the bonds of *maya*."

The two stood up and began to sing:

Why this witchery of the eyes, O false charmer!

The eyes of all the topers were fixed on them, while the two went on singing, lost in themselves.

Then they began to dance. They bounced and jumped, reeled and wriggled, mimed and mimicked.

And in the end they fell down—dead drunk.

Translated by Madan Gopal

Resignation

THE office clerk is a dumb animal. Frown at a workman and he will frown back, swear at a coolie and he will throw off his load, insult a beggar and he will find a way of making you feel small; even a donkey will kick up his hind legs if you torment him too long. But not the office clerk. Frown at him, snub him, insult him, hit him, he will bear it all in silence. He has a control over his feelings that even a Yogi cannot acquire after years of penance and self-control. He is a picture of contentment, a paragon of patience, a personification of loyalty, a model of respectfulness. He is a combination of all the virtues. In spite of this, fortune never smiles on him. Even the straw roof of a miserable peasant's hut has its turn of luck. On Diwali night, the night of the Festival of Lamps, it is illuminated. It enjoys a shower of rain and takes pleasure in the sight of changing seasons. But the monotony of a Babu's life is never relieved. There is never a ray of light in his darkness. There is never the light of a smile on his face. Lala Fateh Chand was a member of this dumb species of humanity.

They say that the name affects the character to some extent. Now the name Fateh Chand means "The Moon of Victory," but from our hero's character it would be more appropriate to call him "The Slave of Defeat." He had failed in his office, he had failed in his private life, he was a failure among his friends, there was disappointment and defeat all around him. He had no son, but three daughters, no brothers but two sisters-in-law, and not a penny to fall back on. He was kind and generous by nature, which means that he was taken advantage of by everybody. On top of this his health was always poor. At the age of thirty-two his hair was like pepper and salt. His eyes were lustreless, his digestion ruined. His face was pale, his cheeks were sunken, his shoulders drooped. There was neither courage in his heart nor strength in his blood. He went to his office at nine in the morning and returned at six in the evening. After that he never had the energy to leave the house. He had no idea what was happening in the world outside the four walls of his home and office. His present life and future life, his heaven and hell was his office. He had no interest in religion, none in entertainment, not even in sin. It was years since he had even played a game of cards.

It was winter. The sky was slightly clouded. When Lala Fateh Chand returned from his office at half past five the candles had already been lit. As usual, he lay quietly on a charpoy in the dark room for about twenty minutes, before he could summon enough energy to open his mouth. He was still lying there when there was a noise outside. Someone shouted for him. His young daughter went out to look and reported that it was a peon from the office. At this moment his wife Sharda was scrubbing some utensils with ash before serving her husband's food. She told the girl: "Ask him what is the matter. He is just back from the office. Why do they want him again?"

The messenger replied: "The Sahib wants him. He says it's very important."

Lala Fateh Chand's forty winks were disturbed. He raised his tired head from the charpoy and asked, "Who is it?"

"It's the Chaprasi from the office," said Sharda.

"The Chaprasi? Why, does the Sahib want me?"

"Yes, he says he wants you urgently. What sort of man is this Sahib of yours? He always seems to want you. Hasn't he had enough out of you all day? Tell him you can't come. The worst he can do is to take this wretched job from you. Let him!"

Fateh Chand muttered as if talking to himself: "I had

finished everything. What does he want me for? It's funny."
And then he shouted to the Chaprasi who was still standing
outside the house: "I am coming," and got ready to go.

"Have something to eat. Once you start talking to the
Chaprasi you'll forget everything else," said Sharda.

She brought him a bowl of lentil porridge. Fateh Chand
had got up to go. When he saw this refreshment he sat down
again, watched it hungrily for some time and then asked his
wife, "Have the children had some?"

Sharda retorted angrily, as if she had been expecting this
question: "Yes, yes! They have had their share. Now you eat
some."

At this moment the youngest daughter appeared from
somewhere and stood nearby. Sharda looked daggers at her.
"What are you doing here? Go and play outside," she said.

"Don't frighten the child," said Fateh Chand. "Come,
Chunni, come and sit here. Have a little of this."

Casting a look of fear at her mother Chunni ran into the
street.

Sharda said: "There's not much of it as it is. Not enough
for you to start giving it away. If you give it to her the other
two will be asking for it as well."

At this moment the Chaprasi again shouted from outside:
"Babuji, it's getting late!"

"Why don't you tell him you can't come at this time of
night?" said Sharda.

"How can I when I depend on him for my livelihood?"

"You're letting him work you to death! Have you looked at
your face in the mirror? You look as if you'd been ill for six
months."

Fateh Chand ate a few spoonfuls of the porridge, quickly
drank a glass of water and hurried away. He did not even
wait for Sharda to finish a paan for him.

The Chaprasi said on seeing him, "You've taken a long
time, Babuji. Now let us hurry. Otherwise Sahib will start
swearing as soon as he sees you."

Fateh Chand tried to run for a few paces. Then he gave it up.

"He can swear if he likes," he said. "I can't run. Is he at his bungalow or at the office?"

The Chaprasi said: "Why should *he* be at the office? Is he a king or is he a clown?"

The Chaprasi was used to walking fast. Babu Fateh Chand on the contrary was used to walking slowly. But how could he confess this? He had a little pride left. He made efforts to keep abreast, but it was no use. He felt a pain in his ribs and he could not breathe easily. His head swayed and his whole body broke into a clammy sweat. Fireflies flitted before his eyes. The Chaprasi warned him bullyingly: "Walk a bit faster, Babuji! You're too slow."

Fateh Chand had difficulty in speaking. "You get along. Tell him I'll be there presently."

And he sat down on a platform at the side of the road. He held his head between his hands and drew deep breaths. When the Chaprasi saw him like this, he said nothing and went on. Fateh Chand was afraid of what this devil might go and tell the Englishman. He got up with an effort and started again. A child could have knocked him down. Somehow he stumbled along and reached the Sahib's bungalow.

The Sahib was walking up and down in the verandah. He looked again and again at the gate and was furious to see nobody coming. When he saw the Chaprasi he shouted: "Where have you been all the time?"

Standing on the steps of the verandah, the Chaprasi replied, "Huzoor, Fateh Chand took so long that I couldn't wait any longer. You can see I have run all the way back."

"What did the Babu say?" said the Sahib in his bad Hindustani.

"He's coming. He took nearly an hour getting out of the house."

In the meantime Fateh Chand entered the spacious compound of the bungalow, came near and salaamed to the

Sahib, bowing very low. The Sahib snapped at him: "Why are you so late?"

When Fateh Chand saw the Sahib's expression his blood ran cold.

"Huzoor, I left the office only a short while ago. But as soon as the Chaprasi called I left the house, as quickly as I could."

"You are telling a lie. I've been waiting here for an hour."

"Huzoor, I am not lying. Perhaps it has taken me more than the usual time to walk because I am not feeling very well, but I left the house as soon as the Chaprasi called for me."

The Sahib brandished the cane he was holding. He was obviously drunk. He shouted, "Shut up you swine! I've been standing here waiting for over an hour. Hold your ears and ask forgiveness."

Fateh Chand controlled himself as if he were swallowing blood. He said: "Huzoor, I worked today for more than ten hours in the office—I never . . ."

"Shut up, you swine! Hold your ears!"

"I have done nothing wrong."

"Chaprasi, you pull this swine's ears!" bawled the drunken Englishman.

The Chaprasi answered in a low but firm voice: "Huzoor, he is also my superior. How can I pull his ears?"

"Pull his ears, I say! If you don't I'll thrash you!"

The Chaprasi replied: "Huzoor, I came to the office to serve, not to be beaten. I, too, have my self-respect. Huzoor can take my job from me. I am prepared to obey all your orders but I cannot lay hands on another's self-respect. I shan't keep this job forever. I cannot make enemies with the world for its sake."

The Sahib could not control his anger. He rushed at the Chaprasi with his cane. The Chaprasi knew it was no longer safe to wait and took to his heels.

Fateh Chand stood silent, transfixed. When the Sahib

could not get at the Chaprasi he came at him. He caught both his ears and shook him. "You swine! You're insubordinate! Go and bring the file from the office."

Fateh Chand said, nursing his ears, "Which file, sir?"

"Which file . . . which file . . . Are you deaf? I want the file. . . . Do you hear?"

Fateh Chand mustered some courage and asked with some disgust: "Which file do you want?"

He was at a loss. But he did not have the courage to pursue the question. The Sahib was by nature a bad-tempered man, on top of that he was drunk with power, and on top of that he was drunk with whiskey. No one could predict what he would do next. So he started walking quietly towards the office.

"Run!" shouted the Sahib.

"Huzoor, I cannot run," said the clerk.

"You're getting lazy, are you? I'll show you how to run. Run, will you, run." He kicked him from behind.

Fateh Chand was an office clerk, but he was also a human being. If he had had any strength he would not have borne so much indignity from a drunkard. But as it was it was useless to resist. He ran out of the gate and reached the road.

Fateh Chand did not go to the office. The Sahib had not even told him exactly which file he wanted. Perhaps he was too drunk to think it necessary to mention it. He started walking home, slowly, because the pain and anguish of this unwarranted humiliation had put chains on his feet. It is true that the Sahib was much stronger physically, but could he not at least have given him a piece of his mind? Why had he not taken off his shoe and hit him on the face?

But there was really no help for it, he thought. The Englishman could have shot him dead. At the most they would give him a light sentence of a couple of months, or a fine of three or four hundred rupees. But *his* whole family would be ruined. There was no one who would look after his children. Perhaps they would die of starvation in the streets.

Oh, why wasn't he a bit richer? If he had even a little money to fall back on he would not tolerate this treatment. He wouldn't have minded being killed after he had given a proper lesson to that bully. He wasn't afraid for his own sake. There were no great pleasures in life he would be sorry to leave. Only his wife . . . his children . . .

He thought of all sorts of things as he went along. Why had he neglected his health so badly? He ought always to carry a knife. He ought to have slapped the Sahib on the face. Perhaps the Sahib's khansamas and other servants would have thrashed him till he was unconscious, maybe till he was dead. Then it would have got round that someone had really stood up against oppression. After all, he had to die someday, and he woudn't be able to look after his family then. There would have been some honor in that kind of death. This last thought fired him so much that he turned back and took a few steps towards the bungalow, but then he faltered again.

Very likely the Sahib had left for his club. What was the use of inviting more trouble? What had already happened was enough.

As soon as he got back home Sharda asked: "Why did he call you? You are very late."

Lying down on his charpoy Fateh Chand said: "He was drunk; he abused me, the devil; he insulted me. The only thing he kept on repeating was, 'Why are you late?' He asked the peon to pull my ears."

Sharda answered angrily, "Why didn't you hit him on the face with your shoe?"

Fateh Chand continued: "The Chaprasi is a good fellow; he said quite plainly, 'Huzoor, I am not in your service in order to humiliate respectable people.' And then he salaamed him and went away."

"That really was brave of him. Why didn't you give the Englishman a piece of your mind?"

"But I did. I gave him more than a piece of my mind. He

rushed at me with his stick. I took off my shoe, he beat me with his stick, I beat him with my shoe."

Sharda was thrilled. She said: "Really? His face must have been a sight!"

"His face looked as if somebody had been over it with a broom."

"You did well! If I was there I wouldn't have left him alive."

"Well, I've given him a beating but things won't be simple now; I don't know what's coming. I shall lose my job, of course, and maybe I shall be put in prison as well."

"Why should you be put in prison? Is there no justice in the world? Why did he abuse you? He hit you first, didn't he?"

"Nobody will listen to me. Even the judges will be on his side."

"Never mind. You'll see now, no English officer will dare to treat his subordinates like that."

"He might have shot me."

"Somebody would have seen him."

Fateh Chand said with a smile: "What would have happened to you then?"

"God would have looked after us. The biggest thing for a man is to keep his honor; if you lose your honor, you don't deserve to look after your children. Since you have beaten that devil, I am proud of you. If you had borne the insult silently, I would have hated to look at your face; maybe I would not have said anything to you, but in my heart I would have lost all respect for you."

In a calm, cool voice Sharda went on: "Now, whatever the consequences are, I shall face them joyfully. Hey, where are you going? Listen, listen . . ."

Like a madman, Fateh Chand ran out of the house. Sharda kept shouting after him, but he did not reply. He was going towards the bungalow; no longer cringing with fright, but holding his head up with pride. There was iron resolution in his face. He was a changed man. Instead of that weak, lifeless pale office clerk, here was a man, an active, brave, strong human being, walking with a purpose. He first went to a friend's house and borrowed a good strong stick. Then he went on to the bungalow.

It was nine o'clock. The Sahib was at dinner, but today Fateh Chand did not wait for him to finish his meal. As soon as the khansama had finished serving the meal and gone back to the kitchen he lifted the curtain and went inside. The room was flooded with electric light. The floor was covered with a carpet, so beautiful, so expensive that Fateh Chand had not seen the like even on the day of his marriage. The Sahib looked at him with furious eyes.

"Get out. Why have you come in without permission?"

Fateh Chand raised his stick and said: "You wanted the file; I have brought the file. Finish your meal and then I'll show it to you. Till then I shall sit here. Have a good meal, maybe it will be your last."

The Sahib was stunned. He looked at Fateh Chand with an expression half of fear and half of anger. He realized that the man was desperate. Physically he was weak, but it was certain that he had come prepared to return a stone for a brick; no, not a stone, but iron. The Sahib was afraid. It is easy to beat a dog so long as he does not growl; but when he snarls back at you you lose your determination. That was exactly what the Sahib felt. So long as he knew that Fateh Chand would bear abuses and even kicks silently he felt tough, but now that he was in a different mood and was watching every one of his movements like a cat, the Sahib's resolution failed him. He knew that one insulting word would bring a blow from that stick. True, he could dismiss him. True, he could even get him sent to jail; but he knew that he could not escape scandal and trouble. So, like a far-sighted man, he became mild and diplomatic, and said: "My dear man, you seem to be annoyed with me. Why are you annoyed? Have I said anything to upset you?"

"Half an hour ago you pulled my ears and called me a

damn fool a hundred times. Can it be that you have forgotten so soon, Sahib?"

"I pulled your ears! You must be joking. Do you think I am mad?"

"The peon is a witness. And your servants were watching, too."

"When did I do all this?"

"Only half an hour ago. You sent for me and then you pulled my ears and kicked me."

"Really! The fact is, Babuji, I must confess that I was a bit drunk. The bearer gave me too much whiskey. I don't remember anything. My God! Did I do that?"

"If you had shot me while you were drunk, would I not have died? If everything is forgivable to a drunkard then just now it is I who am drunk. And my decision is that you shall hold your ears and ask my forgiveness, and swear that you will not treat people again like that. Otherwise, I will teach you a lesson. And don't you dare to move. The moment you leave your chair, I'll crack your skull. Now hold your ears."

The Sahib tried to laugh and said: "Well, Babuji you have a sense of humor, haven't you? Well, if I have said something rude to you, please forgive me."

"Hold your ears," said Fateh Chand, brandishing his stick.

The Englishman was not willing to go through this humiliating ritual so lightly. He jumped from his chair and tried to snatch the stick from Fateh Chand's hands, but Fateh Chand was prepared for this. Before the Sahib had left the table, he gave him one full blow on his bare head. The Sahib's skull started singing. For a minute he held his head in both hands and then said: "I shall dismiss you."

"I don't care. But today I shan't leave until you hold your ears and swear that you won't behave towards people as you behaved to me. And if you don't do it straight away the second blow is coming." So saying he lifted the stick high.

The Sahib had not yet forgotten the first blow. He immediately put his hands on his ears and said: "There! Are you satisfied now?"

"You won't swear at people any more?"

"No."

"If you ever do so, remember that I shan't be far away."

"I'll never swear at anybody," said the Sahib in his bad Hindustani.

"Good. And now I shall leave you. From today I am no longer your clerk. I shall send in my written resignation tomorrow, explaining that because of your bad manners I am not willing to serve under you."

"But why resign? I won't dismiss you."

"I don't want to serve under an ill-mannered bully like you any longer. That is why."

And having said this Fateh Chand left the room and with an easy mind started walking back home. He had a sense of true victory and personal freedom. Never in his life had he experienced such happiness.

Translated by D. Anand

MULK RAJ ANAND

Mulk Raj Anand was born December 12, 1905, in Peshawar, North West Frontier Province. His father came from the Silver and Coppersmith Craft but later joined the British-Indian army; his mother was a peasant woman from Central Punjab.

In his own words, he was "badly educated in the schools and colleges of the Punjab; made up some arrears of understanding while researching for a doctor's degree in philosophy in University College, London, and at Cambridge." He writes that he has been influenced by Tagore, Iqbal, Tolstoy, Gorki, E. M. Forster, Malraux, Céline, Henry Miller, and the Chinese writer Luhsun.

He writes in English and his novels include, Untouchable (*1935*), Coolie (*1936*), The Black Waters (*1940*), The Sword and the Sickle (*1942*), Seven Summers (*1948*), *and* The Private Life of an Indian Prince (*1951*).

For several years Anand has been editor of MARG, *an English-language monthly devoted to the arts. He was for a time Tagore Professor of Art and Literature at the University of Punjab in Chandigarh.*

Anand considers the major achievement of modern Indian literature to be the "synthesis of Western and Indian values resulting in renascent efforts towards the making of 'modern' sensibility and consciousness."

The Barber's Trade Union

(*To John Lehmann*)

MULK RAJ ANAND

AMONG the makers of modern India, Chandu, the barber boy of our village, has a place which will be denied him unless I press for the recognition of his contribution to history. Chandu's peculiar claim to recognition rested, to tell the truth, on an exploit of which he did not know the full significance. But then, unlike most great men of India today, he had no very exaggerated notion of his own importance, though he shared with them a certain naïve egotism which was sometimes disconcerting and sometimes rather charming.

I knew Chandu ever since the days when he wore a piece of rag in the middle of his naked, distended-bellied body, and when we wallowed together in the mire of the village lanes, playing at soldiering, shopkeeping, or clerking and other little games which we invented for the delectation of our two selves and of our mothers, who alone of all the elders condescended to notice us.

Chandu was my senior by about six months, and he always took the lead in all matters. And I willingly followed, because truly he was a genius at catching wasps, and at pressing the poison out of their tails, at tying their tiny legs to cotton thread and flying them, while I always got stung on the cheeks if I dared to go anywhere near the platform of the village well where these insects settled on the puddles to drink water.

When we grew up he still seemed to me the embodiment of perfection, because he could make and fly paper kites of such intricate design and of such balance as I could never achieve.

To be sure, he was not so good at doing sums at school as I was, perhaps because his father apprenticed him early to the hereditary profession of the barber's caste and sent him out haircutting in the village, and he had no time for the home tasks which our schoolmaster gave us. But he was better than I at reciting poetry, any day, for not only did he remember by rote the verses in the textbook, but he could repeat the endless pages of prose in that book so that they seemed like poetry.

My mother resented the fact that Chandu won a scholarship at school while I had to pay fees to be taught. And she constantly dissuaded me from playing with him, saying that Chandu was a low-caste barber's son and that I ought to keep up the status of my caste and class. But whatever innate ideas I had inherited from my forefathers, I certainly hadn't inherited any sense of superiority. Indeed, I was always rather ashamed of the red caste mark which my mother put on my forehead every morning, and of the formalized pattern of the *uchkin,* the tight cotton trousers, the gold-worked shoes, and the silk turban in which I dressed; and I longed for the right to wear all the spectacular conglomeration of clothes which Chandu wore—a pair of khaki shorts which the retired Subedar had given him, a frayed black velvet waistcoat, decorated all over with shell buttons, and a round felt cap which had once belonged to Lalla Hukam Chand, the lawyer of our village.

And I envied Chandu the freedom of movement which he enjoyed after his father died of plague. For then he would do the round of shaving and haircutting at the houses of the high-caste notables in the morning, bathe and dress, and then steal a ride to town, six miles away, on the footrest of the closed carriage in which Lalla Hukam Chand traveled to town.

But Chandu was kind to me. He knew that I was seldom taken to town, and that I had to trudge three weary miles to a secondary school in the big village of Joadiala with the fear of God in my heart, while he had been completely absolved from the ordeal of being flogged by cruel masters as he had left school after his father's death. So he always brought me some gift or other from the town—a paint brush, or gold ink, or white chalk, or a double-edged penknife to sharpen pencils with; and he would entertain me with long merry descriptions of the variety of things he saw in the bazaars of civilization.

He was particularly detailed in his description of the wonderful English styles in clothes which he saw the Sahibs and the lawyers, the *chaprasis* and the policemen wearing at the District Court, where he had to wait for the journey home at the back of Lalla Hukam Chand's phaeton. And, once or twice, he expressed to me a secret wish he had to steal some money from the pitcher where his mother kept the emoluments of his professional skill, to buy himself a rig-out like that of Kalan Khan, the dentist, who, he said, performed miracles in the town, fitting people with rows of teeth and even new eyes. He described to me the appearance of Kalan Khan, a young man with hair parted on one side, and dressed in a starched shirt, with an ivory collar and bow tie, a black coat and striped trousers, and a wonderful rubber overcoat and pumps. And he recounted to me the skill with which this magician unpacked an Angrezi leather handbag and flourished his shining steel instruments.

Then he asked my advice on the question of whether, as a barber educated to the fifth primary class, he would not look more dignified if he, too, wore a dress in the style of Dr. Kalan Khan, "for though I am not a highly educated doctor," he said, "I learnt how to treat pimples, boils, and cuts on people's bodies from my father, who learnt them from his father before him."

I agreed with his project and encouraged him with the

enthusiasm I felt for everything that my hero thought or did.

One day I was thrilled to find Chandu at the door of my house in the morning. He was dressed up in a white turban, a white rubber coat (a little too big for him, but nevertheless very splendid), a pair of pumps in which I could see my face reflected in clear silhouette, and he had a leather bag in his hand. He was setting off on his round and had come to show me how grand he looked in his new rig-out.

"Marvelous!" I said. "Marvelous!"

And he rushed off towards the house of the landlord, whom he shaved every morning, myself following admiringly behind.

There were not many people in the street at this time. So I alone witnessed the glory of Chandu, dressed up as a doctor, except, of course, that he himself seemed rather self-conscious as he strutted up the street, carefully avoiding the taint of cow-dung cakes which the village women stuck to the walls, and the dirty water which flowed through the drains. But as we entered the home of the landlord we met Devi, the landlord's little son, who clapped his hands with joy and shouted to announce the coming of Chandu, the barber, in a beautiful heroic dress like that of the Padre Sahib of the Mission School.

"Ram! Ram! Ram!" said Bijay Chand, the burly landlord, touching the sacred thread which hung over his ear since he had just been to the lavatory. "The son of a pig! He is bringing a leather bag of cowhide into our house and a coat of the marrow of, I don't know, some other animal, and those evil black Angrezi shoes. Get out! Get out! You son of a devil! You will defile my religion. I suppose you have no fear of anyone now that your father is dead!"

"But I am wearing the clothes of a doctor, Jagirdar Sahib," said Chandu.

"Go away you, swine, go away and wear clothes befitting your low status as a barber, and don't let me see you practicing any of your newfangled notions, or else I will have you flogged!"

"But Rai Bijay Chand Sahib!" Chandu appealed.

"Get away! Get away! You useless one!" the landlord shouted. "Don't come any nearer, or we will have to treat the whole house with the sacred cow dung to purify it."

Chandu returned. His face was flushed. He was completely taken aback. He did not look at me because of the shame he felt at being insulted before me whose hero he knew he was. And he rushed towards the shop of Thanu Ram, the Sahukar of the village, who kept a grocer's store at the corner of the lane.

Devi, the landlord's son, had begun to cry at his father's harsh words, and I stopped to quieten him. When I got to the head of the lane I saw the Sahukar with one end of the scale in which he had been weighing grain lifted in one hand, abusing Chandu in the foulest way. "You little swine, you go disguising yourself as a clown when you ought to be bearing your responsibilities and looking after your old mother. You go wearing the defiled clothes of the hospital folk! Go, and come back in your own clothes! Then I shall let you cut my hair!" And as he said so he felt for the ritual tuft knot on top of his head.

Chandu looked very crestfallen, and ran in a wild rage past me, as if I had been responsible for these mishaps. And I nearly cried to think that he hated me now just because I belonged to a superior caste.

"Go to Pandit Parmanand!" I shouted after him. "And tell him that these garments you are wearing are not unclean."

"Ho, so you are in league with him," said Pandit Parmanand, emerging from the landlord's home, where he had been apparently summoned to discuss this unholy emergency. "You boys have been spoiled by the school education which you have got. It may be all right for you to wear those things because you are going to be a learned man, but what right has that low-caste boy to such apparel? He has got to touch our beards, our heads, and our hands. He is defiled enough by God. Why does he want to become more defiled? You are a high-caste boy. And he is a low-caste devil! He is a rogue!"

Chandu had heard this. He did not look back and ran in a flurry, as if he were set on some purpose which occupied him more than the abuse which had been the cause of his flight.

My mother called to me and said it was time for me to eat and go to school, or I should be late. And she could not resist the temptation to lecture me again about my association with the barber boy.

But I was very disturbed about Chandu's fate all day, and, on my way back from school, I called in at the hovel where he lived with his mother.

His mother was well known for a cantankerous old woman, because she, a low-caste woman, dared to see the upper-caste people as they never dared to see themselves. She was always very kind to me, though she spoke to me too in a bantering manner, which she had acquired through the suffering and humiliations of sixty-odd years. Turning to me she said: "Well, you have come, have you, to look for your friend. If your mother knew that you were here she would scratch my eyes out for casting my evil eye on your sweet face. And you, are you as innocent as you look or are you a sneaking little hypocrite like the rest of your lot?"

"Where is Chandu, then, mother?" I said.

"I don't know, son," she said, now in a sincere simple manner. "He went up town way and says he earned some money shaving people on the roadside. I don't know what he is up to. I don't think he ought to annoy the clients his father served. He is a child and gets funny notions into his head and they ought not to be angry with him. He is only a boy. You want to see him and go out playing, I suppose. Very well, I will tell him when he comes. He has just gone up the road, I think!"

"All right, mother," I said, and went home.

Chandu whistled for me that afternoon in the usual code whistle which we had arranged to evade the reproaches of interfering elders that our association often provoked.

"Come for a walk to the bazaar," he said. "I want to talk to you." And hardly had I joined him when he began: "Do you know, I earned a rupee shaving and haircutting near the court this morning. If I hadn't had to come back on the back bar of Hukam Chand's carriage early in the afternoon, I should have earned more. But I am going to teach these orthodox idiots a lesson. I am going on strike. I shall not go to their houses to attend to them. I am going to buy a Japanese bicycle from the gambling son of Lalla Hukam Chand for five rupees, and I shall learn to ride it and I will go to town on it every day. Won't I look grand, riding on a bicycle, with my overcoat, my black leather shoes, and a white turban on my head, specially as there is a peg in front of the two-wheeled carriage for hanging my tool bag?"

"Yes," I agreed, greatly thrilled, not because I imagined the glory of Chandu seated on a bicycle, but because I felt myself nearer the goal of my own ambition; since I felt that if Chandu acquired a bicycle he would at least let me ride to town on the elongated bolt at the back wheel or on the front bar, if he didn't let me learn to ride myself and lend me the machine every now and then.

Chandu negotiated the deal about the bicycle with an assurance that seemed to me a revelation of his capacity for business such as I had never suspected in him, from the reckless way he spent his money. And then he said to me in a confidential voice: "You wait for another day or two. I shall show you something which will make you laugh as you have never laughed before."

"Tell me now," I insisted, with an impatience sharpened by the rhythm of the excitement with which the spirit of his adventure filled my being.

"No, you wait," he said. "I can only give you a hint at the moment. It is a secret that only a barber can know. Now

THE BARBER'S TRADE UNION 101

let me get on with the job of learning to handle this machine. You hold it while I get on it, and I think it will be all right."

"But," I said, "this is not the way to learn to ride a bicycle. My father learned to ride from the peg at the back, and my brother learnt to ride by first trying to balance on the pedal."

"Your father is a top-heavy baboon!" said Chandu. "And your brother is a long-legged spider."

"I," he continued, "was born, my mother tells me, upside down."

"All right," I said. And I held the bicycle for him. But while my gaze concentrated with admiration on the brilliant sheen of the polished bars, I lost my grip and Chandu fell on the other side with a thud, along with the machine.

There were peals of laughter from the shop of the Sahukar, where several peasants congregated round the figure of the landlord. And then the Sahukar could be heard shouting: "Serve you right, you rascally son of the iron age! Break your bones and die, you upstart! You won't come to your senses otherwise!"

Chandu hung his head with shame, and muttered an oath at me, "You fool, you are no good!" though I had thought that he would grip me by the neck and give me a good thrashing for being the cause of his discomfiture. Then he looked at me, smiled embarrassedly, and said: "We will see who has the last laugh, I or they."

"I will hold the machine tightly this time," I said earnestly, and I picked it up from where it lay.

"Yes, break your bones, you swine," came the landlord's call.

"Don't you care!" Chandu said to me. "I will show them." And he mounted the bicycle as I exerted all my strength to hold it tight. Then he said: "Let go!"

I released my grip.

He had pressed the pedal with a downward pressure of his right foot, hard, and, as the wheels revolved, he swayed dangerously to one side. But he had pushed the other pedal

now. The machine balanced, inclining to the right a little, so
that I saw Chandu lift his rump from the saddle in the most
frightening manner. He hung precariously for a moment.
His handles wobbled dangerously. He was tottering. At this
juncture a mixed noise of laughter and sarcasm arose from
the congregation at the shop and I thought that Chandu
would come to grief with this confusion, if not on account of
his utter incapacity. By a curious miracle, however, Chandu's feet had got into the right rhythm for pedaling and his
handle had adjusted itself to his stiff hands, and he rode off
with me running behind him, bursting myself with enthusiastic "Shabashes."

A half a mile run and he repeated the trick.

Though I was very eager to share the joy of his newly
acquired skill, I didn't see Chandu the next day, as I was
being taken to see my aunts in Verka, straight from school.

But on the third day he called for me and said that he
would show me the joke he had talked of the other day. I
followed quickly, asking the while: "Tell me, what is it all
about?"

"Look," he said, hiding behind the oven of the village
potter. "Do you see the congregation of men in the Sahukar's
shop? Try and see who's there."

I explored the various faces and, for a moment, I was
quite baffled.

"Only the peasants sitting round waiting for the landlord,"
I said.

"Look again, idiot," he said, "and see. The landlord is there,
his long-jawed face dirtied by the white scum of his un-
shaved beard."

"Ha! Ha!" I shouted hilariously, struck by the contradic-
tion of the big thick moustache (which I knew the landlord
dyed) with the prickly white bush on his jowls. "Ha! Ha!"
I roared, "a sick lion! He looks seedy!"

"Sh!" warned Chandu. "Don't make a row! But look at the
Sahukar. He looks like a leper with the brown tinge of

tobacco on his walrus moustache which I once used to trim.
Now you run past the shop and call 'Beavers, beavers!' They
can't say anything to you!"

I was too impetuous a disciple of the impish Chandu to
wait to deliberate.

"Beavers! Beavers! Beavers!" I shouted as I ran past the
shop to the edge of the platform by the banyan tree.

The peasants who were gathered round the shop burst out
laughing, as they had apparently been itching to, for they
had noticed the strong growths on the elders' faces, though
they had not dared to say anything.

"Catch him, catch him, the little rogue!" shouted the
Sahukar. "He is in league with that barber boy, Chandu!"

But, of course, I had climbed up the banyan tree, from
which I jumped on to the wall of the temple and shouted my
slogan at the priest.

The rumor about the barber boy's strike spread, and jokes
about the unkempt beards of the elders of the village became
current in every home. Even those who were of high castes,
even the members of the families of the elders, began to
giggle with laughter at the shabby appearance of the great
ones and made rude remarks about their persons. And it
was said that at least the landlord's wife threatened to run
away with somebody, because, being younger than her husband by twenty years, she had borne with him as long as he
kept himself in trim, but was now disgusted with him beyond the limits of reconciliation.

Chandu did good business in town during these days and
saved money, even though he bought new clothes and new
tools for himself and gave me various presents.

The village elders threatened to have him sent to prison
for his offences, and ordered his mother to force him to obey
before they committed him to the police for a breach of the
peace.

But Chandu's mother had for the first time in her life
touched the edge of prosperity, and she told them all what

she thought of them in a language even plainer than that in which she had always addressed them.

Then they thought of getting the barber of Verka to come and attend them, and offered him an anna instead of the two pice they had usually paid to Chandu.

Chandu, however, had conceived a new notion this time, newer than those he had ever thought of before. Having seen the shop of Nringan Das, the barber of the town, he had applied his brain to the scheme of opening a shop on the wayside at the head of the bazaar, in partnership with his cousin, the barber of Verka, and with Dhunoo and the other barbers within a range of seven miles from his village. He proposed his new idea to his cousin and Dhunoo and all the other barbers at a special meeting of his craft, and, by that gift of the gab which he had, besides his other qualities of Head and Heart, he convinced them all that it was time that the elders of the village came to them to be shaved rather than that they should dance attendance upon their lords and masters.

Rajkot District Barber Brothers' Hairdressing and Shaving Saloon has been followed by many other active trade unions of working men in our parts.

The Informer

THERE were seven of us, or rather six, because the seventh behaved merely as a cipher, or follower, doing what we did, saying what we said. If, for instance, we had an all-night session to discuss ways and means of contacting our friends in different parts of the country, he would never make an original suggestion but sit up all night, even though he had to be fighting sleep in order to keep awake; and if any of us said anything, whether silly or profound, he would repeat the last part of the sentence exactly, to signify agreement, somewhat in this way:

"Anxiety is like a tangled undergrowth of fear," I said.

"Anxiety is like a tangled undergrowth of fear," he repeated in a falling, bored voice.

"Every one of us should show what a man can be," our secretary said.

"Yes, every one of us should show what a man can be," he said.

And yet he was no mere yes-man, because somewhere in him, amid the large silences of lethargy, he seemed to be retreating his steps to the narrow lanes where he had been born and among which he brooded, as though he were sitting among the ruins of his heritage and as though he heard the rumble of his father's voice admonishing him for some default, while his mother was consoling him with affectionate words and the proverbial sweets. . . .

He was singularly handsome to look at, with a tallish frame which made up for his lack of grace, his narrow chest, the rounded shoulders, and the shuffling gait: his face was a dark brown moon visage with a small forehead, a shapely nose, full lips, and a pair of enormous brown eyes which, though rather furtive and withdrawn, as though he were hiding them, were mellow with gentleness.

Altogether, the effect of his personality was that of an individual weighed down by some unknown fear or obsession into the dull reiteration of the ox mind, whose viciousness lay rather in the unconscious malice of stupidity than in any deliberate intent to hurt anyone.

For viciousness indeed it was on his part to tell the police everything about us when the house we lived in at Lahore was raided, and where we were charged with "conspiring to deprive His Majesty the King Emperor of his Suzerainty in India, and for plotting the overthrow of the Government as constituted by law, etc." Thus, the person whom we did not count at all, whom we regarded as a mere nothing because of his abject and unintelligent echoing of every phrase of ours, became the important person, the key to our destiny.

It was a ghastly experience:

For the police arrived at dawn and stunned us by their presence on the top of the house we inhabited in Kutchery Road: we had not been expecting such a sudden visitation, as we had been fairly careful about our movements and had left no traces of the literature we were distributing. A little rubbing of the eyes, however, a somnolent stretch or two, accompanied by sighs of regret for the beautiful sleep in the nimble breeze of the cool early morning of which we had been deprived, and we surrendered ourselves without a fuss, though after we had demanded that the warrants for our arrest be produced and expressed our intention to plead "not guilty" when charged. But Gopal, the seventh member of our cadre, seemed not so much stunned as ready to break, to lose his head altogether. From being the indifferent, ineffectual, lackadaisical person that he had always seemed, he became quite impassioned and hysterical.

He jumped off his bed and, with a curious jolt, began to somersault across the length of the roof in a series of unending movements, frothing at the mouth, weeping large tears from his large eyes and hissing like a serpent, even as he shook his head as if to cast off the deadening weight of thoughts which had hung his head down for years. After he had slipped from the grasp of the policemen three or four times and he was finally brought to his bed, and we were all trying to pacify him with kind words, remonstrances, and anger, he jumped off again, somersaulted and sat in the middle of the roof, beating his head, grinding his teeth, and frothing profusely, shaking his head up and down. Then, throwing himself back, he fell with a thud and lay in a morose silence. We all wondered if it was epilepsy or whether he was shaking off the troubles of a million years of pain.

But as the police forcibly lifted him with a roughness, aroused by, what they called, his obstinacy, he began to blurt out confessional statements, emotional vaporings, and pleas for mercy, and accusations against us which might be useful to the police.

"You planned it fine," he said, "with no thought to the consequences of your designs, with never a thought that we should be hanged on the gallows by the Sarkar! Freedom and Liberty, you said! But you did not even suspect that the people of whom you talked are crude, peasant boors, incapable of appreciating—"

"Shut up and don't be such a petit-bourgeois fool!" Hans said.

"You thought you were all being very clever in evading the law and I was a fool to fall in with you!" he ejaculated. "I will spill the beans now, you scheming old devils. You didn't even have the courage to call for blood; you were little bureaucrats waiting for the judgment day! . . ."

"You are mad," was all we said, and let him "spill the beans."

During our trial we thought he would turn approver and

get off lightly. But curiously, apart from the crazy snatches of defiant abuse he hurled against us, punctuated with gentle smiles, whimpering, and hurricanes of uncontrolled temper, he merely repeated the evidence we gave in his familiar manner of our old confederate days.

We were all given ten years' penal servitude each, a sentence accompanied by a statement from the judge that though there was no evidence to show that we had committed any violence, we had been suspiciously underground for a year and had tried to organize Labor for purposes which might have been detrimental to the peace of the realm.

Needless to say, the severity of this sentence came as a shock to us, but all we could do was to accept it and hope that our friends would file an appeal on our behalf.

Gopal did not break down as he had done at the time of our joint arrest. In fact, he remained particularly calm. But, as we were embracing each other, because we thought we might not meet again for many years if we were sent to different gaols in the country to serve our respective sentences, he came over to us and flung himself on the ground before us, and made obeisance with joined hands. Then he touched the dust at our feet with his hands, smeared it on his forehead, joined his hands again and in the most tender, supplicating voice said:

"Forgive me, please, forgive me, brothers."

We lifted him hastily and told him there was nothing to forgive.

"There is nothing to forgive." He repeated the tail end of our exhortation as was his wont to do.

R. K. NARAYAN

*R. K. Narayan was born in 1906, at Madras. He
was one of nine children in a family of high-
caste Brahmins. His father was a schoolmaster.
Narayan had his schooling at Madras, but he
"loathed school and never learnt anything there."
He took his B.A. at the Maharaja's College in
Mysore in 1930 at the age of twenty-four. He married in 1934 and lost his wife in 1939.*

*From childhood, Narayan wanted to be a writer.
He read the Russian novelists but is not an ad-
mirer of Tolstoy. He does admire the work of
Hugo, Dumas, H. G. Wells, E. M. Forster, and
D. H. Lawrence.*

*With the backing of Graham Greene, his first
novel,* Swami and Friends, *appeared in London in
1935. In his introduction to Mr. Narayan's second
book,* The Bachelor of Arts, *Graham Greene wrote,
"It was Mr. Narayan with his* Swami and Friends
*who first brought India, in the sense of Indian
population and the Indian way of life, alive to me.
. . . His novels increase our knowledge of the
Indian character, certainly, but I prefer to think
of them as contributions to English literature, contributions of remarkable maturity."*

*Narayan was introduced to American readers
in 1952 by the Michigan State University Press,
which began to publish his earlier books. These
include, besides* Swami and Friends, The Bachelor
of Arts *(1937),* The Dark Room *(1938),* An Astrologer's Day and Other Stories *(1947),* Mr. Sam-
path *(1949),* The Financial Expert *(1954),* Waiting for the Mahatma *(1955). His more recent*

books are The Guide *(1958),* The Man Eater of Malgudi *(1961), and* Gods, Demons and Others *(1964).*

His novel The Guide *won for him in 1961 the Sahitya Akademi Award, the most coveted literary honor in India. His writing is distinguished by humor, an unoffending irony, a unique Indianness, and a simplicity which is utterly charming and authentic. His work is free from all isms; he does not preach or moralize, but observes and records. A maddeningly modest man, Narayan once said, "If one pauses to think, one realizes that there is little one could say about one's self."*

An Astrologer's Day

R. K. NARAYAN

PUNCTUALLY at midday he opened his bag and spread out his professional equipment, which consisted of a dozen cowrie shells, a square piece of cloth with obscure mystic charts on it, a notebook, and a bundle of palmyra writing. His forehead was resplendent with sacred ash and vermilion, and his eyes sparkled with a sharp abnormal gleam which was really an outcome of a continual searching look for customers, but which his simple clients took to be a prophetic light and felt comforted. The power of his eyes was considerably enhanced by their position—placed as they were between the painted forehead and the dark whiskers which streamed down his cheeks: even a half-wit's eyes would sparkle in such a setting. To crown the effect he wound a saffron-colored turban around his head. This color scheme never failed. People were attracted to him as bees are attracted to cosmos or dahlia stalks. He sat under the boughs of a spreading tamarind tree which flanked a path running through the Town Hall Park. It was a remarkable place in many ways: a surging crowd was always moving up and down this narrow road morning till night. A variety of trades and occupations was represented all along its way: medicine sellers, sellers of stolen hardware and junk, magicians, and, above all, an auctioneer of cheap cloth, who created enough din all day to attract the whole town. Next to him in vociferousness came a vendor of fried groundnut, who gave his ware a fancy name each day, calling it "Bombay Ice Cream" one day, and on the next "Delhi Almond," and on the third "Raja's Delicacy," and so on and so forth, and people flocked to him. A considerable portion of this crowd dallied before the astrologer too. The astrologer transacted his business by the light of a flare which crackled and smoked up above the groundnut heap nearby. Half the enchantment of the place was due to the fact that it did not have the benefit of municipal lighting. The place was lit up by shop lights. One or two had hissing gaslights, some had naked flares stuck on poles, some were lit up by old cycle lamps, and one or two, like the astrologer's, managed without lights of their own. It was a bewildering crisscross of light rays and moving shadows. This suited the astrologer very well, for the simple reason that he had not in the least intended to be an astrologer when he began life; and he knew no more of what was going to happen to others than he knew what was going to happen to himself next minute. He was as much a stranger to the stars as were his innocent customers. Yet he said things which pleased and astonished everyone: that was more a matter of study, practice, and shrewd guesswork. All the same, it was as much an honest man's labor as any other, and he deserved the wages he carried home at the end of a day.

He had left his village without any previous thought or plan. If he had continued there he would have carried on the work of his forefathers—namely, tilling the land, living, marrying, and ripening in his cornfield and ancestral home. But that was not to be. He had to leave home without telling anyone, and he could not rest till he left it behind a couple of hundred miles. To a villager it is a great deal, as if an ocean flowed between.

He had a working analysis of mankind's troubles: marriage, money, and the tangles of human ties. Long practice had sharpened his perception. Within five minutes he understood what was wrong. He charged three pies per question, never opened his mouth till the other had spoken for at least ten minutes, which provided him enough stuff for a dozen answers and advices. When he told the person before him, gazing at his palm, "In many ways you are not getting the fullest results for your efforts," nine out of ten were disposed to agree with him. Or he questioned: "Is there any woman in your family, maybe even a distant relative who is not well disposed towards you?" Or he gave an analysis of character: "Most of your troubles are due to your nature. How can you be otherwise with Saturn where he is? You have an impetuous nature and a rough exterior." This endeared him to their hearts immediately, for even the mildest of us loves to think that he has a forbidding exterior.

The nuts vendor blew out his flare and rose to go home. This was a signal for the astrologer to bundle up too, since it left him in darkness except for a little shaft of green light which strayed in from somewhere and touched the ground before him. He picked up his cowrie shells and paraphernalia and was putting them back into his bag when the green shaft of light was blotted out; he looked up and saw a man standing before him. He sensed a possible client and said: "You look so careworn. It will do you good to sit down for a while and chat with me." The other grumbled some reply vaguely. The astrologer pressed his invitation; whereupon the other thrust his palm under his nose, saying: "You call yourself an astrologer?" The astrologer felt challenged and said, tilting the other's palm towards the green shaft of light: "Yours is a nature . . ." "Oh, stop that," the other said. "Tell me something worthwhile. . . ."

Our friend felt piqued. "I charge only three pies per question, and what you get ought to be good enough for your money. . . ." At this the other withdrew his arm, took out an anna, and flung it out to him, saying: "I have some questions to ask. If I prove you are bluffing, you must return that anna to me with interest."

"If you find my answers satisfactory, will you give me five rupees?"

"No."

"Or will you give me eight annas?"

"All right, provided you give me twice as much if you are wrong," said the stranger. This pact was accepted after a little further argument. The astrologer sent up a prayer to heaven as the other lit a cheroot. The astrologer caught a glimpse of his face by the matchlight. There was a pause as cars hooted on the road, *jutka* drivers swore at their horses, and the babble of the crowd agitated the semidarkness of the park. The other sat down, sucking his cheroot, puffing out, sat there ruthlessly. The astrologer felt very uncomfortable. "Here, take your anna back. I am not used to such challenges. It is late for me today. . . ." He made preparations to bundle up. The other held his wrist and said: "You can't get out of it now. You dragged me in while I was passing." The astrologer shivered in his grip; and his voice shook and became faint. "Leave me today. I will speak to you tomorrow." The other thrust his palm in his face and said: "Challenge is challenge. Go on." The astrologer proceeded with his throat drying up: "There is a woman . . ."

"Stop," said the other. "I don't want all that. Shall I succeed in my present search or not? Answer this and go. Otherwise I will not let you go till you disgorge all your coins." The astrologer muttered a few incantations and replied: "All right. I will speak. But will you give me a rupee if what I say is convincing? Otherwise I will not open my mouth, and you may do what you like." After a good deal of haggling the other agreed. The astrologer said: "You were left for dead. Am I right?"

"Ah, tell me more."

"A knife has passed through you once?" said the astrologer.

"Good fellow!" He bared his chest to show the scar. "What else?"

"And then you were pushed into a well nearby in the field. You were left for dead."

"I should have been dead if some passer-by had not

chanced to peep into the well," exclaimed the other, over-whelmed by enthusiasm.

"When shall I get at him?" he asked, clenching his fist.

"In the next world," answered the astrologer. "He died four months ago in a far-off town. You will never see any more of him." The other groaned on hearing it. The astrologer proceeded:

"Guru Nayak—"

"You know my name!" the other said, taken aback.

"As I know all other things. Guru Nayak, listen carefully to what I have to say. Your village is two days' journey due north of this town. Take the next train and be gone. I see once again great danger to your life if you go from home." He took out a pinch of sacred ash and held it to him. "Rub it on your forehead and go home. Never travel southward again, and you will live to be a hundred."

"Why should I leave home again?" the other said reflectively. "I was only going away now and then to look for him and to choke out his life if I met him." He shook his head regretfully. "He has escaped my hands. I hope at least he died as he deserved." "Yes," said the astrologer. "He was crushed under a lorry." The other looked gratified to hear it.

The place was deserted by the time the astrologer picked up his articles and put them into his bag. The green shaft was also gone, leaving the place in darkness and silence. The stranger had gone off into the night, after giving the astrologer a handful of coins.

It was nearly midnight when the astrologer reached home. His wife was waiting for him at the door and demanded an explanation. He flung the coins at her and said: "Count them. One man gave all that."

"Twelve and a half annas," she said, counting. She was overjoyed. "I can buy some jaggery and coconut tomorrow. The child has been asking for sweets for so many days now. I will prepare some nice stuff for her."

"The swine has cheated me! He promised me a rupee,"

said the astrologer. She looked up at him. "You look worried. What is wrong?"

"Nothing."

After dinner, sitting on the *pyol*, he told her: "Do you know a great load is gone from me today? I thought I had the blood of a man on my hands all these years. That was the reason why I ran away from home, settled here, and married you. He is alive."

She gasped. "You tried to kill!"

"Yes, in our village, when I was a silly youngster. We drank, gambled, and quarreled badly one day—why think of it now? Time to sleep," he said, yawning, and stretched himself on the *pyol*.

The Blind Dog

IT was not a very impressive or high-class dog; it was one of those commonplace dogs one sees everywhere—color of white and dust, tail mutilated at a young age by God knows whom, born in the street, and bred on the leavings and garbage of the marketplace. He had spotty eyes and undistinguished carriage and needless pugnacity. Before he was two years old he had earned the scars of a hundred fights on his body. When he needed rest on hot afternoons he lay curled up under the culvert at the Eastern gate of the market. In the evenings he set out on his daily rounds, loafed in the surrounding streets and lanes, engaged himself in skirmishes, picked up edibles on the roadside, and was back at the market gate by nightfall.

This life went on for three years. And then occurred a change in his life. A beggar, blind of both eyes, appeared at the market gate. An old woman led him up there early in the morning, seated him at the gate, and came up again at midday with some food, gathered his coins, and took him home at night.

The dog was sleeping near by. He was stirred by the smell of food. He got up, came out of his shelter, and stood before the blind man, wagging his tail and gazing expectantly at the bowl, as he was eating his sparse meal. The blind man swept his arms about and asked: "Who is there?" At which the dog went up and licked his hand. The blind man stroked its coat gently tail to ear and said: "What a beauty you are. Come with me—" He threw a handful of food which the dog ate gratefully. It was perhaps an auspicious moment for starting a friendship. They met every day there, and the dog

cut off much of its rambling to sit up beside the blind man
and watch him receive alms morning to evening. In course
of time observing him, the dog understood that the passers-
by must give a coin, and whoever went away without dropping a coin was chased by the dog; he tugged the edge of
their clothes by his teeth and pulled them back to the old
man at the gate and let go only after something was dropped
in his bowl. Among those who frequented this place was a
village urchin, who had the mischief of a devil in him. He
liked to tease the blind man by calling him names and by
trying to pick up the coins in his bowl. The blind man helplessly shouted and cried and whirled his staff. On Thursdays
this boy appeared at the gate, carrying on his head a basket
loaded with cucumber or plantain. Every Thursday afternoon it was a crisis in the blind man's life. A seller of bright
colored but doubtful perfumes with his wares mounted on a
wheeled platform, a man who spread out cheap storybooks
on a gunny sack, another man who carried colored ribbons
on an elaborate frame—these were the people who usually
gathered under the same arch. On a Thursday when the
young man appeared at the Eastern gate one of them remarked, "Blind fellow! Here comes your scourge—"

"Oh, God, is this Thursday?" he wailed. He swept his arms
about and called: "Dog, dog, come here, where are you?" He
made the peculiar noise which brought the dog to his side.
He stroked his head and muttered: "Don't let that little
rascal—" At this very moment the boy came up with a leer
on his face.

"Blind man! Still pretending you have no eyes. If you are
really blind, you should not know this either—" He stopped,
his hand moving towards the bowl. The dog sprang on him
and snapped his jaws on his wrist. The boy extricated his
hand and ran for his life. The dog bounded up behind him
and chased him out of the market.

"See the mongrel's affection for this old fellow," marveled
the perfume-vendor.

One evening at the usual time the old woman failed to turn up, and the blind man waited at the gate, worrying as the evening grew into night. As he sat fretting there, a neighbor came up and said: "Sami, don't wait for the old woman. She will not come again. She died this afternoon—"

The blind man lost the only home he had, and the only person who cared for him in this world. The ribbon-vendor suggested: "Here, take this white tape—" he held a length of the white cord which he had been selling— "I will give this to you free of cost. Tie it to the dog and let him lead you about if he is really so fond of you—"

Life for the dog took a new turn now. He came to take the place of the old woman. He lost his freedom completely. His world came to be circumscribed by the limits of the white cord which the ribbon-vendor had spared. He had to forget wholesale all his old life—all his old haunts. He simply had to stay on forever at the end of that string. When he saw other dogs, friends or foes, instinctively he sprang up, tugging the string, and this invariably earned him a kick from his master. "Rascal, want to tumble me down—have sense—" In a few days the dog learnt to discipline his instinct and impulse. He ceased to take notice of other dogs, even if they came up and growled at his side. He lost his own orbit of movement and contact with his fellow creatures.

To the extent of this loss his master gained. He moved about as he had never moved in his life. All day he was on his legs, led by the dog. With the staff in one hand and the dog-lead in the other he moved out of his home—a corner in a choultry veranda a few yards off the market: he had moved in there after the old woman's death. He started out early in the day. He found that he could treble his income by moving about instead of staying in one place. He moved down the choultry street, and wherever he heard people's voices he stopped and held out his hands for alms. Shops, schools, hospitals, hotels—he left nothing out. He gave a tug when he wanted the dog to stop, and shouted like a bullock-driver when he wanted him to move on. The dog protected his feet from going into pits, or stumping against steps or stones, and took him up inch by inch on safe ground and steps. For this sight people gave coins and helped him. Children gathered round him and gave him things to eat. A dog is essentially an active creature who punctuates his hectic rounds with well-defined periods of rest. But now this dog (henceforth to be known as Tiger) had lost all rest. He had rest only when the old man sat down somewhere. At night the old man slept with the cord turned around his finger. "I can't take chances with you—" he said. A great desire to earn more money than ever before seized his master, so that he felt any resting a waste of opportunity, and the dog had to be continuously on his feet. Sometimes his legs refused to move. But if he slowed down even slightly his master goaded him on fiercely with his staff. The dog whined and groaned under this thrust. "Don't whine, you rascal. Don't I give you your food? You want to loaf, do you?" swore the blind man. The dog lumbered up and down and round and round the marketplace on slow steps, tied down to the blind tyrant. Long after the traffic at the market ceased, you could hear the night stabbed by the far-off wail of the tired dog. It lost its original appearance. As months rolled on, bones stuck up at his haunches and ribs were reliefed through his fading coat.

The ribbon-seller, the novel-vendor, and the perfumer observed it one evening, when business was slack, and held a conference among themselves: "It rends my heart to see that poor dog slaving. Can't we do something?" The ribbon-seller remarked: "That rascal has started lending money for interest—I heard it from that fruit-seller—he is earning more than he needs. He has become a very devil for money—" At this point the perfumer's eyes caught the scissors dangling from the ribbon-rack. "Give it here," he said and moved on with the scissors in hand.

The blind man was passing in front of the Eastern gate. The dog was straining the lead. There was a piece of bone lying on the way and the dog was straining to pick it up. The lead became taut and hurt the blind man's hand, and he tugged the string and kicked till the dog howled. It howled, but could not pass the bone lightly; it tried to make another dash for it. The blind man was heaping curses on it. The perfumer stepped up, applied the scissors, and snipped the cord. The dog bounced off and picked up the bone. The blind man stopped dead where he stood, with the other half of the string dangling in his hand. "Tiger! Tiger! Where are you?" he cried. The perfumer moved away quietly, muttering: "You heartless devil! You will never get at him again! He has his freedom!" The dog went off at top speed. He nosed about the ditches happily, hurled himself on other dogs, and ran round and round the fountain in the market square barking, his eyes sparkling with joy. He returned to his favorite haunts and hung about the butcher's shop, tea-stall, and the bakery.

The ribbon-vendor and his two friends stood at the market gate and enjoyed the sight immensely as the blind man struggled to find his way about. He stood rooted to the spot waving his stick; he felt as if he were hanging in midair. He was wailing. "Oh, where is my dog? Where is my dog? Won't someone give him back to me? I will murder it when I get at it again!" He groped about, tried to cross the road, came near being run over by a dozen vehicles at different points, tumbled and struggled and gasped. "He'd deserve it if he was run over, this heartless blackguard—" they said, observing him. However, the old man struggled through and with the help of someone found his way back to his corner in the choultry veranda and sank down on his gunnysack bed, half faint with the strain of his journey.

He was not seen for ten days, fifteen days, and twenty days. Nor was the dog seen anywhere. They commented among themselves. "The dog must be loafing over the whole earth, free and happy. The beggar is perhaps gone for-ever—" Hardly was this sentence uttered when they heard the familiar tap-tap of the blind man's staff. They saw him again coming up the pavement—led by the dog. "Look! Look!" they cried. "He has again got at it and tied it up—" The ribbon-seller could not contain himself. He ran up and said: "Where have you been all these days?"

"Know what happened!" cried the blind man. "This dog ran away. I should have died in a day or two, confined to my corner, no food, not an anna to earn—imprisoned in my corner. I should have perished if it continued for another day— But this thing returned—"

"When? When?"

"Last night. At midnight as I slept in bed, he came and licked my face. I felt like murdering him. I gave him a blow which he will never forget again," said the blind man. "I for-gave him, after all a dog! He loafed as long as he could pick up some rubbish to eat on the road, but real hunger has driven him back to me, but he will not leave me again. See! I have got this—" and he shook the lead: it was a steel chain this time.

Once again there was the dead, despairing look in the dog's eyes. "Go on, you fool," cried the blind man, shouting like an ox driver. He tugged the chain, poked with the stick, and the dog moved away on slow steps. They stood listening to the tap-tap going away.

"Death alone can help that dog," cried the ribbon-seller, looking after it with a sigh. "What can we do with a creature who returns to his doom with such a free heart?"

RAJA RAO

Raja Rao was born in 1909, at Hassan, Mysore, South India, in a Brahmin family. His father was a professor of Canarese in Hyderabad and Raja Rao had his schooling in that city. From 1925 to 1927 he studied French at Aligarh University in North India, then he returned to complete his B.A. at Nizam College, Hyderabad. He was selected Government of Hyderabad Scholar to the University of Montpellier, in France, and later studied at the Sorbonne. He lived in France from 1929 to 1939 and again from 1946 to 1956.

Raja Rao wrote his first short story when he was still in his teens. His first novel, Kanthapura, *was published in England in 1938 and received high praise. A collection of short stories,* The Cow of the Barricades, *appeared in 1947 and* The Serpent and the Rope, *for which he received the Sahitya Akademi Award was published in England in 1960, and in the United States in 1963. His later work,* The Cat and Shakespeare (1965), *is, like* The Serpent and the Rope, *a metaphysical novel.*

He is equally at home in India and the West. His knowledge of classical Sanskrit and modern European literature is profound. On the one hand he has been influenced by the Ramayana, *the* Mahabharta, *the* Gita, Vedanta, *and on the other by W. B. Yeats, Gide, and Malraux. "Gide influenced my literary form and Malraux my literary expression."*

Like most intellectuals of his generation, Raja Rao came under the spell of Mahatma Gandhi. In

1942 he spent some months at Gandhi's Ashram in Central India.

Recently, Raja Rao has lectured at various American universities on Indian philosophy.

The Little Gram* Shop

RAJA RAO

EVERYBODY hated him, hated him. "That swine of a bania,"
they would say, spitting and thumping on the floor, "that
son of a prostitute, he'll soon eat mire and vomit blood. Oh!
you son of a donkey!" They would spit again, draw a puff
from the tip of the hookah and continue swearing and
blustering. It was hardly a week since Ananda's family had
moved to the Cornerhouse, and already he had heard a great
deal about "bania Motilal." Narasimha, his class-fellow,
hated him and always had curses upon his lips whenever he
passed by Motilal's gram shop. One day, as Ananda was in
no hurry, he slipped into Narasimha's house to have a little
chat. Narasimha was furious. That bania had called him a
dog, and had spat on him!

"Why?" asked Ananda, curious.

"Why? What will a dog do but bite?"

"I don't understand," the other managed to mutter.

"You don't! Then you do not know the story?"

"No."

"Then I'll tell you!" cried Narasimha triumphant, and this
is what he told him.

That Motilal, the wretched bania, was poor as a cur—
poor as a cur in a pariah street. A copper pot in his hand,
with nothing to wear except the rags they had on them, he
and his wife Beti Bai started from their little village in
Gujarat, when? nobody knows, but it must have been some
fifteen, twenty, or forty years ago. They tramped from vil-

* A cereal grown widely in North India.—Ed.

lage to village, singing and begging, eating the food they got, and knotting in the doles they received. And within a year or two they had actually managed to save a hundred rupees, yes, ten times ten, a hundred rupees. Now with that sum in hand, they had only to find a town to settle down in. His wife, poor Beti Bai, was terribly worn out by this errant life, and she swore she would go no further than Badepur. But Motilal was ambitious. What? A great-grandson of Bhata Tata Lal of Khodi to settle down in a dirty hole like Badepur! Never! It was true, misfortune on misfortune had pulled them down. But they had to rise up again. They had to become great and rich like Bhata Tata Lal of Khodi. It pleased Beti to be the wife of the great-grandson of so great a man. And she would do anything to be great like that famous ancestor of her husband. Herself poor—so poor that she drank water out of the street gutters, added Narasimha —herself poor, with a widowed mother who did manual work in a bania's house, Beti Bai had grown ambitious too with the stories that Motilal told her about his great-grand-father. "What do you think," he had assured her once, in the serai of Badepur when she was sick and unwilling to go any further, "what do you think, Beti? Bhata Tata Lal had a house as big . . . no, about as big as this town. He had hundreds and hundreds of servants, and a byre that con-tained at least a thousand cattle. Oh! if only these dirty red men had not come, he would have been rich, rich like the Maharaja of Bhavan. Beti, we too shall be rich like that . . . some day . . . one day. . . ."

"But you said," objected Beti Bai, "but you said it was your grandfather who wasted it all."

"Yes, Beti. My grandfather had ten concubines and he squandered his property among them, among all the ten of them. And the little that remained, my father wasted it on his own mistresses."

"And the red man . . ."

"Yes, the red man! Concubines and the red man. It is they

together that plundered my great-grandfather's treasury. Oh! I wish I had been born then! To be born as I was, between cotton sacks on one side and the cattle on the other . . . in such poverty. . . . Oh! Beti! what a life for the great-grandson of Bhata Tata Lal of Khodi!"

He had tears in his eyes.

"No, no, do not weep, brother. As you say we will go far, far, as far as you like . . . to Hyderpur. You say there one can become rich in the twinkling of an eye. All right, I'll go with you, I will."

"What an angel for a wife!" beamed Motilal, "how wonderful! We shall go to Hyderpur and become rich in a day, fabulously rich in the twinkling of an eye. And when we go back to our town they will treat us like veritable gods. They will say 'Look! look at them, sister, look at Bhata Motilal! His father died before he was born and his mother died but two months after he saw light, and yet look how rich he has become! The gods have helped him, surely. He lived, sister, like a sacred bull of the street which wanders wild and eats what it finds. He lived by begging, and now he is rich, so rich.' They will envy and fear me, Beti." Beti could not help weeping. She was so happy.

"Yes! When we go and tell mother we are rich, how splendid it will be! She shall toil no more. And she shall live with us."

"We shall see. . . ." Motilal looked towards the town, which was sinking away into the darkness. Here and there a light shone, and he lay down beside Beti and slept.

"So, after many, many months," continued Narasimha, "still begging and still wandering, sick or lame, they reached Hyderpur. They found that dirty hovel they now live in. It had neither roof nor walls. They went to the owner and asked him for an honest deal. He was but too happy to get rid of it. And with the necessary hagglings he was willing to part with it for—how much do you think?—fifty rupees, a damned pittance of fifty rupees. They bought it, and while they were trying to put up the wall, and lay the roof, they still sang and begged. Once a dog begins to eat filth," said Narasimha contemptuously, "you cannot ask him to stop. So, after a month's work—still begging—they were able to have a thatch over their heads. Then with the rest of the money they went and bought a few seers of gram and sugar and thus started their shop. Now, as everybody knows, they are overflowing with money, and yet how they live, these dogs, these curs, they live like pariah's pigs . . ."

Ananda said nothing. He listened to the story with great interest; but to join the other in his anger was beyond his inmost feelings. He had just come to go to Motilal's shop. His stepmother wanted sugar for the evening dinner. Bidding an indifferent goodbye to Narasimha, he ran out. He ran to Motilal's gram shop.

The shop could not have changed much in its appearance since they had settled down there. The roof was of zinc sheets, with a few beams that had at least half a century of life. The only addition to the house was a little wooden byre that they had put up for the cow they had newly bought. The fodder was carefully piled upon the roof, and nobody seemed to remember if ever it had been pulled down these two years. The cow wandered all day from one dustbin to another, eating chips of vegetables that were thrown away, or, as it was rumored, actually entered latrines and cleared them. Anyway she gave the seer of milk she had to, which with a little generosity under the tap became a seer and a half, and Beti Bai always had helpless clients to buy it. Ananda himself had once paid eight pice for a quarter of a seer—half water and half God knows what! But it was a good thing to have some sort of milk. If not, what shame! What would the guests think!

To come back to the shop itself; it consisted of a small verandah, some ten feet by fifteen, which opened directly on the road. In one corner was the grocery. Small drawers, some fifty or so, were fixed into the wall, each filled with pepper, ginger, or sesame seeds. Just by it, between four open boxes of rice, wheat, salt, and tamarind, was an oily seat where Motilal usually sat. When people had to wait, they generally squatted down by one of the boxes and thus swept away the dust that had been gathering for some considerable time. On the other side, projected into the road, was a wooden platform—an old bedstead perhaps, with a few planks on either side—which contained the various grams in bamboo baskets. There was the sugared gram, the fried gram, the Bombay gram cakes, and occasionally perfumed gram balls, and sticks of sugar and almonds. It was Beti Bai who usually sat in the gram shop. She had made a duster out of an old cloth, and she kept off the flies by flicking it now here, now there. But, in spite of this, the dust that came from the road carefully settled down upon the grams. It did not matter much, as Beti once half seriously confessed to a friend from the bazaar; it added to the weight.

Behind Beti, by the kitchen door on the left, was a small platform on which lay almost all the things they possessed. A bed, always folded and carefully arranged, used to lie prominently on it. From the many holes in the carpet, one could easily guess what the bedding may have contained. Perhaps a blanket, a sheet, and an old mattress, thin like the skin of a cow. Beside the bed were a few big vessels that were used for frying and baking the grams. Nobody had as yet seen where the safe was. There were rumors that they kept it in a hole in the earth, which was covered by the seat of Motilal in the grocery.

Between the gram platform and the platform where the bed lay was a narrow space that served now for eating, now for grinding and now for sleeping. It opened on the kitchen —a small tin shed that had protruded, much against the Municipal Inspector's warnings, into the little lane. One of these days, the Inspector was going to come again. But his servants were clever fellows. They had been given more than an anna's worth of grams some three or four times, and they had informed the boss that it was all perfectly in order. Well, if he came, if he actually came, a rupee or two in his hands and everything would go well. Motilal had known ten such inspectors, and had sweet well silenced them.

The one happy thing in the shop was the little green parrot in the cage, which cried out "Ram, Ram" to all the clients who entered. Everybody who came in offered a few grams to her, and thus she had always more than enough to eat. Beti Bai loved her as though she were her own child. Especially since their son Chota had run away with that woman, they had found the little parrot to be their only solace. She cost nothing, and was always so alive and affectionate. When Beti quarreled with Motilal, which happened almost every day, she had only to turn to the parrot and call "Mithu, Mithu," and little Mithu would reply, hopping round and stretching her feathers, "Ram, Ram, Mai . . . Ram," "Pyari, Mithu," "Ram, Ram, Mai . . . Ram."

Motilal must now have been over fifty. He was tall, thin, and rather wrinkled in the face. His steel-black eyes had something wanting in lustre. They seemed seated in their sockets like rats in a hole. And, too, like rats in a hole they were shrewd when you least observed them. His wiry hands, with bulging blue veins, shivered at every shake or touch. For ages asthma had kept him awake night after night, and but for his hookah, life would have been intolerable. The hookah was comforting for the moment. But in the long run, it had almost completely ruined his health. In spite of Beti Bai's constant quarrel about it, he smoked almost every minute of the day. In fact he sometimes smoked so much that the very water of the hookah began to stink. But he coughed away, spat away, and smoked on, careless of all but the warm caress of the smoke in his throat. It was so delicious to have a friend like that. When he had to weigh things, he reluctantly put it aside for a moment. And no sooner had he finished his weighing than he would snatch it back with the eagerness of a miser, and begin his "*gud . . . gud . . . gud . . .*" It made such a queer gurgling noise. Children who came to buy a few peppermints or sugar candy would usually sit and listen to the gurgle. And when they went out they would clap their hands, gurgle deeply in their throats and laugh. Behind them Motilal would still be at his hookah and it would still be gurgling, "*gud . . . gud . . . gud . . .*"

Nobody was sure what it was that had made Motilal so nervous and irritable. Some said it was Beti, but others insisted it was the hookah. Beti, of course, complained against the hookah, and had once got so disgusted and jealous of it that she thrust it behind the fuel in the kitchen and kept quiet as a stone. Motilal searched all over the place, and swore at every client in terrifying despair. But the clients could say nothing at all. They took their sugar, or their rice, and thanking the stars that for once he was less nauseating, they went their way. At last he could bear it no more. He thrust his fists at Beti and swore he would damn well skin her to death. But she smiled, sent a few prayers to the helpful gods and feigned ignorance. He went here, went there, upset the whole house, and still he could not find it. But there was still the kitchen. And in a moment he had discovered it. He jumped and swore and in a mighty fury he flung Beti to the ground and, clack-clack, beat her with a piece of firewood he had brought from the kitchen. She shrieked and she wept, her big breasts pressed to the floor and her hair all scattered about. The clients who came could do nothing. They stood in the shop silent and pitiful. Some who were more sensitive hid their eyes with their saris, unable to bear the sight of the blood flowing down Beti's back. Motilal still stood beside her, the thorny stick in his hand.

After a moment's suspense, he went to his seat in the grocery, lit his hookah and attended to the clients. They were happy to have got out, and he the happier to have got rid of them. Everybody had gone and Beti still lay there, prostrate on the floor, and weeping. The blood that oozed from her back was trickling down and a few flies—it was summer—had already settled to their orgy. The dust in the street rose—and fell. Now it was a bullock cart, and another time a motor car. The sun was hot, iron-melting. It was Ananda who entered. "Ram, Ram, . . ." cried the parrot. Smoking his hookah Motilal flared up at him. It was frightening to see him flare up like a lion.

"What do you want?" he growled in a hoarse, frenzied voice.

"Just a seer of sugar," murmured Ananda, trembling. He looked towards Beti and it sent a shiver through his back.

"Bapuji . . . Bapuji . . . save me . . . save me!" she begged.

"Save you! Go to hell, you dirty dragon! Go and sell yourself in a house of prostitution, you wretch, you devil! You witch, you donkey's kid, you bloody . . .!" He growled like thunder. Beti breathed heavily and sobbed.

"What do you want . . . hukk . . . hukk," he coughed, "what do you want? Sugar?"

"Yes."

"How much?"

"A seer."

"Bapuji . . . Bapuji . . . save me . . . save me!"

Motilal leapt from his seat and, kicking her right happily on the back, banged her with the thorny piece of firewood.

"Ayyo . . . ayyo . . . ayyo . . . Mai, mother . . . ayyo . . . ooo," she yelled, then rolled forward and writhed.

"Dog, whore, wench, devil, you witch! Shriek, shriek, as much as you like. Nobody will come to help you. No! Nobody . . ."

He grinned, wiped away his perspiration with his right arm, and drew a puff from his undenying hookah.

"Ha . . . Haa . . . ," she breathed, and became unconscious.

Ananda was in tears. He wanted to run away. But he was

afraid Motilal would catch him, and break his thirty-two teeth. He looked so enraged. He seemed ready to beat the whole world. Ananda shivered and stood, gazing unwillingly at the parrot.

Fortunately, the fear that she would die entered Motilal's head, and it horrified him. He went into the kitchen, brought a pailful of water, and sitting beside her threw a handful upon her face. Her mouth was wide open, and her tongue half visible. She was as red as the inside of a pumpkin. After a moment she opened her eyes and smiled. He smiled back tenderly, compassionately. His hookah was with him . . .

In the evening when Ananda was coming back from school, Beti was sitting on the gram platform, whisking away the flies.

The morning was fresh as usual. For Beti and Motilal, days followed one another, and each day was as fresh and good as the other. They had got up as usual at five, and while she had gone to the street pipe to get a pailful of water, Motilal had dusted a part of the grocery and had seen to the folding of the bed. Then he went and removed the door planks one by one, tried to dust them too and laid them aside by the kitchen door. Beti had come back with water, and began to wash the vessels, in the street. They were not many. Just a few pots and the two bell-metal plates they ate in. She took a handful of sand from the street, and with a tuft of coconut fibre rubbed them till they shone like gold. Motilal, who had nothing to do for the moment, sat on the steps, his hookah in his hands. He had not slept very well the previous night, and his head was maddeningly heavy. He closed his eyes and sank into a quiet doze. People began to move about in the street, and the morning carts were rattling along. Beti Bai was thinking of her native village and she began to weep. Her mother was dead, and now there was nobody to go there for. And even if she wished, would Motilal ever make such an expensive journey? Never. . . .

The first client woke Motilal. She had come for a quarter

of a seer of rice. A quarter of a seer of rice! What a sinister thing to begin a day with!

"Nothing else?" he bawled, furious.

"Nothing else. Just a quarter of a seer of rice."

"Oh! this world, this world! We'll soon die starving, with your damned quarter of a seer of rice! A quarter of a seer of rice . . . A quarter of a . . ."

"I must be going, Seth *."

"You want to go? Why, woman, you can go and drown in the next well! Or better still, go and lie with a licking male dog . . . Woman, you . . ."

"Very well," she grunted, and walked away.

"I say . . . I say . . ." roared Motilal. To let go the first client . . . the first client, by God, and ruin the whole day . . . "I say!!!"

The client walked away. She hastened along. Motilal ran swearing after her.

"I saaay . . . I saaay . . ."

The client shrugged her shoulders, and hurried on faster than ever.

"I say . . . ," he cried gasping, and stood threateningly in front of her. She tried to slip away. But he caught her hands and held them fast. She shrieked. But there was not a soul to come to her rescue. And she ambled back helplessly and, grumbling, bought her quarter of a seer of rice. Motilal gave a broad smile. He was victorious.

"I am not going to let go my first client like that," he muttered to himself.

"Then you had better learn to be more polite to them," she suggested, with an indulgent smile. She was not so angry now. And perhaps if she was good to him, she would get a handful more.

"But a quarter of a seer of rice! Just imagine!" He coughed, and laughed disdainfully.

"Oh! I cannot buy any more, Seth. Don't you know my

* A polite way of addressing the owner of a business establishment.

husband has run away with another woman, and I am poor?"

"Is it so?" he asked nervously. His son had done the same. This sadness turned into a strange pity. And, asking her to open her bag, he threw in a handful of rice. She was happy, so happy. And she walked away with many a blessing on the generous Motilal.

In the meanwhile, Beti Bai had finished washing the vessels, and had even come back from her daily bath beneath the public tap. She was muttering to herself the songs of Krishna, which she chanted every morning, doing her household work. The fire was to be lit, and the cow to be milked, and the milk boiled. All this before eight o'clock, when the customers would begin to come in numbers, one after the other. This morning, her fire too would not take well. It had been twice dead. What a bad sign to begin a day with, she said to herself, and she resolved to bear quietly any threats or beatings from Motilal. A bad day, for her, meant that. At last the fire slowly lit up, and, placing a pot of water on the oven, she went to milk the cow. The calf somehow had managed to slip away from its noose, and half the milk was gone. She banged the calf in fury, and thrusting it aside, beat the teats in the hope of getting even half a seer of milk. Fortunately there was a little left—in fact there was a great deal left—and driving the cow onto the street, she went back to the kitchen. The fire was but feebly burning, and the water was not warm. She cursed herself, cursed the fuel, cursed the calf, and blowing air into the oven, she sat thinking of all that might happen that unfortunate day—that dark day to be. Even a cough from Motilal would disturb her and send a shiver through her spine. But in a moment, as though to console her, the fire made the luck-bringing hiss. She was happy about it. So it was not going to be a bad day! The fire god had prophesied . . . Motilal entered. He too was happy.

"Beti," he cried enthusiastically, "do you know, a lizard fell upon my right shoulder!"

"Really!"

She had tears in her eyes.

"Yes! Just now. I was sitting in the grocery and it fell on my right shoulder and disappeared. I wonder what it will bring us!"

He drew two long puffs from his hookah and let them go into the air with a pouted mouth, like a child that is blowing bubbles.

"Perhaps Chota will come back," murmured Beti, turning away toward the fire.

"Chota . . . Chota . . . You still dream of him! I will not let him set his foot in this house. No! But really, Beti, I think we shall get something, something wonderful. Who knows? Perhaps the Nawab Sahib will accept my terms. Fifteen per cent interest. . . . It is nothing for a rich man like him."

"Perhaps he will," she muttered mechanically.

"He will," he assured himself. "Yesterday when I saw his secretary, he said he would see to it. You see, Beti, as I told you fifty rupees to the secretary and fifteen per cent interest. Imagine how much it will bring us, on twenty thousand rupees! We shall be rich, Beti!"

"What for? My mother is dead, and Chota . . ."

"Shut up, you donkey's child!" he cried, and walked away to the grocery, calculating again and again how much he would make out of this affair.

The morning slowly rolled along, and the afternoon too creaked heavily away, and yet nothing had happened. Every moment Motilal was expecting a servant from the Nawab Sahib or even the Nawab Sahib himself. Twice in the day he had counted his money, and put the twenty thousand rupees—all in thousand-rupee notes—aside. Every car that passed in the street looked like the Nawab Sahib's, and every client who came looked like a messenger from him. At lunch he did not eat at all. He said he was not hungry, and poor Beti was so sad to see him anxious. Her own heart was beating hard. She too was expecting something wonderful to happen. But what? Naturally, the idea of Chota coming back filled her with strange happiness and fear. Oh! if he should come back! Oh! if he really should. He would go to Gujarat and marry Bapan Lal's daughter. She was meant for him, she was. Hardly had she seen the light of the sun, than she had been engaged to Chota, to her dear child Chota. It seemed the girl had now grown up into a charming little maid. And she was still meant for Chota. To have a daughter-in-law at home, how very fine, how good! Half the work in the house would be done by her, and then Beti would have but little to do. Yes! Chota would come back. He would! Chota! . . . Chota! . . . She wept. Motilal entered the kitchen to get some fire for his hookah and he asked her why she was in tears.

"I was afraid . . . I was afraid . . . ," she blurted between her sobs, "I was afraid you would die before me . . ."

"Poor thing!" he murmured, caressing her hair, and went back to the grocery.

Now the sun was setting, and it being Saturday, Motilal had to go to Maruthi's temple. Usually he went in the afternoon, but today he had intended to take a larger present to the god on hearing of his success with the Nawab Sahib. And so he waited and waited. But now he had to go. If not, the door of the temple would be closed. And it was at least three miles away. So, sad and still expectant, he put on his old velvet coat and, placing his wiry turban upon his head, stood yawning for a moment, went and lighted his hookah, talked to the parrot, and yet . . . and yet . . . now there was no hope and he started. "If the Nawab Sahib comes," he ran back and told Beti, "tell him I'll see him this very night if he likes."

"All right," she answered drily. The Nawab Sahib, always the same story. . . .

She was still dreaming of her son coming back and her good daughter-in-law-to-be, when the sun suddenly sank, and going in she lighted the shop lantern, and chanted her usual lighting-time prayers. She even lit the little oil lamp by the picture of Rama that hung in the kitchen. A little oil now, but perhaps it would bring luck. The gods after all are not so cruel. They might make you wait. But they will surely answer your prayers.

It was about eight o'clock. In an hour or so Motilal would be back. So Beti went into the kitchen and sat cooking. Somebody coughed outside. She turned round. It was just darkness, dense darkness, and not a sign of any living soul. But still the cough strangely disturbed her. How? She did not know. But it gave her some unnatural joy. She would have got up and gone to see who it was. But then, the person had surely gone. And the darkness was so heavy. . . . Unconsciously she dozed away. She was accustomed to it. Suddenly somebody seemed to call her in a familiar voice. "Mai, mai . . . Mother . . . Mai. . . ." Before she opened her eyes Chota had embraced her. And they wept.

Motilal came back a little earlier than usual. Had the Nawab Sahib . . . ? He howled and blazed in fury. But he let Chota stay. After all he had come back. That was enough.

Mata Bapan Lal was happy that Chota had come back. So, in three weeks' time, he came down to Hyderpur to settle about the dowry. Motilal insisted on fifty thousand rupees. Chota was the great-great-grandson of Bhata Tata Lal of Khodi. But Bapan Lal had already married two daughters and had two more to marry. No, he could not pay that heavy sum. Anyway, as Beti was less ambitious and but too happy to have her son marry the daughter of Mata Bapan Lal—yes, of Mata Bapan Lal of Gorakhpur—she forced Motilal to accept only thirty thousand. So, it was all agreed, and the marriage took place with all pomp and generosity. The expenses were all met by Mata Bapan Lal and the bridegroom's party had everything they wanted. Beti had a three-hundred-rupees' Benares sari, Motilal a Calcutta dhoti, and there was actually a marriage procession with a bridal Rolls-Royce car, beginning at the corner of the Badé Bazaar and ending at the market square, by the clock tower. When Beti saw her son with a gold-laced turban, a filigree-worked achkan, garlanded from head to foot, and followed by thousands and thousands of people as the procession moved along amidst illumination and fireworks, she could not control her tears, and repeated a thousand times to herself, that now she could die, happily, contentedly. And the daughter-in-law was such a sweet creature. She looked healthy and strong, and she would work so well.

A week later everything went on as usual. Only, each time Ananda—or in fact any customer—went into the shop, Beti repeated from beginning to end all about the clothes and clang and grand hospitality of marriage. In the meanwhile the young daughter-in-law—rather plump and big-breasted, with thick voluptuous lips and eyes that showed an iron will and unasking calm—the daughter-in-law would be grinding rice or wheat behind the gram platform. And Chota was hardly ever to be found in the shop. It was understood that he spent his whole day, except when he had to go and get provisions from the Central Grain Market, with his mistress in her cigarette shop beside the mosque. Whenever Beti wanted him, she sent her little daughter-in-law—they called her Rati—to the cigarette shop to fetch him. Only once Venku, Chota's mistress, had mocked at Rati and called her "a village kid." Otherwise they were on polite, indifferent terms. Chota's child through Venku sometimes came into the gram shop, to get something to eat from his grandmother, and Rati herself had often washed and fed him. But after a few months a strange jealousy broke in her. She was pregnant.

Now Motilal was really getting old. By next Dassera, he would be fifty-eight or sixty. And that awful asthma had grown worse than ever. Night after night he had sat sleepless, smoking his hookah and waiting for the dawn to come, when it would suddenly grow less painful, and he would lie down to have a short nap. These sleepless nights had greatly weakened his already feeble nerves. He felt like beating everybody he saw, and lately there had actually been a boycott among his clients, because of his extreme irritability. They had all agreed—it was his rival Mohanlal of the little shop by the banyan who was behind it—they had all agreed that they would never go to him again. For three or four days, so few set foot in the shop that Beti, who had a vague idea about it, went to ask Ananda's stepmother and the short clerk's wife as to why they had become so cruel towards her. They did not hide the cause, and assuring them that she would see that her husband would lose his temper no more, she came back and scolded him. He coughed away and listened, and sat as furious as ever. The parrot's noise bothered him and the sight of his daughter-in-law was unbearable. Sometimes he closed his eyes, and sat telling himself that the whole world wanted to kill him. Once he had threatened Ananda with his hookah for having touched the rice before he gave it. But Ananda had come to have a strange affection for poor Beti, and he always went to buy things there. And there was one little secret that nobody knew except Ananda and Beti. On Saturday evenings, when Motilal was not there, Ananda always went into the shop and Beti would give him a handful of salted grams with such trust and tenderness! "That thing is an orphan," she would say to herself, "and I too have been an orphan." And in her heart she felt Ananda liked her. They were secret friends. But Motilal was never to know of it. Never.

Of late the transactions of Motilal had extended not only throughout Hyderpur but even to the districts. He had many friends amongst the clerks and secretaries and their bosses always wanted money, more money. The District Collector of Sundarpur had taken a loan of ten thousand rupees to buy his new car and pay off a few old debts. The King's brother-in-law, who had just come of age to inherit his property, about which there was a lot of trouble, had borrowed twenty thousand rupees to pay his Bombay advocates. When he should win the case, which was sure, Motilal would get back the money, with twenty per cent interest. It was not known to many people, but it was a fact—there were documents to show it—that the great Prime Minister, having lost a great deal of money in a jute firm in Calcutta, had borrowed from him fifty, yes, five and zero, fifty thousand rupees at seventeen per cent interest. In a few months, that money with interest was to come back. There was but one sour unfortunate affair. A certain clerk whom he had known for years had duped him. That scoundrel of a fellow had taken him to a man who wanted only two thousand rupees. Yes, only two thousand rupees. He was, Motilal was told, a zamindar who owned many villages in Tikapur District. He lived in such a big house, with so many servants and cars, that Motilal was but too willing to lend the necessary amount. It was only for a short time. Six months at the most with twenty-two per cent. The agreement was duly registered, and Janki Ram—for that was the name of the man —thanked Motilal profusely for rescuing him from an old creditor. The next harvest would make him rich. But creditors are so cruel. They talk to everybody about your private affairs! A few weeks passed and somebody casually mentioned to Motilal the awful scandal of a fellow who had called himself Zamindar of Kotyapalli, and had suddenly disappeared from the city, leaving his cars unpaid for, his servants unpaid, his house rent unpaid. Hardly did Motilal hear that than he fell on the floor, shrieking like a child, and tearing his hair in utter despair. Beti ran to him, and the whole quarter came to see what they could do. But there was nothing to be done. Days passed. Sometimes he would suddenly cry out "The Zamindar of Kotyapalli! Two thousand rupees at twenty-two per cent interest. Do you know him, brother?" Or in the middle of the night he would wake up and going out into the street he would shriek out, as loud as he could, that the house was on fire, that the two thousand rupees had come back with a hundred per cent interest. More often he sat in the grocery, weeping and laughing, muttering things to himself in strange and different voices. But he was scrupulous as ever with his rice or salt, and weighed things exactly, nothing less, nothing more, just as though he were normal. He now stopped beating Beti and sometimes fondled her at unusual hours. He still hated Rati, but twice or thrice he suddenly embraced her and wept, crying what a sinner he was, what an old brute. But it was strange, very funny, as the short clerk's wife told her neighbor, that he, it seemed, never spoke a word to his son. Even if Chota stood in front of him, he would coolly turn away and smile at the parrot or a client.

After he had "lost his head in the well," as the people in the quarter said, he had taken to the strange mania of collecting bits of paper that blew in the street. Torn envelopes, cigarette boxes, bits of newspaper and even dry banana and banyan leaves that looked like paper. He collected them carefully, and bringing them home he would place them in a corner and ask his wife to admire his riches. Day after day he went out, and sometimes he even left his customers standing, and ran after a rag of paper that rolled down the street with the rising winds. Sitting in his seat, he would often say to himself, "I have paper. I have so much, so much paper. I am rich. If I should sell it I shall get money. Hé! hé! Money! Bank notes!" Or he would shriek out in the middle of his meals that the Zamindar of Kotyapalli had come and brought him twenty thousand rupees, actually twenty thousand rupees. "How do you like it, Beti? Hé?" "Very well," Beti would say, turning away her face. So that was what her husband had come to be.

One afternoon, while he was collecting his papers, a motor ran over him and he was instantly killed.

Beti got ten thousand rupees as damages and she was free.

Now that Motilal was dead, Chota had more responsibilities than before. He had to look to the accounts, go to people and dun them for payments, sign and register new transactions, and in addition he had his usual provisions to buy in the Central Grain Market twice a month. Very often he came back at nine or ten at night, tired and breathless, his head all covered with dust and his eyes pale and lustreless, and Rati would serve him his dinner that was always kept ready for him in the corner. Of course they rarely spoke to each other, and if they had anything to say, it was always communicated through gestures or short-worded statements, muttered as though to oneself. Beti sat by him when he ate and talked about that day's transactions. After dinner he would rest a moment and then go away to Venku, who had always a mouthful of curses to greet him with. He never gave her enough money and yet he would not let her go. That comic actor Mir Sahib was still asking her to come back to him, and Chota knew it was true. They had wrangles about Mir Sahib, who had once been actually found talking to her by the shopwindow. In his fury Chota had beaten her, and she had run away to the other, free as a dog. Chota swore and spat in terrible rage. But there was nothing to be done. She had gone. And that's that. He closed the shop and went home to eat. When Beti talked to him he flared up at her and asked her to mind her own business. Rati served. The soup was not hot, it was not . . . "You daughter of a witch! You bloody whore!" He kicked her so badly on the stomach that she fell on the floor moaning. This was the second time he had kicked her like that, the first time being some months ago when she was pregnant, and the child had died of it. Anyway it was not so great an affair now. Neither operation, nor the police, to be feared. Rati soon recovered and everything went on as usual. Only when he went back to the cigarette shop, it was still closed. That wretched woman had not only run away herself, but had taken his own son. Sour concubine! He felt humiliated, torn. The devout and suffering eyes of Rati seemed so comforting. Why did he think of her? He did not know. He ran back and slept with Rati. She was so happy. She had never been so happy with him. But she knew he would be cold again—the following morning.

Poor Rati! Her life was such a dark affair. Born of rich parents, she had hardly known what it was to do any manual work. The prettiest among her sisters, she was the most loved in the family. Now her parents were dead, and her brother had never as much as written a card to her. Here, a slave of Beti, a casual wife of a husband with a mistress, her existence was worse than anything she had ever heard or known in all her town. Of what use was all the money her husband had? What for? She had to patch her sari almost every week, and she wore silver bangles instead of the gold ones she had in childhood. There was nothing to hope for, nothing to ask. She had even hung a coconut in Maruthi's temple, with vows and prayers that her husband might turn kinder to her. But nothing had so far happened, nothing. Once or twice she had ideas of suicide, but it frightened her. To live alone like this was more comfortable. She bit her lips and determined she would live alone. One day her husband would turn back and come to her. If not, well, one has just to live . . . like Beti. . . .

For some years, the "goddess," as they call the epidemic of plague, used to make annual visits to Hyderpur. October or November would announce her, and processions of corpses would go every day in the streets, till the hot sun of March would fight a battle with her and dethrone her for the moment. During the time the goddess reigned, half the city would be empty. The whole countryside would be filled with little bamboo huts, where people retired for fear of being the chosen ones. Only the medical men, the big sahibs with their spacious and clean bungalows, the banias, and the crippled and the starving would stay in their haunted homes. From the time the sun beamed forth in the morning till he speedily sank away by the evening, the whole town would be busy. They said the goddess could work only at night. The camps would be practically empty except for the mothers and the aged. Then, hardly would the dusk throw her torn blanket over the town than the street would be a desert again. The dogs too had lessened in number. Now and again, however, a car rushed past as though in holy fear that the goddess might peep through it even for a moment, or a crowd of people would be seen following a corpse with shrieking and hell-moving cries. Only the stars hung in the sky full of purity and strength. They alone seemed to know life was eternal.

There was another place where life was unchanging. It was the little gram shop. There everything went on as usual. And as many merchants had died in the city, so the prices had gone up and Beti naturally profited by it. One sold milk at eight pice a pau instead of at six. Even rice had increased in price. In one month they had earned one and a half times what they usually made in other seasons. Beti sat in her seat on the gram platform as though the goddess herself would be whisked away with her little fly duster.

But it was not to be. The goddess had left them safe for two years, and now she was not going to leave them. One night Rati got a terrific fever. Of course there was no doubt, it was plague. The next morning the municipal servant came and cleaned the house with tar and burned sulphur in the rat holes. At eleven the Municipal Inspector came and asked Beti to send her daughter-in-law to the Isolation Hospital. No, she would not go. Rati when asked began to weep. She would rather die in that house than in a hospital. The idea of the hospital horrified her. All that they did there, nobody knew. They cut you, pierced your flesh, and did a million unholy things. Death were better. But by some strange power that Rati had developed, death seemed nothing to her. Not that it did not matter. But that it would not touch her. It would not. The will in her seemed stronger than any death. She knew she could not die. . . . But on the second day the fever increased. The bubo became bigger. And she was unconscious half of the time. But when she was awake she seemed so confident of her life that even the visiting doctor, who had been sent by the Plague Defense Committee, was struck by the fearlessness and confidence she showed. She had assured him she *would* not die. The goddess would not take her away.

It was the third day. Ananda, who had come to town to get some clothes from the deserted house, naturally went to see Beti and have his pice-worth of gram. Rati lay unconscious by the grocery, her eyes full of stagnant tears, her body stiff and uncovered, one hand upon her heaving breasts and the other upon the floor, her mouth wide open, with a legion of buzzing flies, some that went in, some that flew around, and some that sat upon her palpitating nostrils, and amidst all this she moaned forth, raucous and breathless, "Mother, mother, mai . . . Mai . . . My mother, mai . . ."

Need it be said, Rati died the fourth day towards dawn and was burnt that very afternoon. She was gone. Her will seemed brittle before the fire that consumed her. Death was the victor.

Years later, when Ananda came back from the north, he passed by his favorite gram shop. It was still so familiar to him. Only they said Beti had died a few months ago of old age, and it was Venku who sat on the gram platform. Buying the usual pice-worth of gram, he gave a few grains to the parrot, that had survived all. "Mithu! Mithu!" "Ram Ram . . . Babu Ram. . . ." "Pyari Mithu!" "Ram Ram . . . Babu Ram. . . ." In the street the dust rose—and fell.

Nimka

I MET Nimka in Paris yesterday. Nimka (or Nimotchka) is a White Russian of Caucasian origin, but she prefers to call herself Circasian—it gives her mystery distinction. Nimka has green mongoloid eyes, and a soft lolling tongue that contains rounded sweetness. When I knew her first, about twenty years ago, she served in some restaurant of the Quartier Latin, which gave her food and function and the few hundred francs that were necessary to make her mother live, from week to week. Nimka's mother was of course brought up at the Smolny, and the Smolny courtyard seemed to play a more important part in their family history than the revolution and the civil war. For in the Smolny courtyard, everyone on their walks *de jeunes filles* dreamt, and they dreamt such glorious dreams—that some Grand Duke of course went to a ball, and of course the Circasian beauty was the most ravishing of all that he had ever seen (and Smolny taught such rare bashfulness, it made even the horses at the sledges neigh) and the *Impératrice,* naturally, would hear nothing of it all, but some high priest intervened, and as the Court loved escapades, the couple fled to Switzerland, and the Emperor was duly white and red with ire, but what was, was, and after all the Circasian beauty had a father who was a general, and he was made bigger and brought to the Court, and the fault was of course laid on Count Tolstoy who destroyed every vestige of Society, and Tolstoy wrote a letter to the Countess Straganza Boriloff, a letter which is still a treasure in the little room—*troisième à gauche, escalier de droite,* as the concierge says, and you knock at the door and this Circasian princess opens the door to you, with a smile that would warm your heart even on this cold and wet summer of 1953. When I say, you are warmed by Nimka's heart, I mean it, for I have sat hour after hour, in her little room Rue Fossé Saint Jacques, where no sun ever shone, and even the concierge's cat had to go and sit by the sill to see if there's sun shining anywhere in the sky. Nimka, of course, made such lovely borscht for her mother—they lived on the ground floor that opened on the yard, and students went in and out of the main door, casting mysterious glances at this young princess who fed the concierge's cat. Some of them had read Gorki's "Twenty-Six Men and a Girl," and the thought went through their minds, that this princess may well be their inviolable deity. Nimka had naturally never read Gorki—how could she—but she knew what was right from what was wrong without her mother saying anything. The Tolstoy letter, duly framed and hung on the wall —the Ikon from Kiev stood a little further down in the corner—gave every advice that anyone could ever need. Tolstoy had said, in his rough flourishing hand—there were many French words in his letters which showed to whom he was addressing himself—"Il n'y a pas de doute que—Auguste Comte dit quelquefois—d'autre part il faut bien le dire—je suis, etc., etc. . . ." Tolstoy's flourishing hand said that the evil must be met with good. The good is what had distinction, and the bad what is successful. Even the cat knew what is good—one hadn't to call the cat when mother's soup was finished and one brought the rest to the courtyard; the cat waited there, as though the right thing would come from the right place at the most appropriate time. He who knows himself good is known by the animals he has. The cat never miaowed—you hadn't like the concierge to call out Minou, Minou, the little white streaked black thing was ever furrily present with uplifted gratitude. The old princess even left her small portion to the cat, and so the young Nimotchka left some of her foods for her mother. That is goodness, if goodness needs a definition. Nimotchka was good, very good, and of a simple true beauty, as though you cannot efface it even were you to cut her face with many crosses. Her beauty had certainty, it had a rare equilibrium, and a naughtiness that was feminine and very innocent. It projected a quality of assurance that you were good, even were you bad, for this beauty could not be had, so you had to be good. It was beauty—it always will be, and you cannot take it, and as such you cannot soil yourselves. How could you, for when you contemplate beauty, you end in contemplation —you may even have a cup of tea. Nimotchka loved tea— of course—and I loved it because she loved it.

I used to go to Nimotchka—I was a student too, and at the Sorbonne—and, on Sunday mornings when she came back from church, she loved to have friends visiting her. That day, the lunch service was later, so you had an hour more. Nimka was gay, and when she came back, I read to her some text from the Ramayana or the Mahabharata, the story of Nala and Damayanti, and the exile of the royal couple always moved her. She made a link between the Smolny courtyard and the palace of Damayanti, and she had only to invent the Swan. I was the Swan then—I was the Swan now. Nimka knew the Indian saying that the swan knows how to separate milk from water—the good from the bad, and as I knew her to be good, she recognized me a swan. The swan sailed in and out and India became the land where all that is wrong everywhere goes right there. In India, the Smolny courtyard exists—it could not but exist—look at the number of Maharajas, the Maharaja of Kapurthala and His Highness the Aga Khan, all Indians and you saw their pictures in the newspapers. They assured you of your very existence—you had a right to exist in righteousness, for they existed and their decorous faces lit up the pages of the newspapers. Nimka, whom I had once taken to the Théâtre des Champs Élysées to see Uday Shankar dance, actually met the Yuvaraja of Mysore. I introduced her to him, and she gave such a curtsey and a smile—it made her certain her assuredness was right. The mother was all grateful for my kindness. And in a few months a new picture went up on their wall. It was the picture of Mahatma Gandhi, for Tolstoy was a friend of Mahatma Gandhi (I read her the full text of Tolstoy's letter to Mohandas Gandhi—the one in Romain Rolland's *Life of Gandhi*, éditions Stock). And so Tolstoy was right and India was right, and since she could not put up a picture of me on the wall, she put up Mahatma Gandhi's. It gave great beauty to Tolstoy's face—the one looked the disciple, and the other the master. Since I was a son of India, I was as it were, a sort of grandson, and she was, so to say, of the same status as I. That made everything possible, the conversation, the gentle looks, and a dinner now and again—one had an afternoon off every fortnight, in those days—which made affinity permissible. I could also take her out to Chinese restaurants, and she loved to be the Princess. She had her mother's mink coat, of course, and a pearl necklace they had saved against all odds—it was to be her marriage gift. Nimka, I think, loved me, but somehow that necklace came in the way. She could not imagine me and the necklace altogether—that necklace was made of pain, it stood there as a reminder of man's inner strength against outer odds—it meant struggle and passion and poverty—the bow of Rama is easier to break than to twist the screw of that Russian necklace, the hand that could twist it, needed a more masculine grasp, a more painful nobility, a graver happiness. The Indian is too simple in his depth—if there's no concierge and the cat, there's no goodness. Success is sin. Gandhi is poverty. The Maharaja is proof of truth. Truth is unnaked. Love is unsaid. So, Nimotchka fell in love with Michel.

Now, Michel was a friend of mine. He was nineteen, and had a fine mask of dignity. He had gone through the École Normale, and was at the rue d'Ulm. I knew him for he'd taken Sanscrit for his "aggrégation" and I often met him at the Institut de la Civilisation Indienne at the Sorbonne. He

was pale, with a nervous twitch of the nose, and his hands
ever trying to adjust his eyeglasses, as though however much
he wanted to see clearly, he just could not see clearly. He
said to me, "When my teachers say green, I just do not know
what green is—when they say red, I just do not know what
red is—I know them as names of colors. All my life I just
wanted to see—see it, the object, the object as reality, and
my friend, what can I do? I just cannot look at it. I am a
failure. I am damned. My father died in the war, and left my
mother a widow of twenty-one. I am the hope of the family
—hope indeed, he who cannot distinguish between red and
green. Color, yes, a name. A name is everything. Abélard,
that old sensualist was right. We are all nominalists. The
object exists because of its name. Remove the name, and the
object is space. Remove the space, and the object is the
Reality. Poetry must be made of reality. Vocables are volun-
tary creations. We just invent language as we invent breath.
Breath," he said, opening his waistcoat, as though he wanted
more air, and he stopped. Nimka who served us, would wait
with her plate till the speech was over. She loved his dignified voice and his love for scribbling all over the tablecloth.
He wrote vocables. He invented vocables.

And one day when I'd gone out on Easter holidays and returned, I saw Nimka and Michel arm in arm. They smiled
to me very sweetly. Michel was a poet. The poet is sacred.
Tolstoy was not a poet. He was a writer. But then he was a
poet all right. Michel wrote beautiful things. He said beautiful things. How he laughed, when Nimka laughed. I was
their saint and protector. Since Michel lived in rue d'Ulm
and she couldn't take him to rue Saint Jacques, they met in
my room, rue du Sommerard. Michel read to her his poems.
She never wore the pearl necklace for him. She became
grave. I knew she never allowed him to touch her. Thus
she respected me. Only once, said Michel, she allowed him
to kiss her, and that was in a church. (The Rumanian one,
behind rue du Sommerard.) She thought it improper—it had

to do with the flesh—and she had to hide it from her mother. She decided then to marry, marry anyone. She could not marry me—I was too far, too distant and different. She could not marry Michel—he had kissed her. Michel was so desperate. Nimka married, almost a month after that, Count Vergilian Kormaloff, who ran the vegetarian restaurant, off the Pantheon. She bore him a child very soon, and though there was so much warmth in her heart, her face was infinitely sad. Sorrow seemed to sit on her brow, for the noble count, apart from being twenty years her elder and a widower, was interested in betting on horses. He lost everything he ever had on horses. Then he started borrowing from his clients. One day his restaurant too had to be sold. He left Nimotchka during the days of the Czechoslovak crisis, and ran to Monte Carlo to make money. Boris, his little son, never saw him again.

When Hitler occupied France, I wondered what would have happened to Nimka and her mother. When the Hitler police saw the picture of Tolstoy and Gandhi, they never worried her, wrote Nimka. During the war, she said, she became, for Boris' sake, a mannequin. She knew nothing wrong could happen to her. Success she despised most of all. She liked to live as her mother had taught her to live. The mother had died during the occupation. She believed that one day truth would reign in the world. She hoped Mahatma Gandhi might still save the world. She liked Hitler, for he liked India . . . Mahatma Gandhi was shot, and Nimka knew that was the price of righteousness. At seventeen Boris studied at the Lycée Louis le Grand. Boris knew all was good. So when the Russians invited the Russians from all over the world to return, he was so proud (anyway he did not like to do military service in France) and he went, hoping to come back and take his mother. Boris never returned, of course.

Nimka lives in rue des Écoles, not far from rue du Sommerard, and she knits pullovers for the "Grand Magasins".

She sold her pearl necklace and put the money into a little cloth shop off rue Poitou (for food and clothing are essentials of life and you cannot lose on that) and the returns are not too bad. The Ikon and the Tolstoy letter, still adorn the walls, and the picture of Mahatma Gandhi has gone up above the bed. He knows, does Mahatma Gandhi, the pinching pain of mankind. With every scrub of the floor, and with every cry of the child in the street, there's a voice that responds, and that is Mahatma Gandhi. Mahatma Gandhi, said Nimka to me yesterday, is not a man, he is not a saint, he is a country. Green fields must billow into the bright sun, and men must bend to collect the corn. The swan must fly there, and goodness is good for it is not success. Virtue is the woman's privilege, man is the undiscoverable. Nimka was not sad. Her heart contained an intimacy of sorrow that was almost kin of joy. She was warm, of course, and spoke beautifully. Her French accent had that silvery touch of the Slavs that makes the language almost sing. Nimka asked nothing of life. She asked nothing of me. When I said goodbye, she did not say, when shall I see you again? She knew the life that has ended is eternal. When you are shot you become immortal.

P. B. BHAVE

P. B. Bhave was born at Dhulia in 1910, into a family of doctors and educators. He received his B.A. and L.L.B. degrees from the University of Nagpur.

He began writing while still in high school. "Self-expression was the driving motive." He read classical Indian literature and was influenced by the Ramayana, *the* Mahabharat, *and the works of Kalidas. He admires Shakespeare, Dostoevski, Chekhov, de Maupassant, Hugo, and Thomas Hardy.*

Bhave is among the foremost short story writers in the Marathi language. During the past twenty years he has written about a dozen novels, hundreds of short stories, and many plays.

Bhave is considered by critics to be one of the pioneers of the new short story movement in Marathi, which like Bengali is alive and active. His view is that the Indian writer's vision is somewhat narrow and has to be broadened.

Bhave combines literary activity with practicing law.

The Mystery

P. B. BHAVE

DINU was very much disturbed that day. He was not himself at all. Something in him had risen in a little rebellion against him. The perfume of *attars* and scents hung thick around him like a cloud. For this had been his main job, for the last few days; sprinkling rosewater and scents at the guests and visitors, who came for the marriage reception.

"Well, young man," someone asked, "your cousin has already done it. How about you?"

"If he managed it at twenty-three, why could you not do it at twenty-one? This is a tropical country, this India," another remarked.

And a third one said,

"Well, prince, it is just not enough that this lovely place of yours serves the purpose of a marriage pandal for the relatives. It's where your marriage ceremony would eventually come off, we imagine. And what was that you said? 'Taking the B.A. exam, this year'. . . No, no, and no. Examination! So what? Even the great men of the past were married, when they were just children in fact. They got through their exams all right, eh!"

M-A-R-R-I-A-G-E . . . Everyone talked with him in the same manner, and gave him the same searching looks. It was as if Vasant, the new bridegroom, had already been bundled out and all were now anxiously waiting for Dinu's turn to face the music. He had attracted a lot of attention of the parents of a number of eligible young girls, when he moved about smartly as man-in-waiting. In fact, the bridegroom himself was of no consequence at all. The visitors had already taken a careful look at the palatial bungalow and the beautiful limousine of the young man's father, and the fact that Dinu was just a young college student reading for his B.A. exam made hardly any difference. Wrinkled hands were folded before Dinu's father. The high and mighty talked in soft and sweet tones, and polite questions were asked: when could the daughter's photograph be sent, when could some precious time be spared, when could the girl be brought along for a meeting? Everyone seemed to be talking about marriage. Not about Vasant, the bridegroom, who was in the marriage pandal, mind you, but about Dinu who was just not ready to think of it for a couple of years or more.

Dinu too felt a certain attraction for the opposite sex, just what a normal young man would ordinarily feel. But he had surely never thought of marriage seriously till that moment. For the last three days, however, things had changed. He moved in an atmosphere so surcharged with it, and so many fingers had pointed in the one and only direction that he gradually became more and more conscious about what was happening. Greatly startled, as if at some mysterious happening, his attention was now concentrated in one direction. He began to see there something he had never seen before.

Someone played classical music outside on the *shahnai,* and it had an exquisite charm about it. Luckily, the fellow had not fallen for the temptation to play some cheap film song, and had chosen some real masterpiece. As he lay in his room, Dinu could see the picture of the player before his eyes. A little cyclonic world of music and emotions was being created, and Dinu was being sucked into the cyclone.

How wonderful were the three days that had gone by? The magic tunes of the *shahnai* had woven together the delicate world that existed during the last three days. The smoke of the incense, the rising flame of the sacred fire, columns of banana trees, the offshoots of the mango tree, heaps of flowers, beautiful garments, attractive ornaments, gay faces, precious carpets, and about all the *mantras*—sacred, compact with beautiful words and meaning.

And then there were faces too; of people coming from somewhere, and going some place. Faces that were approaching and vanishing, raised and drooping. But all were smiling, happy. His house had undergone a transformation in the last few days. It was not just a stone and mortar building any more, it was turned into a temple of marriage. New hopes were flowering. New expectations and a novel joy were blossoming forth. The whole thing was magical, exceedingly magical. Vasant Patwardhan and Leela Paranjape—where had they come from? They came from far-off places. They had never cast their eyes on each other before in their lives. A couple of months back, they did not even know of each other's existence. And now, the two had come together, for ever, into a lifelong union. They were now going to share each other's lives with their joys and griefs, hopes and disappointments. They had a common future before them, and lives of these two, who were unknown to each other just a few days back, had now merged into a single life. This unknown woman was now to be as near and dear to him as his own parents. Perhaps even more than the parents in a sense. The parents might part company, but not this young girl who was just a stranger to him the day before. Without rhyme or reason, she had become his partner for the rest of his life. Just after taking seven steps together in the marriage ceremony, they had become united for seven lives. How wonderful and how mysterious?

The men and women outside laughed loudly. Dinu could imagine what was happening. The ritual bath was going on, and certainly there could be no better occasion for fun and frolic. Vasant was a handsome young man and Leela was a beauty. But the charm that surrounds a couple on the occasion of marriage itself has something special about it. Right from the time they entered the pandal, some flame from within had lighted up their bodies, their faces, their whole beings in fact. At the time when they sipped *kheer* from the same vessel, when he whispered her new name in her ears and wrote it down on the grains of rice with his ring, when they garlanded each other, when she worshipped, and when they took the seven steps together, and then at the time of the ritual bath, his face had brightened up and she too had bloomed. Beautiful was hardly the word for it. It was something ethereal.

The *shahnai* played some fine melody outside. Occasionally, the music was submerged by loud guffaws, and one could hear the splashing of water. Then the new bride was asked formally to pronounce her husband's name, and when she did, there was an explosion. The laughing gas was on once again. The thick voices of men, soft voices of women, tingling sounds of bangles and vessels were in the air. Dinu was trying to snatch some rest after the heavy and strenuous work of attending to the guests. As he lay in his bed in his room, various scenes in the marriage ceremony flashed before his eyes. In that half-awakened and half-sleepy state, a number of voices jostled together asking him, "Well, young man, when does your marriage come off?"

"What's up, eh!" Dinu said and staggered to his feet looking in the direction of the door for some seconds. Hira was standing there on the doorstep. Hira—the daughter of father's friend, who had come to attend the marriage function. Hira—a young, unmarried girl. She probably had come round to his room for the last two days intentionally, and quite often too, when he was in there. She had given up partaking of the fun that was going on outside, and had come in.

"Will you just get up for a moment, please?" she asked.

"Well, what brings you here?"

"Oh, I'm sorry. My sari is lying there on the bedstand. Would you mind if I just take it away?"

Dinu was up in a flash. Her costly sari, with the border

of golden thread, was lying on his bed. The heavy meals, the pressure of ceaseless work had made Dinu pretty drowsy and as soon as the bath-ritual had begun outside he had made his escape into his room. This was what was happening all these three days. He came last night to his room, completely fagged out, all ready to go to sleep straightaway, only to find that this girl and another one were already sleeping there on his bed. Perforce, he had to spend the night outside on a bench and he was only lucky that it was not cold out there. Otherwise, he would surely have caught cold, thanks to these intruders in his room.

He took the sari, and handed it over to her.

"Excuse me please. I never seemed to notice it, you know."

"Oh, not at all. My mistake in fact." Her tone was apologetic.

"Well, that's nothing. In a crowded place like this," he said. The delicate damsel then withdrew, her eyes still lingering on the young man.

Dinu looked at her receding figure. He looked at his bed and at the room which appeared to have been completely transformed. It did not look like one belonging to a collegian, but more like a women's dressing room. It was not just the sari that was lying on the bed. There was a new sari thrown on the back of his chair, and then there was an old one which someone had changed, and which was lying on the floor. There were brassieres, and there were powder tins, combs, hairpins, flowers, and sundry other things. A complete outfit for any fashionable young lady. His room had been turned into a godown. Without a word of permission or consent, the girls and ladies had taken charge of his room. In the bookcase there, Shakespeare and Ruskin stood, their faces looking small.

Dinu had never come in such close contact with women. And what was that? Woman's hair on his table! He was upset, and marching angrily up to the table, he picked them up. They were very soft to the touch. At once, Dinu understood. These were the hair of Vimal Joshi—the golden-haired damsel. She was one of the bridegroom's marriage party. Though a college student, she was not as bold as the other girl, Hira. She never appeared in his presence on purpose. She was beautiful and modest, her hair—long, soft, and golden. And her father, too, had talked with Dinu's father—his hands folded, courtesy incarnate.

Dinu was all excitement. Again the boisterous laughter echoed from outside. His eyes surveyed once again the riot of toilet articles, powder tins, nailpaints and lipsticks, combs, the folded new sari hanging from the back of the chair, the used one that was lying on the floor, and finally they rested on the old lemon-colored sari with the red borders. At the same time, the *shahnai* unwound a delicate melody outside.

The marriage pandal had become empty and deserted by now. The chairs and carpets had been removed. Dried plantain and betel leaves, petals of flowers, empty cigarette packets lay scattered on the floor. The kids in the house, who had not left yet, were playing with the plantain leaves, from which they had prepared little trumpets. The pandal itself would soon be removed. The drops were being taken out, the strings wound up, and the "kitson" lamps taken away. The big gathering of people, that had assembled for the occasion, quickly disappeared. The house that bustled with activity, had now regained its original sobriety and calm. But this was unbearable to Dinu any more. Ceremony and bustle seemed to him the natural atmosphere of the place.

Hira and her mother, the Joshi couple and their daughter Vimal left that evening by train. Hira's mother talked for quite a while with Dinu's mother in private. Till the train left, Hira looked searchingly at Dinu. Vimal's father again talked with Dinu's; his hands folded when he did so. Before the train left, Vimal bade goodbye to him, and how much did she blush then? She appeared to have guessed what her father must have talked to Dinu's.

"Well, goodbye then, and when do you invite us to visit here once again?" Vimal's mother had said, when Dinu had offered her *namaskar*.*

"Anytime. You are welcome, always," he replied.

"Well, try and give us the opportunity, young man," Vimal's father had remarked, meaningfully, looking through his glasses.

"The opportunity is there, for your asking," the young man replied.

"OK then. Don't hesitate afterwards, when the time comes. Your dad says, everything is up to you to decide," the Rao-bahadur said, following it up by loud laughter.

"Well, do invite us for your marriage party. Won't you?" Hira whispered looking at Vimal.

"And the invitation would be mutual, I suppose," Dinu replied.

"Oh . . . Uh . . ." Hira said, coyly. But she actually wanted to add if possible, "Could it not be so that our marriage parties will be just one? . . ." But there was no time to elaborate on this.

The green signal was on, and the guard whistled with shrill impatience. Back came the long whistle from the engine driver, and the train left. Dinu returned home after listening to the open and veiled hints about his marriage.

The marriage pandal was completely vacant by now, and the house seemed deserted. Now his room was not occupied by women, nor had been left behind any single thing belonging to them. Dinu flung his coat and cap on to the bed and reclined in the easy chair. From there, the marriage pedestal with the picture of Lord Ganesha painted on it, the columns of banana trees created for the auspicious occasion —all came into view. He had seen all these things before, but now they seemed to take a magical appearance. It was a great transformation undoubtedly. Hardly a week before,

---

* Respectful greetings.—Ed.

he was alone. He had moved about alone, lunched and lived all by himself. Now a young woman had appeared from somewhere, and had become part and parcel of his life. One can always understand the love of parents, of brothers and sisters. They are one's blood relations after all, and one has the advantage of living together with them under the same family roof. But how about this one? From where does this fountain of eternal love spring? What magic is this? Vasant was never before acquainted with Leela. His was just a simple marriage in strict, orthodox fashion. There was no question of the couple knowing each other beforehand, nor of friendship before marriage. Even so, Vasant had been greatly distressed when some blighter had stepped on Leela's foot, at the time of the marriage procession. His brow had cleared only when she began to smile. How does this feeling appear? From where does this pure love spring— love that resembles rain falling from a clear blue sky? M-A-R-R-I-A-G-E! How wonderful is the mystery of marriage? Somewhere a boy is born and a girl is born at someplace else. They do not know about each other's existence at all, but then they are born for each other's sake nevertheless. From among the countless girls, this is the one that he gets, and she too gets him from among the countless young men. The same way as Leela had found Vasant, and Vasant had found her. They were able to unravel the mystery, and find out the treasures for themselves. But how about this Hira? Who must be the man intended for her by God? And Vimal too! To whom would she belong? If I wish, indeed, I can have her for my wife. But then, I don't want to get married, not now. What is the big hurry after all? No, no sir, I am not getting married to Vimal, and Hira is just not the girl for me.

Dinu got up from the easy chair and sat on the bed. But he could not bear sitting on the bed. His emotions had blossomed forth in the last few days and his imagination had run riot. Garlands, flowers, saris, toilet sets—there was nothing of them in his room now. Hira wasn't there and

Vimal wasn't there too. His room was completely vacant—deserted. He alone was there, entirely and coldly alone.

He remembered Vimal's long hair, Hira's lingering, unsteady glances. He remembered the yellow sari with the red borders, that lay on the floor of his room. And the one question that the garlands and bouquets, scents and *shahnai*, and many others had suggested in many ways and had even asked openly began to echo in his ears. The question he had never seriously thought of, so far; the question he had not understood in fact till now. Like a rainbow emerging clearly from the mist, the question confronted him. And its colorful mystery enchanted him, and he was restless.

Who would that be, he thought: She who would worship the marriage-idol for him, whose name he would write with his ring, who would garland him and take his hand in marriage? Well, she must be someone. One with whom he would spend his whole life. She was going to arrive from somewhere one day, and stand before him. Who could that be? If Hira was not going to be his wife, who then was it to be? She must be there some place, but where was that place? What does she look like, what is her name? Sometime, he was going to know all about this. She would then step into his life and would be one with all that it would bring. He would then be able to talk to her; she would not just remain a dream, but will be real. But how did it happen that he knew just nothing about this one: who was going to be his, who was going to give him lifelong company, with whom he would spend the beautiful days and nights, happy and stormy days of the future?

Could she be Hira after all? Or maybe Vimal? The one who was going to change her name for his, the one who was going to arrive in any case, one among a million; who was she? Why should this secret about him be a secret to himself also? She might, in fact, be proceeding in his direction now, at this moment, in fact. Did he not have a right to know her after all?

This was the question. A question, the answer to which he was going to find out some day, but not now. Dinu was very much disturbed and excited. He felt like shouting at the top of his voice, for the girl that existed somewhere. He wanted her to come from wherever she was. "You are going to arrive after all. I shall then be able to look at you to my heart's content. Sometime I am going to feel your delicate touch on my body. I feel a great longing for you. I want to know who you are, where you are, and what you look like. How mysterious and wonderful! The partner for the rest of my life—but as yet unknown and unseen. I crave to tear off this curtain of the unknown and find out the mystery behind it. Won't you come? For a moment, at least?"

It was as mysterious as the dawn and the sunset, the morning sun and the stars, but he had never before felt any eagerness or anxiety to probe the mystery. He had just accepted its existence so far; but now, he longed to solve the mystery.

His thoughts began spinning around the girl who was going to step into his life sometime, though her person was still misty and unidentified. He felt suffocated inside the four walls of the room, eternally watched by the paper ghosts of Shakespeare and Ruskin. It was slowly getting dark and the exciting mystery became as much more attractive as it became deeper.

In a flash Dinu was out of his room. Swiftly, he walked across to where his bike was kept, leaning against the garage wall. He put on the light, and the next moment the vehicle went racing down the road.

Soon he crossed the river-bridge, Regent Square, and the YMCA Hostel. The moon-bathed trees in the big city garden stood still like the all-attentive audience at a public meeting. The Law College building, and the C. P. Club, flashed past as his bike went rushing along. The fields near the club exuded cold due to the lake waters nearby, that had seeped in. Though there was the cosy warmth of February in the city, the winter cold still lingered here, on the city's outskirts. The hills, fields, and the lake shivered in the biting cold and the moonlight too appeared to have been frozen by it.

But Dinu wasn't himself. A heat wave was blasting through his veins, and a stormy current of blood was surging up to his head. His bike still went dashing down and its shadow skimmed the road, as it ran.

It seemed that Dinu was not going to give up the chase until he had completely solved the mystery that had maddened him so.

Translated by Bal Gadgil

KRISHAN CHANDAR

Krishan Chandar, a leading Urdu short story writer and novelist, was born in 1913, at Lahore. His father was a doctor in Kashmir, where Krishan Chandar spent his childhood and youth. He was educated at the University of the Punjab, where he received both an M.A. in English and a bachelor's degree in law.

Krishan Chandar began his literary career in the post-Prem Chand era and was soon caught up in the "Progressive" movement. He rapidly became one of its most important exponents. He has been influenced by Marx, Freud, Tagore, and Prem Chand and admires the works of Chekhov, Balzac, Gorki, and Hemingway.

He has written about a dozen novels, some 300 short stories, and several one act plays. His books have been translated into English, German, Russian, Chinese, Japanese, Arabic, Persian, Danish, Italian, Czech. He lives in Bombay, and when not writing books he directs films. He writes both in Hindi and in Urdu.

In Krishan Chandar's view, the major achievement of modern Indian literature is "its attempt to modernize itself and to view India's attempt at modernization with sympathy and understanding."

The Soldier

KRISHAN CHANDAR

ZAMAN KHAN and Shahbaz Khan belonged to the same battalion. Friends and comrades-in-arms, who understood each other thoroughly. Theirs was not a friendship born of joint visits to cafes, drinking houses, and dance halls. It was something more enduring—a friendship grown slowly to maturity under the menacing wings of war planes, under the deafening barrage of guns and the creeping shadows of death. There was nothing soft or refined about their friendship; it was coarse-grained and wild, like animal exuberance. Deep, firm like the Jung tree, nurtured by the rocky soil of the tableland. Such friendship has no place for sentiments, nor any scope for mutual bickerings, and it is completely devoid of the flights of fancy or the poetry of life. But it has a surprising element of mutual trust. It is an attachment which has no tongue, but nevertheless understands the language of the heart. Zaman Khan and Shahbaz Khan greeted each other in abusive terms, and had frequent rows. They would go to the extent of reporting against each other to the havaldar of their unit. But when it came to facing danger, they acted as one and no sacrifice was too great for them. The officers and other ranks of the battalion knew about it, and out of fun, often tried to drive a wedge between them, but without success.

The war was over. After five years of active service they were returning home. Shahbaz Khan belonged to Chaklala and Zaman Khan came from Jhelum. They sat in the train facing each other, looking out of the window, at the acacia trees and the shrubs of jund and shrah. Their hungry, eager eyes roved over the high rocky cliffs and the red-brown earth, on which nothing grew except millet and men with sinews of steel.

The train cutting its way through a long range of high cliffs entered a sloping valley. In the distance, a little above them, a thin meandering path swept past the feet of a maiden who was carrying a pot on her head, and whose gait seemed to sway to the beat of an invisible drum. "Come, my sweetheart, my soldier, whose face is like the moon," Shahbaz hummed. He suddenly stopped humming and bit his thin lips. "Over there, across that hill, is Abdulla's village."

Below the range of hills lay huddled a small valley, through which flowed a small stream. Across the stream lay a village, a village over which stretched the sky—Abdulla's village. Abdulla, who would never return. He had died fighting in an Italian village and his body lay buried in alien soil.

"And Nisar," Zaman Khan said.

"And Nisardad Khan!"

"Bhatta!"

A long row of faces flit past their eyes—red and white faces, laughing faces, frowning faces. Faces, fearless, wild, cruel, innocent. They were human faces, the faces of their brethren; faces which had sprung from the same soil, had lived in the same environments and were now watching their native land through the eyes of Shahbaz and Zaman.

Gone, all gone.

Nisar, Karamdad, Bhatta, Abdulla . . .

Shahbaz said, "Why do we have wars?"

"Ask the Havaldar," Zaman replied and he looked at the medals spread on his breast.

"Why do soldiers die?"

Zaman Khan was silent.

"Suppose all the soldiers in the world refuse to fight," Shahbaz said. "Then . . ."

"Then the enemy would win!" Zaman replied.

"Enemy? Where would the enemy be?"

"Better ask the Havaldar," Zaman repeated.

Shahbaz became silent. The train went hurtling through the rocky gorge.

"My Jhelum is getting nearer," Zaman Khan said with pride.

"But my Chaklala is still a long way off," Shahbaz said a little sadly. Then a faint smile spread on his face, like the first rays of the sun. "My wife may come to meet me at the station."

"Huh!" Zaman's tone was harsh. He was still unmarried.

"And my son . . . When I joined the army he was hardly one year old. He must have grown tall."

"Yes, as big as the barrel of your rifle," Zaman said.

"I wonder if he will recognize me," Shahbaz said as if talking in a dream.

"He won't, if he is a bastard," Zaman replied.

Shahbaz hit him in the chest. Zaman rolled with laughter.

"You son of a pig!" Shahbaz roared. "—your mother! — your sister!"

They were still abusing each other when they arrived at Jhelum.

Zaman Khan, nicknamed Jamma, climbed out of the train, leaning on his crutch. The coolie took down his luggage and put it by his side. Zaman counted his belongings—a heavy bedroll, and a large trunk. That was all. After six years of war, that was all that he possessed. And he had returned minus one leg, lost somewhere in the battle front. His thick, black moustache bristled, the color of his face had turned to copper and his blue eyes were filled with hate. He scratched his chin, turned round and stood to attention before the carriage window.

"God be with you, Baje," he said.

"God be with you, Jammi."

"Write to me."

"Yes, I will."

There was an awkward pause.

"Will you be able to manage? Or should I reach you to your village?" Shahbaz cast a quick glance at Zaman's crutches.

Zaman thought that Shahbaz's sympathy was tinged with mockery. His body stiffened.

"No, I'll manage," he said vigorously pumping Shahbaz's hand for the last time. "I'll be home in the twinkling of an eye."

The train started moving. "Jamma, my boy."

"Yes, Baje!"

"The war was not so bad, after all. If you had only come back whole. I feel sorry for your lost leg, my friend."

With a frown on his face, Zaman kept looking at Shahbaz's laughing face, till the train had left the platform. He stamped the crutch on the platform in anger.

"Brother!" the coolie said.

"Bastard!" Zaman Khan fumed at Shahbaz.

"Did you call me a bastard?" the coolie exploded. "Bastard you, and bastard your father! Soldiers like you sell here at two a pice. Don't put on airs or I'll shove this crutch of yours up your pipe. I belong to the Buldayal tribe. Buldayal, you know?"

"I am also Buldayal, you son of a stick!" Zaman grinned with pleasure. "Pick up my luggage, you son of a drum! I'm your brother. Where do you come from?"

"Koh Murree."

Zaman Khan patted him on the shoulder. "Our tribe is unique," he said to the coolie effusively, tracing the coolie's ancestry to pigs. "By God, all the Buldayal jawans of our regiment were bastards. Brave bastards, all. They fought like lions, and each one decorated for valor!"

The coolie placed the trunk on his head, and put the bed-roll under his arm. "Here, give me the crutch also!" he said.

"And how will I walk then? with your legs? son of a pig?"

The coolie laughed. They came out of the station. Zaman Khan wanted to pay him. "Not from you," the coolie said. "Not from a Buldayal, who is like a brother to me. You are back from the war and . . ." He looked at the crutch and suddenly stopped on seeing the expression on Zaman's face. "Go in peace, jawan. May you live long to enjoy your pension."

Zaman's lips were curled in a thin smile—a strange, sweet, imperceptible smile which had more tears than joy, more pity than tears, and more helplessness than pity. The smile said, "This is my land, here is my village, which used to ring with my childhood days, whose beautiful sky is still studded with the stars of my dreams and in whose soil still lies embalmed the dance of my beloved's soft feet." He slowly descended the steps of the railway station and heaved himself into the tonga with the support of the crutch.

"To the city, jawan?" the tongawalla asked.

"No."

"To Gatalian, jawan?"

"No, I'm bound for the small village, this side of the Jhelum. If you drive fast we shall be there before nightfall."

"Get going my beauty!" The tongawalla twisted the tail of the horse. The bells round its neck jingled and the red plume on its head bobbed in the breeze. Zaman Khan, holding his crutch in one hand, and with one foot planted on the trunk was on his way to his village.

When the village came in sight, Zaman Khan asked the tongawalla to slow down a little. Before him was the boundary wall of the village and beyond it the bank of the river Jhelum. Across the river ran the boundary line of Kashmir state and on it the Octroi post of Gatalian. He heard the soft murmur of the flowing river and the faint smell oozed from the dank grass growing along its banks. The crops had been gathered and the bare stubbles of the field suddenly reminded him of those graves on which thousands of tiny white crosses had been planted. The war too had gathered in its gruesome harvest—which, incidentally, also included a sizeable portion of his precious leg.

The evening had descended and the last batch of village girls with pitchers filled from the well were hurrying towards the village. There was a time when standing behind the sreh tree Zaman eagerly used to look forward to Zena's coming. He would wait for her interminably till the afternoon stretched into the evening. The valley would be filled with a grey haze and a stillness would descend over the village, as if love had enveloped everything in its sweet languor. But he would keep his eyes glued to the path which meandered through the fields till he saw her hurrying towards him with sweet mincing steps. With every step she took, his heart would pound faster. Occasionally, when Zena failed to turn up, the silence would become oppressive, and returning to his village with a heavy heart, he would pick up his benjali, his folk bagpipe, and sit upon the bank of the Jhelum, where the lilting melody of the instrument would merge into the sound of the swirling water, every note proclaiming the name of Zena—Zena, whose complexion was the color of gold, whose voice was sweet as the music of the benjali, whose body was lithe as the branches of the bunj tree. A multitude of thoughts about Zena came crowding into Zaman's mind, some real, of this earth, others enveloped in an unearthly halo. The night had deepened and the village wall was left behind. On the outskirts of the village he saw the wrestling arena, where the boys of the village used to wrestle. Like the other boys of the village he came here to exercise, and when healthily tired, he would go to sleep on the soft earth under the banyan tree and then take a dip in the Jhelum.

Zaman was a spirited village youth, a champion wrestler and an expert swimmer. On seeing the wrestling arena, his hand unconsciously fell on his thigh to thump it in the manner of a wrestler, and slid over the rump of his missing leg. Painfully he withdrew his hand, and stood defiantly erect.

The tongawalla stopped the tonga and asked him for direction.

"Take me first to the tomb of the pir, and from there about a hundred yards to the right."

Before joining the army, he had come to the tomb along with Zena to invoke the favor of the pir that they should remain true to their love. They had made a votive offering of five annas each at the tomb and tying the money in small cloth bags had hung them on the branch of the big plum tree. Zaman Khan got down from the tonga at the tomb of the pir and reverently bowed his head in prayer. The prayer over, he moved his hands across his face and looked around. A dim earthen lamp burning in the niche of the wall cast its pale rays on a girl kneeling at her prayers, her beautiful face half covered with a black apron cloth. Zaman started. He limped towards her and cried, "Zena!"

The girl got up in confusion and looked at Zaman in surprise.

"Excuse me, sister," Zaman said realizing his mistake. "I thought you were my Zena."

The girl stood silent. Holding his crutch Zaman got into the tonga. The tonga moved on and the girl knelt again to finish her prayers.

The tonga finally stopped after going another hundred yards. Zaman had reached home. There was smoke coming out of the house and the smell of meat being cooked. He heard the shrill laughter of children punctuated by heavy male voices which floated above the din, and an occasional softly cooing woman's laughter. Above it all rose the sound of a gramophone playing *Mahiya*. They seemed so happy, and comfortable. Although he had not informed them about his coming he wished that they had been standing lined up before the house in silent greeting. He had joined the army for their sake and had even sacrificed one leg for them. He had burnt the candle of his youth before a barrage of guns and a hail of bullets. And here, unmindful of his absence the house rang with laughter, the gramophone played all the time, and life went on as usual. For all they knew there had been no war, Zaman Khan had never joined the army, and his leg had never come to grief. He felt like a stranger in his own village.

Zaman gave a twirl to his moustache and asked the tongawalla to fetch Miraj Din from the house. "Tell him Zaman is here."

In a moment his tonga was surrounded by the members of his family. They carried his bedroll and trunk into the house. They even lifted him and carried him in. He respectfully bowed before his father, was embraced by his weeping mother, and greeted by his younger brother, who like him had grown into a strapping youth. He pressed his young sisters to his shoulder and patted them on the head. Then he sat down on the cot and started talking merrily. But there was no joy in his heart and his talk seemed hollow and sapless to him.

In a trembling voice his father asked Miraj to fetch uncle Hashmat and tell the people of the village that his son had returned from the war covered with glory.

His mother wept on seeing his amputated leg. "Why didn't you write to us that you had lost your leg?"

"Mother, it makes no difference," he consoled her. "I've got another leg—an iron leg. I can walk with it."

He got up, walked a few steps and again sat down on the cot.

"I will kill a cock," his elder brother said. Scratching his head he disappeared from the courtyard.

His younger brother looked closely at the medals. "In which campaign did you win these?" he made bold to ask, highly impressed.

"In Africa—at the siege of Karen. It was a major campaign. Even the white regiments had fallen back. And then our platoon was ordered to press forward. It was we, the jawans of the 10th Punjab Regiment, who won the battle of

Karen. There was terrible fighting. I and Shahbaz Khan were required to climb about two hundred yards and silence a machine gun embattlement with hand grenades. We were below and the embattlement right over our heads, and the enemy had riddled our soldiers to pieces with machine gun fire. Under cover of some shrubs I crawled forward, inch by inch, and at last making a mad sortie cleared up the enemy pocket."

"And this . . ." the brother hesitated, "this leg was lost in that battle?"

"No." Zaman Khan twirled his moustache. "This was lost on the Italian front. Our Officer Commanding had ordered us to make a bayonet charge. There was a hand to hand skirmish with the Germans. This leg . . ." He laughed. "I would have been killed. But Allah is great."

Zaman suddenly fell silent. The people of the village had started coming. He received all of them with great courtesy and then uncle Rahmat. Momentarily overwhelmed with sadness at the sight of his crippled leg, each visitor tried to hide his tears behind a smile, and gently fondled Zaman's head. But Zaman all the time feigned cheerfulness, as if to have his leg amputated was an everyday affair with him. While recounting with gusto his war experiences to the visitors he would try to divert their minds from his leg by rambling into other subjects. But his listeners could not keep their eyes off his leg, and to make matters worse, his mother would start crying before each new visitor, making her son's missing leg the subject of her piteous narration. All the people from the village came to see Zaman. Men, women, and children; even those children who were born after Zaman had joined the army. One of these children was the boy Zena carried in her lap. She had come to see Zaman.

When she entered a hush fell over the room. Zaman's sister suddenly stopped playing the gramophone. Everyone held his breath. Zaman sighed.

Seeing Zena, Zaman's mother hurriedly said, "Zena is

now married to Kher. This is her child by him. Give her your blessings, my son. Kher . . ."

Zaman took the child from Zena and began fondling it. "How are you?" he asked Zena.

Zena kept standing with downcast eyes. And then everybody started talking, the gramophone again started playing, and Zena with the child in her lap joined the ladies of the house. Zaman had again busied himself with the guests, regaling them with his bantering talk. One by one, the visitors left. Zaman sat down to dinner with other members of his family and enlivened the dinner with more anecdotes about his army friends. When the dinner was over, the big hurricane lantern was extinguished and they retired for the night. In the dim light of the earthen lamp which had been kept burning in the room, he lay awake for a long time, counting the beams of the ceiling.

His mother opened her trunk with trembling hands and came to him with an old photograph. This photograph had been taken before he was recruited into the army. It was the same Zaman—erect, broad-chested, trim-moustached. But in this photograph he had two legs.

His mother sighed.

Zaman kept gazing at the photograph for a long time, particularly at the leg which had now parted company with him. Then he returned the photograph to his mother. "Go to sleep, mother," he said. "There's nothing wrong with me. I am quite happy as I am."

His mother went away crying and he again started counting the beams. Unable to sleep, he got up from his bed and picked up the benjali from the shelf. Indicating to his mother that he was going to the riverside, he took up his crutch.

When he played the benjali by the bank of the river, the air was filled with echoes of days gone by, and gloomy shapes began to fill the void of his heart. Images from his past returned vividly to him, memories . . . his first meeting with Zena, their first kiss, their going together to the fair in Jhelum city. The sound of the benjali grew sharp and piercing like the point of a bayonet, and pricking the heart of his memories trailed into silence. The reeds whispered in the breeze, and occasionally chunks of earth fell into the river with a soft thud.

Zaman sat there a long time throwing lumps of sand into the river. Then he heard footsteps and a shadow fell across the ground.

He got up and veered round on his crutch. Zena was standing before him.

"I have sinned against you," Zena said.

Zaman watched her silently. But something terrible seemed to have exploded in his mind, shattering like the boom of guns.

"I am still yours," Zena whispered.

Zaman was still silent. He could feel her trembling words —suspended above the moans of the swaying reeds.

"Nobody knows that we are here," Zena said again. "Strangle me and throw my body into the river. But, please, please, say something. Your silence is unbearable."

Zaman raised his head. There was a faint smile on his face. He gently took Zena's hand into his own. "Sister, let me see you home," he said in a soft voice. "Your child and your husband must be waiting for you."

When Zaman returned from Zena's house the earthen lamp was still burning in the niche of the pir's tomb. A maiden from the hills was sitting before the tomb, her hands raised in prayer. In the surrounding darkness the lamp shed its meagre light on her closed eyes. There was a benign glow on her face.

Quietly, Zaman sat down by her side. He raised his hands in a gesture of prayer, but no words of prayer came to his lips. His soul was voiceless, his heart empty of words. Only a few tears trickled down his cheeks and fell on the sand.

Translated by Jai Ratan

Kalu Bhangi

I HAVE often wanted to write about Kalu Bhangi, but what *can* one write about him? I have looked at his life from all sorts of angles and tried to assess and understand it, but I could never find anything out of the ordinary on which I could base a story, or even a plain, uninteresting photographic sketch of him. And yet, I don't know why, every time I start to write a story I see Kalu Bhangi standing there in my imagination. He smiles at me and asks: "Chote Sahib, won't you write a story about *me*? How many years is it since you started writing?"

"Eight years."

"And how many stories have you written?"

"Sixty—sixty-two. Sixty-two."

"Then what's wrong? Can't you write one about me, Chote Sahib? Look how long I've waited for you to write about me. I have been a good servant to you all these years —your old sweeper Kalu Bhangi. *Why* can't you write about me?"

There is nothing I can say in reply. His life has been so dull and uninteresting that there is simply nothing I can write about it. It's not that I don't want to write about him; for ages I've really wanted to write about him, but I could never do it, try as I might. And so today too, Kalu Bhangi is standing there in the corner of my mind, holding his old broom, with his big bare knees, his rough, cracked, ungainly feet, his varicose veins standing out on his dried-up legs, his hipbones sticking out, his hungry belly, his dry, creased, black skin, the dusty hair on his sunken chest, his wizened lips, wide nostrils, wrinkled cheeks, and bald head shining above the dark hollows of his eyes. Many characters have told me their life stories, asserted their importance, impressed upon me their dramatic quality, and disappeared. Beautiful women, attractive fancies, loathsome faces—all of these I have painted, all have left their impression and faded away. But Kalu Bhangi is in his old place, standing there in just the same way, holding his old broom. He has seen every character that has come into my mind, watched them weeping and beseeching, loving and hating, sleeping and walking, laughing, making speeches—seen them in every aspect of life, on every level, at every stage from childhood to old age and from old age to death. He has seen every stranger who has peeped through the door, and, seeing that they were coming in, swept their path before them, himself moved to one side, as a sweeper should, and stood respectfully by until the story has begun to be written, until it has ended, until both characters and spectators have taken their leave. But even then Kalu Bhangi has gone on standing there; and now he has simply taken a step forward and come into the center of my imagination, so that I may see him clearly. His bald pate is shining and an unspoken question is on his lips. I have been looking at him a long time, and I just can't think what I can write about him. But today this apparition is not to be put off. Year after year I have fobbed him off. This time perhaps I can get rid of him.

I was only seven years old when I first saw Kalu Bhangi. Twenty years later when he died he looked exactly the same. Not the slightest change. The same knees, same feet, same complexion, same face, same bald head, same broken teeth, same broom. His broom always looked as though he had been born with it in his hand, as though it were a part of him. Every day he used to empty the patients' commodes, sprinkle disinfectant in the dispensary, and then go and sweep out the doctor sahib's and the compounder sahib's bungalows after which he would take the doctor sahib's cow and the compounder sahib's goat out to graze. Towards evening he would bring them back to the hospital, tie them up in the cattle shed, go off to prepare his food, eat it, and go to bed. I watched him at these tasks every day for twenty years—every day without fail. During this whole time he was never ill for so much as a single day, which was something to wonder at—but still not so wonderful that you can write a story about it. Well, I'm writing this story under pressure. I've been fobbing him off for eight years, but the old man wouldn't let me alone. He kept on pressing me to write a story, and that was unfair both to me and to you—to me because now I'm having to write it, and to you because you're having to read it—this in spite of the fact that there is nothing much in him to justify all this labor. But what can I do? There is such a shy, imploring sort of persistence in his silent gaze, such a mute helplessness, such a depth of feeling asking for expression, that I am compelled to go on writing, though even as I write I keep on thinking, "What *can* I write about such a life as his?" There is no facet of it which is interesting, no part of it about which there is any mystery, no angle which has anything to attract one's attention. True, he's kept cropping up in my imagination continually for the last eight years—God knows why—but I can't see what that proves, except his obstinacy. Even in the days when I was writing romantic stories,* painting scenes of silvery moonlight, when my outlook on the world was a very milk-and-watery one—even then Kalu Bhangi was standing there. When I got beyond romanticism, and seeing both the beauty of life and its bestial passions, began to touch its broken strings, then too he was there. When I looked down from my balcony and saw the poverty of those who give us our food, and when I saw rivers of blood flowing on the soil of the Punjab and realized that we are savages, then too he was standing on the threshold of my mind, silent and mute. But

---

* The lines which follow indicate the main phases of the author's development. *Broken Strings, Givers of Food,* and *We Are Savages* are the titles of collections of the author's stories.

now I shall surely get rid of him; now he'll *have* to go; now I'm writing about him. Please, listen to his dull, flat, uninteresting story, so that I can send him packing and be rid of his unclean presence. If I don't write about him today and you don't read about him, he'll still be there another eight years hence—perhaps, indeed, for as long as I live.

But what bothers me is the difficulty of knowing what to write. Kalu Bhangi's father and mother were sweepers, and I should think that all his ancestors were sweepers too and lived in this same place for hundreds of years just like him. And then Kalu Bhangi never got married, never fell in love, never traveled very far—in fact, believe it or not, he never even went out of his own village. All day he would work, and at night he would sleep, and next morning get up again to busy himself with the same tasks. And from his very childhood this is what he had done.

Oh yes, there is one quite interesting thing about him. He used to love to get some animal, a cow or buffalo for example, to lick his bald head. I have often seen him at midday under the blue sky, sitting on his heels on the low earthen wall of some field near the hospital in the bright sunshine, with the green velvet carpet of the grass behind him, and a cow licking his head, again and again, until the soothing feeling has sent him off to sleep. I used to feel a curious thrill of pleasure whenever I saw him sleeping like this, as though I had caught a glimpse of the drowsy, languid, all-prevailing beauty of the universe. In my short life I have seen the most beautiful women, the freshest flowers in bud, the world's most entrancing scenery, but—why I don't know—never in any other scene have I felt such innocence, such beauty and tranquility, as I used to feel when I was seven years old and that field used to seem so huge and the sky so blue and clear, and Kalu Bhangi's bald head shone like glass, and the cow's tongue, gently licking his head as though to soothe him, made a dreamy rustling sound. I used to feel like getting my own head shaved like his, so that I could sit beneath the cow's tongue and drop off to sleep like him. In fact once I tried it out, and what a thrashing I got from my father! And Kalu Bhangi got it even worse. My father thrashed him so hard that I was afraid he would be kicked to death, and cried out in alarm. But he suffered no ill effects at all, and next day turned up as usual, broom in hand, to sweep our bungalow.

Kalu Bhangi was very fond of animals. Our cow was devoted to him, and so was the compounder sahib's goat, although goats are very fickle creatures, worse even than women. But Kalu Bhangi was a special case. It was he who watered them, fed them, took them to graze, and tethered them in the cattle shed at night. They could understand his every sign as well as a man understands a child. On several occasions I have followed him. Whether in the open or on the road, he used to let them loose, but they would still walk along beside him, suiting their pace to his, as though they were three friends out for a walk. If the cow stopped to take a mouthful of green grass, the goat would stop too and begin to nibble the leaves of some bush; and as for Kalu Bhangi, he would pluck the *sanblu* and start eating it—eating it himself and feeding it to the goat too, and talking to himself. Not only to himself; talking to them too. And the two animals would join in the conversation, grumbling, flapping their ears, shuffling their feet, lowering their tails, curvetting, and in all manner of ways. I'm sure *I* couldn't understand what they used to talk about. Then after a few moments, Kalu Bhangi would start off again, and the cow too would leave off grazing, and the goat would leave his bush and go along with him. If they came to some little stream or some pretty little spring, Kalu Banghi would sit down there and then, or rather lie down, and put his lips to the surface of the water and begin to drink, just like an animal does. And the two animals would begin to drink in just the same way, because after all they weren't human and didn't know how to drink from their hand.

Then if Kalu Bhangi lay down on the grass, the goat too would lie down by his legs, drawing her legs in and going down on her knees as though she were saying her prayers; and the cow would sit down near him with such an air that you would think she were his wife and had just finished cooking the dinner. A sort of tranquil, homely air showed itself in every expression which passed over her face, and when she began to chew the cud she looked to me for all the world like some capable housewife settling down to her crotchet or to knitting Kalu Bhangi a pullover.

Besides this cow and goat there was a lame dog with whom Kalu Bhangi was very friendly. Because of his lameness he couldn't roam about much with other dogs and would usually get the worst of it in a fight. He was always hungry and always getting hurt. Kalu Bhangi was always busy tending his wounds and generally dancing attendance upon him—bathing him in soap and water or getting the ticks out of his coat, or putting ointment on his wounds, or feeding him on bits of dried maize bread. But the dog was a very selfish creature. He'd only show up twice a day, once at midday and once in the evening, when he would eat his meal, get his wounds dressed, and be off again. His visits were always very brief and would absorb all Kalu Bhangi's attention. I didn't like the animal at all, but Kalu Bhangi always received him with great affection.

Moreover, Kalu Bhangi knew every living creature of the forest. If he saw an insect at his feet he would pick it up and put it on a bush. He would answer the mongoose with its own cry. He knew the call of every bird—the partridge, the wood-pigeon, the parrakeet, the sparrow, and many more. In this respect he was more learned than Rahul Sankritya-yan * and, at any rate to a seven-year-old like myself, the superior even of my own parents.

He used to roast corn on the cob beautifully, parching it carefully over a low fire so that every grain would gleam like

* A celebrated Indian scholar of Sanskrit and Pali.

gold and taste like honey and smell as fragrant and sweet as the fragrance of earth itself. He would roast the cob slowly, calmly, expertly, looking at it repeatedly on every side as though he had known that particular cob for years; he would talk to it like a friend, treat it as gently and kindly and affectionately as though it were some kinsman, as though it were his own brother. Of course other people used to roast cobs, but who could compare with him? Their cobs used to be so half-baked, so tasteless, so altogether ordinary, that they scarcely deserved the name. And yet the selfsame cob in Kalu Bhangi's hands became completely transformed, and would come off the fire like a new bride gleaming with gold in her wedding dress. I think that the cob itself would get an inkling of the great love which Kalu Bhangi bore it; otherwise where could a lifeless thing acquire such charm? I used to thoroughly enjoy the cobs which he prepared, and would eat them secretly with great delight. Once I was caught and got a real good thrashing. So did Kalu Bhangi, poor fellow, but the next day there he was at our bungalow as usual.

Well, that's all; there's nothing else of interest to be said about him that I can recollect. I grew up from boyhood to youth and Kalu Bhangi stayed just the same. Now he was of less interest to me; in fact you may say of no interest at all. True, his character occasionally attracted my attention. Those were the days when I had just begun to write, and to help my study of character I would sometimes question him, keeping a fountain pen and pad by me to take notes.

"Kalu Bhangi, is there anything special about your life?"

"How do you mean, Chote Sahib?"

"Anything special, out of ordinary, unusual?"

"No, Chote Sahib."

(A blank so far. Well, never mind. Let's persevere. Perhaps something may emerge.)

"All right, tell me then; what do you do with your pay?"

"What do I do with my pay?" He would think. "I get eight

rupees.* I spend four rupees on *ata*,† one rupee on salt—one rupee on tobacco—eight annas on tea—four annas on molasses—four annas on spices. How much is that, Chote Sahib?"

"Seven rupees."

"Yes, seven rupees. And every month I pay the money-lender one rupee. I borrow the money from him to get my clothes made, don't I? I need two sets a year; a blanket I've already got, but still, I need two lots of clothes, don't I? And Chote Sahib, if the Bare Sahib ‡ would raise my pay to nine rupees, I'd really be in clover."

"How so?"

"I'd get a rupee's worth of *ghi* § and make maize *parathas*. ‖ I'd never had maize *parathas*, master. I'd love to try them."

Now, I ask you, how can I write a story about his eight rupees?

Then when I got married, when the nights seemed starry and full of joy, and the fragrance of honey and musk and the wild rose came in from the nearby jungle, and you could see the deer leaping and the stars seemed to bend down and whisper in your ear, and someone's full lips would begin to tremble at the thought of kisses to come—then too I would want to write something about Kalu Bhangi, and I would take a pencil and paper and go and look for him.

"Kalu Bhangi, haven't you got married?"

"No, Chote Sahib."

"Why?"

"I'm the only sweeper in this district, Chote Sahib. There's no other for miles around. So how *could* I get married?" **

* Eight rupees a month. A rupee is about 1sh. 6d. An anna is roughly 1d.
† Coarse flour.
‡ Big Master—the doctor.
§ Clarified butter.
‖ A sort of pancake made of flour and fried in clarified butter.
** He could only marry another untouchable.

Another blind alley. I tried again.

"And don't you wish you could have done?" I hoped this might lead to something.

"Done, what, Sahib?"

"Don't you *want* to be in love with somebody? Perhaps you've been in love with someone and that's why you don't marry?"

"What do you mean?—been in love with someone, Chote Sahib?"

"Well, people fall in love with women."

"Fall in love, Chote Sahib? They get married, and maybe big people fall in love too, but I've never heard of anyone like me falling in love. And as for not getting married, well I've told you why I never got married. How *could* I get married?"

(How could I answer that?)

"Don't you feel sorry, Kalu Bhangi?"

"What about, Chote Sahib?"

After that I gave up, and abandoned the idea of writing about him. Eight years ago Kalu Bhangi died. He who had never been ill suddenly fell so seriously ill that he never rose from his sickbed again. He was admitted to the hospital and put in a ward on his own. The compounder would stand as far away as he could when he administered his medicine. An orderly would put his food inside the room and come away. He would clean his own dishes, make his own bed, and dispose of his own stools. And when he died the police saw to the disposal of his body, because he left no heir. He had been with us for twenty years, but of course he was not related to us. And so his last pay-packet too went to the government because there was no one to inherit it. Even on the day he died nothing out of the ordinary happened; the hospital opened, the doctor wrote his prescriptions, the compounder made them up, the patients received their medicine and returned home—a day just like any other day. And just like any other day the hospital closed and we all went home, took our meals in peace, listened to the radio, got into bed

and went to sleep. When we got up next morning we heard
the police had kindly disposed of Kalu Bhangi's body, whereupon the doctor sahib's cow and the compounder sahib's
goat would neither eat nor drink for two days, but stood
outside the ward lowing and bleating uselessly. Well, animals are like that, aren't they?

What! You here again with your broom? Well? What do
you want? Kalu Bhangi is still standing there.

Come now! I've written down everything about you,
haven't I? What are you still standing there for? Why do
you still pester me? For God's sake go away! Have I forgotten anything? Have I missed anything out? Your name:
Kalu Bhangi; Occupation: sweeper. Never left this district.
Never married. Never been in love. No momentous events
in your life. Nothing to thrill you—as your beloved's lips, or
the kisses of your child, or the poems of Ghalib * thrill you.
An absolutely uneventful life. What *can* I write? What else
can I write? Pay: eight rupees. Four rupees *ata*, four annas
spices, one rupee salt, one rupee tobacco, eight annas tea,
four annas molasses. That's seven rupees. And one rupee for
the moneylender, eight. But eight rupees don't make a story.
These days even people earning twenty, fifty, even a hundred rupees aren't interesting enough to write stories about,
so it's quite certain that you can't write about someone who
only earns eight. So what can I write about you? Now take
Khilji. He's the compounder at the hospital. He gets thirty-
two rupees a month. He was born in a lower-middle-class
family and his parents gave him a fair education up to
Middle,† then he passed the qualifying examination to be
a compounder. He is young and full of life, with all that that
implies. He can wear a clean white *shalwar*,‡ have his shirt
starched, use brilliantine on his hair and keep it well

* Ghalib was a celebrated Urdu poet of the nineteenth century.
† Middle, i.e., elementary education such as an English child re-
ceives to the age of fourteen.
‡ Baggy white trousers, gathered at the ankles.

combed. The government provides him with quarters, like a little bungalow. If the doctor makes a slip he can pocket the fees, and he can make love to the good-looking patients. Remember that business about Nuran? Nuran came from Bhita. A silly young creature of about sixteen to seventeen. She'd be sure to catch your eyes even if she were four miles away, like a cinema poster. She was a complete fool. She had accepted the attentions of two young men of her village. When the headman's son was with her she was his. And when the *patwari's* * boy turned up she would feel attracted to him. And she couldn't decide between them. Generally people think of love as being a very clear-cut, certain, definite thing; but the fact is that it is usually a very unstable, vacillating, uncertain sort of condition. You feel that you love one person and also another person, or perhaps no one at all. And even if you are in love, it's such a temporary, fickle, passing feeling, that no sooner is the object of your affection out of sight than it evaporates.

Your feeling is quite sincere, but it doesn't last. And that's why Nuran couldn't make up her mind. Her heart throbbed for the headman's son, and yet she no sooner looked into the eyes of the patwari's boy than her heart would begin to beat fast and she would feel as though she were alone in a little boat in the midst of a vast ocean, and rolling waves on all sides, holding a fragile oar in her hand; and the boat would begin to rock, and go on gently rocking, and she would grab the fragile oar with her fragile hands just as it was slipping from her grasp, and gently catch her breath, and slowly lower her eyes, and let her hair fall in disorder; and the sea would seem to whirl around her, and ever-widening circles would spread over its surface and a deathly stillness would descend on all sides and her heart in alarm would suddenly stop beating, and then someone would hold her tight in his arms. Ah! when she gazed at the patwari's

* The village official responsible for keeping the records relating to land tenure, etc.

boy that was just how she felt. And she just couldn't decide
between the two. Headman's son, patwari's son . . . patwari's son, headman's son. . . . She had pledged herself to
both of them, promised to marry both of them, was dying
of love for both of them. The result was that they fought
each other till the blood streamed down, and when enough
young blood had been let, they got angry with themselves
for being such fools. And first of all the headman's son
arrived on the scene with a knife and tried to kill Nuran,
and she was wounded in the arm. And then the patwari's
boy came, determined to take her life, and she was wounded
in the foot. But she survived because she was taken to hospital in time and got proper treatment. Well, even hospital
people are human. Beauty affects the heart—like an in-
jection. The effect may be slight or it may be considerable,
but there will certainly be some effect. In this case the effect
on the doctor was slight; on the compounder it was considerable. Khilji gave himself up heart and soul to looking after
Nuran. Exactly the same thing had happened before. Before
Nuran it had been Beguman, and before her, Reshman, and
before her, Janaki. But these were Khilji's unsuccessful love
affairs, because these were all three married women. In fact
Reshman was the mother of a child too. Yes, there were not
only children, but parents, and husbands and the husbands'
hostile glares which seemed to Khilji to pierce right into his
heart, seeking to find out and explore every corner of his
hidden desires. What could poor Khilji do? Circumstances
had defeated him. He loved them all in turn—Beguman,
and Reshman, and Janaki too. He used to give sweets to
Beguman's brother every day; he used to carry Reshman's
little boy about with him all day long. Janaki was very fond
of flowers; Khilji would get up and go out very early every
morning, before it was properly light, and pick bunches of
beautiful red poppies to bring her. He gave them the very
best medicines, the very best food, and the very best of his
attention. But when the time came and Beguman was cured

she went away with her husband weeping; and when Reshman was cured she took her son and departed. And when
Janaki was cured and it was time to go, she took the flowers
which Khilji had given her and pressed them to her heart,
and her eyes were brimming with tears as she gave her
husband her hand and went off with him, until they at last
disappeared beneath the crest of the hill. When they reached
the farthest edge of the valley, she turned and looked in
Khilji's direction, and Khilji turned his face to the wall and
began to weep. When Reshman had left he had wept too,
and when Beguman went he again wept, in the same unre-
strained way, with the same sincerity, overwhelmed by the
same agonized feelings. But neither Reshman, nor Beguman, nor Janaki stayed for him. And now, after I don't
know how many years, Nuran had come, and his heart had
begun to beat faster, in just the same way; and every day it
throbbed for her more and more. At first Nuran's condition
was critical, and there was very little hope for her, but as a
result of Khilji's unflagging efforts, her wounds gradually
began to heal; they began to discharge less, and the bad
smell went away, and the swelling subsided. The lustre
gradually returned to her eyes and the healthy color to her
wan face; and on the day when Khilji removed the bandages
from her arm, then Nuran on a sudden impulse of gratitude
threw herself into his arms and burst into tears. And when
the bandages were removed from her foot she put henna on
her feet and hands and lamp-black on her eyelids, and arranged the long tresses of her hair. And Khilji's heart leapt
for joy to see her. Now Nuran had given her heart to him
and promised to marry him. The headman's son and the
patwari's son had on several occasions come to see her, and
to ask her forgiveness and to promise to marry her; every
time they came Nuran would take fright and begin to
tremble, and look this way and that to avoid their glances;
and she would not feel at ease until they had gone and Khilji
would take her hand in his. And when she was quite re-

covered the whole village turned out to see her. Thanks to the kindness of the doctor sahib and the compounder sahib, their lass was better, and her mother's and father's gratitude knew no bounds. Today even the headman had come, and the patwari too, and those two conceited asses, their sons, who every time they looked at Nuran felt sorry for what they had done; then Nuran went to her mother and leaning upon her, looked towards Khilji, her eyes swimming with tears and lamp-black, and without a word left for her village. The whole village had come to meet her, and the headman's son and the patwari's son were following at her heels. Khilji felt their steps, and more steps, and more steps—hundreds of steps passing across his breast as they went on their way taking Nuran with them, and leaving behind them a cloud of dust hanging over the road. And turning his face to the wall of one of the wards he began to sob.

Yes, Khilji's life was a beautiful and romantic one—Khilji, who had passed his Middle, whose pay was thirty-two rupees a month and who could earn fifteen to twenty rupees over and above; Khilji who was young, who knew what it is to love, who lived in a little bungalow, read the stories of reputable authors, and wept for his love. What an interesting, and romantic, and imaginative life Khilji's was! But what can you say about Kalu Bhangi? Except the following:

1. That Kalu Bhangi washed the blood and pus from Beguman's bandages.

2. That Kalu Bhangi emptied Beguman's commode.

3. That Kalu Bhangi cleaned Reshman's dirty bandages.

4. That Kalu Bhangi used to give Reshman's boy corn-on-the-cob to eat.

5. That Kalu Bhangi washed Janaki's dirty bandages and every day sprinkled disinfectant in her room, and every day towards evening closed the window of the ward and lit the wood in the fireplace so that Janaki shouldn't feel cold.

6. That Kalu Bhangi for three months and ten days regularly emptied Nuran's commode.

Kalu Bhangi saw Reshman departing; he saw Beguman departing; he saw Janaki departing; he saw Nuran departing. But he never turned his face to the wall and wept. At first he would look a bit perplexed for a minute or two and would scratch his head. And then when he couldn't account for what was going on, he would go off into the fields below the hospital and let the cow lick his bald head. But I've already told you about that.

Well, what more am I to write about you, Kalu Bhangi? I've said all there is to say, told all there is to tell about you. If *your* pay had been thirty-two rupees, if *you'd* passed your Middle—or even failed it—if *you* had inherited a little culture, a little refinement, a little human joy and the exaltation which it brings, I'd have written something about *you*. But as it is what can I write about your eight rupees? Time and again I pick up your eight rupees and study them from all angles—four rupees *ata*, one rupee salt, one rupee tobacco, eight annas tea, four annas molasses, four annas spices—that's seven—and one rupee for the moneylender—that makes eight. How can I make a story out of that, Kalu Bhangi? No, it can't be done. Go away. *Please* go away. See, I implore you with folded hands. But he still stands there, showing his dirty yellow, uneven teeth and laughing his cracked laugh.

I see I can't get rid of you so easily. Very well then. Let me rake over the embers of my memory once more. Perhaps for your benefit I'll have to come down a bit below the thirty-two rupees level. Let's see what help I can get from Bakhtyar the orderly. Bakhtyar the orderly gets fifteen rupees a month. And whenever he goes out on tour with the doctor or the compounder or the vaccinator he gets double allowance and traveling expenses too. Then he has some land of his own in the village, and a small house, surrounded on three sides by lofty pine trees, and with a beautiful little garden on the fourth side laid out by his wife. He has sown it with all sorts of vegetables—spinach and radishes, and turnips and green chillies, and pumpkins, which are dried in the summer sun and eaten in the winter when snow falls and there are no greens to be had. Bakhtyar's wife knows all about these things. Bakhtyar has three children, and his old mother, who is always quarreling with her daughter-in-law. Once Bakhtyar's mother quarreled with her daughter-in-law and left home. The sky was overcast with thick clouds and the bitter cold made your teeth chatter. Bakhtyar's eldest boy came running to the hospital to tell him what had happened, and Bakhtyar set out there and then to bring his mother back, taking Kalu Bhangi with him. They spent the whole day in the forest looking for her— Bakhtyar and Kalu Bhangi, and Bakhtyars wife, who was now sorry for what she had done and kept on weeping and calling out to her mother-in-law. The sky was overcast, and their hands and feet were getting numb with the cold, and the dry pine twigs were slippery underfoot; and then it began to rain. And the rain turned to sleet and a deep stillness descended all round, as though the gate to the abyss of death had opened and sent forth line upon line of snow fairies over the earth. The snowflakes kept falling, still, silent, voiceless, and a layer of white velvet spread over valley and hill and dale.

"Mother!" shouted Bakhtyar's wife at the top of her voice.

"Mother!" shouted Bakhtyar.

"Mother!" called Kalu Bhangi.

The forest re-echoed and was quiet.

Then Kalu Bhangi said, "I think she must have gone to your uncle's at Nakkar."

Four miles this side of Nakkar they found her. Snow was falling, and she was making her way along falling and stumbling, panting and out of breath. When Bakhtyar caught hold of her, for a moment she resisted, and then fell senseless into his arms, and Bakhtyar's wife held her up. All the way back Bakhtyar and Kalu Bhangi carried her turn by turn and by the time they reached home it was pitch dark and when the children saw them coming they began to cry. Kalu Bhangi withdrew to one side, and looking about him, began to scratch his head. Then he quietly opened the door and came away. Yes, there are stories to be told about Bakhtyar's life too, beautiful little stories; but what more can I write about *you*, Kalu Bhangi? I can certainly write something about everyone else at the hospital, but as for you—well, after all this rummaging around in my memory I'm at a loss. What can I do? Go away now, for God's sake. You have pestered me too much already.

But I know that he won't go. I shan't be able to get him out of my mind, and in all my stories he'll be standing there with his filthy broom in his hand. Now I know what it is you want. You want to hear the story of something which never happened but which *could* have happened. I will begin with your feet. Listen. You want your dirty rough feet to be washed clean, washed until all the filth has been washed away. You want ointment to be rubbed on their cracks. You want your bony knees to be covered with flesh, your thighs to be strong and firm, the creases on your withered belly to disappear, the dust and grime to be washed from the hair on your weak chest. You want your thin lips to become full and to receive the power of speech. You want someone to put lustre in your eyes, blood in your cheeks, give you clean clothes to wear, to raise the four walls of a little home about you, pretty and neat and clean, a home over which your wife will rule and in which your laughing children will run about.

I cannot do what you want. I know your broken teeth and your half weeping laugh. I know that when you get the cow to lick your head, in your imagination you see your wife passing her fingers through your hair and stroking your head until your eyes close and your head nods and you fall asleep in her kindly embrace. And when you roast the cob for me so gently over the fire and look at me so kindly and affectionately as you give it me to eat, in your mind's eye you are seeing that little boy who is not your son, who has not yet come into the world, and while you live never will come, and yet whom you have fondled like a loving father, and held in your lap while he played, and kissed on the face, and carried about on your shoulder saying "Look! this is my son!" And when you could have none of these things, then you stood aside and scratched your head in perplexity and all unconsciously began to count on your fingers, one, two, three, four, five, six, seven, eight—eight rupees. I know the story of what could have happened. But it didn't happen, because I am a writer, and I can fashion a new story, but not a new man. For that I alone am not enough. For that the writer, and his reader, and the doctor, and the compounder, and Bakhtyar and the village patwari and headman, and the shopkeeper, and the man in authority, and the politician, and the worker, and the peasant toiling in his fields, are all needed—the united efforts of every one of those thousands and millions and hundreds of millions of people. On my own I am powerless; I can't do anything. Until all of us join hands to help one another, this task cannot be carried out, and you will go on standing there on the threshold of my mind, just the same with your broom in your hand; and I shall not be able to write a really great story, in which the splendor of the complete happiness of the human spirit will shine; and the builders will not be able to build that great building in which the greatness of our people will reach its highest achievement; and no one will be able to sing a song in whose depths will be mirrored all the greatness of the universe.

No, this full life will be impossible, so long as you stand there, broom in hand!

Never mind! Go on standing there. It's better that you should; then perhaps the day will come when someone will take your broom from you and gently press your hand and take you beyond the rainbow.

Translated by Ralph Russell

THAKAZHI SIVASANKARA PILLAI

Thakazhi Sivasankara Pillai was born in 1914, at Thakazhi, a little village some ten miles south of Alleppey in the state of Kerala. His father was a farmer, but his home was rich in the traditions of Sanskrit culture and the indigenous arts of Kerala. At dusk the head of the family would sit by the light of the oil lamp and read from the Mahabharata *and the* Ramayana.

Thakazhi Sivasankara Pillai's earliest education was at home. He went to school at Thakazhi and afterwards to the middle school at Ambalapuzha. He later attended the high school at Hariped. For his college education he went to the capital of the state, Trivandrum, where he studied at the law college. Here his reading and his intellectual interests widened. He read English and European literature, including Freud and Marx. His first short stories, "In the Flood" and "The Fair Baby," appeared about this time.

In 1934, a volume of short stories in Malayalam, New Blossoms, *was published. His first novel,* Reward, *came out a little later and was followed by* Fallen Lotus. *Since then he has written fourteen novels and some six-hundred short stories, all in Malayalam. His books have been translated into many Western languages.*

Thakazhi's work has a strong social content and an evident left-wing bias. Of his novels, the most famous is Chemmeen, *which won the Sahitya Akademi Award, and which was written in three weeks. It has been translated into many Indian and foreign languages. His latest novel,* The Children of Ouseph, *deals with the Christian community in Kerala.*

Thakazhi recently wrote in a letter, "I am a farmer by birth, a lawyer by profession and a writer by choice. Flaubert, Balzac, de Maupassant, Hugo, Dostoevski, Gogol, Tolstoy influenced me. No Indian author was directly responsible for my writing. The reason is obvious. I know no other Indian language besides Malayalam. Even Tagore was not responsible for the development of Malayalam fiction."

Father and Son

THAKAZHI SIVASANKARA PILLAI

THE following day the State Director of Public Instruction was due to arrive in the little village to inspect the local school. The Headmaster went from class to class making arrangements to see that the children came the next day properly washed and scrubbed and dressed in their best clothes. Before leaving the school the teachers, too, told the children what they had to do.

The news of the Director's visit became the talk of the village. It was a great event. The only officers who occasionally visited the village were the Police Inspector, the Postal Inspector, who came to inspect the local Post office, and the Inspector of the Co-ops. This was the first time that an officer of the State Government was visiting the village. There was, in the village, in the house of Illikkal, an officer who drew Rs.500/- a month. And his brother was an advocate. But, of course, a Director was a bigger officer than even these two.

That evening the Headmaster went to a house near the school. It was to arrange for milk for the Director. The head of the family asked the Headmaster: "What would his salary be, sir?" The Headmaster replied: "Two thousand rupees a month. He has had his education in England."

The mistress of the house, staggered by the figure, blurted out: "What will he do with all that money?"

Her husband said: "He will be able to spend it. He is a big man."

Their son, Ramu, felt proud that the Headmaster was

visiting his home. When he went to school the next day, he could tell his friends: "The Headmaster came to my house." When he heard that the Director's salary was Rs.2,000/- a month he made a mental calculation. Divide two thousand by thirty. That was what the Director made every day. His own father made one rupee a day—when he worked.

As he was leaving, the Headmaster gave detailed instructions to the woman: "Two measures of milk. Do you understand? Milked clean. Add a couple of spoons of water from the temple well to it. Then boil the milk. Don't let a speck of ash get into the milk. I shall send you my silver tumbler. You send me the milk in that."

The woman asked: "Shall I add any sugar?"

The Headmaster thought for a while. He hadn't considered that. Finally, he said: "No. You might add too much sugar. Perhaps he does not take sugar. What is more, your sugar may have ants in it."

After he had crossed the courtyard, the Headmaster turned round and said again: "Remember everything I said. Clean. Pure. No ash."

The poor woman said: "I shall bathe before I boil the milk . . ."

The Headmaster was at a loss. She had not understood a thing. He was desperate and said: "No, not that. What I said was that everything should be clean. Not that you should have a bath."

Her husband said: "I shall look to everything, sir. I understand."

Ramu was now in a position to show off in front of his classmates at school. First of all, the Headmaster had visited his home. Secondly, it was his people who were to provide the milk for the Director. And there was something else. This was a chance to humble Illikkal Krishnan Kutti. Kutti used to boast that his uncle was a salaried man, and that his house had a tiled roof, not just a thatched one.

The next day every child in the village had a good scrubbing and was dressed in his best clothes for school. Ramu had a pair of blue shorts which his father had got him for Onam. Now the color had faded into patches of white and light blue. He also had a vest with short sleeves. Krishnan Kutti was the best-dressed boy in the class. He was dressed in shorts of shining silk and a smart bush shirt. No boy could help staring at him. They wanted to touch those smooth shorts of his and the fine shirt. Not Ramu. He was determined to humble Krishnan Kutti.

He put him a question: "You belong to a great family. Can you tell us where the Director was educated?"

Krishnan Kutti couldn't. But he wasn't going to be beaten. He accepted the challenge. He pretended he knew.

"At Trivandrum."

Ramu clapped his hands and laughed. Krishnan Kutti was beaten. He blinked helplessly. Ramu stated: "No, no. Not there." He turned to the others and asked them: "Can anyone tell me?"

No one could. Ramu puffed out a little. Then he said: "I can tell you. In England!"

But Ramu wasn't satisfied with the way he had humbled Krishnan Kutti. He hurled another question: "What is the salary of this Director?"

Krishnan Kutti felt very small. He said nothing. Ramu stated, with complete authority: "Two thousand rupees a month."

Krishnan Kutti had to do something in the face of such humiliation. He said: "That is nothing. My father gets Rs.2,250/-."

That was Rs.250/- more than the Director.

Ramu again clapped his hands and laughed as if it were a big lie. He said, "Go on. Don't lie." He then turned to the others and said: "Did you hear that, that his father gets Rs.2,250/- a month? Fancy old Sankummaman, who hobbles about the field on a walking stick in the mornings, wrapped up in a green shawl, getting Rs.2,250/-!"

Krishnan Kutti had an answer for that: "He is my grandfather—my mother's father, though I call him father."

Ramu asked: "How is it then that none of us has seen your father?"

Krishnan Kutti answered: "My father—he is up in the North."

Without a second's pause Ramu asked: "Where—in the North?"

Krishnan Kutti did not know. He was at a loss for an answer. He stood there, his eyes wide open, holding back the tears. If he batted his eyelids just once, the tears would roll down. The children hooted. Krishnan Kutti had told a lie. He was boasting. That was what they said. And Krishnan Kutti stood there, humiliated, holding back the tears with an effort.

Ramu asked him a cruel question: "Why is it that you are making out that someone else is your father?"

Krishnan Kutti stretched out his hand to scratch Ramu. But Ramu withdrew.

Ramu did not stop his taunting: "Where is your father?"

Krishnan Kutti could not stand it any longer. He ran to his teacher, crying helplessly, to complain about Ramu. Ramu ran away.

That day Krishnan Kutti went home, broken and dejected. As usual, his mother was waiting for him at the gate. When he saw his mother he burst out crying. Bhawani Amma ran to her son and took him in her arms. He sobbed helplessly on his mother's breast. The mother too cried. He was her all in all. He was the only thing she had. She didn't ask him why he was crying. It was as if she had accepted the fact that their life was one of tears. There was never any need to ask why.

Sankummaman and his wife ran out. Worry and disappointment were written all over the grandfather's face. Every wrinkle told its tale. He lived in the perpetual fear that something catastrophic might befall him at any moment. He tried to pull the boy away from the mother, but the boy was holding fast. He wouldn't let go.

Rubbing his chest uneasily, Sankummaman said: "Nara-yana, Narayana, what has happened to the child? Bhawani tell me."

Bhawani said nothing. It was a sorrow that was shared by the mother and son alone. No one else, not even Sankum-maman, could partake of it.

Sankummaman said: "Narayana, Narayana, have you kept all this sorrow for my old age?"

That night, in bed, the son lay close to his mother. The mother would lie awake every night, thinking and thinking, before she would doze off to sleep. Once, a man used to share that bed and that room with her. And she used to fall asleep in no time and sleep peacefully. But that was years ago. Now she could hardly sleep. She would lie awake for hours, thinking. Gradually her eyes would close. Sleep ulti-mately won in that contest. But every night, even now, she would still lie awake, thinking, thinking. That night Krish-nan Kutti, too, was thinking. And he couldn't sleep.

"Why is it, mother, that father is not with us?"

Bhawani Amma was just dozing off to sleep. That ques-tion pierced her heart.

She bit her teeth and suppressed the sob that came from deep down within her being. Krishnan Kutti did not know it. He repeated his question: "Why, mother?"

The mother replied: "That is our fate, son!"

By now Bhawani Amma could not hold back her tears. Krishnan Kutti realized his mother was crying.

He could not understand what fate meant. But he didn't ask her. In the still darkness of the room, he asked her some-thing else.

"Mother, will you show me the picture of my father?"

He asked hesitantly, as if he felt she might find some ex-cuse for not showing it to him. But there was something in his childish, beseeching voice which showed his deep-seated and urgent desire to see it.

The mother got up and wiped her tears. She lit a lamp.

Sankummaman who was sleeping in the next room called out to her: "Why are you lighting a lamp, Bhawani?"

She answered after a moment's hesitation: "Because Krishnan Kutti wants it."

"Isn't he asleep yet?"

"No."

"Good God!"

Bhawani Amma took out from the bottom of a box a photograph wrapped up carefully in silk. She looked at the photograph intently. Tears filled her eyes.

From the next room Sankummaman could be heard repeating to himself: "Narayana, Narayana."

Krishnan Kutti took the picture from his mother and gazed at it, devouring it greedily, as it were. His face brightened. And, as he looked at it, his little face lighted up. He said: "It was like this that the Director was dressed. Coat and tie. But he didn't have a walking stick or a hat." A moment later he lifted his face and, looking his mother in the eye, asked: "Mother, may I take this picture to the school with me tomorrow?"

"Why, son?"

"To show Ramu. He says I haven't got a father like this."

The mother said: "This is a picture we have to look after carefully. We should not soil it."

"I shall not spoil it, mother. This is my father's picture!"

He kept looking at the picture and, unable to hold himself back, gave it a little kiss.

In the next room, Sankummaman kept repeating the words, "Narayana, Narayana," in the belief that God would answer his call some time or other.

Krishnan Kutti wrapped up the picture carefully and put it away. His mother put out the light. Mother and son once again went to bed.

Hours passed. The whole world was fast asleep. But from the bottom of Krishnan Kutti's heart came a question:

"Won't father ever come to us mother?"

In answer, Bhawani Amma could only hold him tight in her arms. How could she answer him?

Illikkal Sankummaman was a farmer on whom fortune smiled. By his own efforts he had earned enough to live fairly well. He had two sons and a daughter who was his favorite. The two boys were very bright and clever. It was a prosperous home, blessed with an abundance of good things. It had seen only laughter and playfulness and high spirits. The shadow of depression had never crossed its threshold. Nobody could have imagined that such a state would ever change. That home was like a bit of heaven.

Of all his children, it was the daughter that Sankummaman was most fond of. No one minded that. Bhawani was the darling of her brothers', too. There was never any occasion for Bhawani's face to be other than cheerful. Her least little wish was like a command to them. And she was lovely to look at. Sankummaman's one great desire in life was to give her away in marriage to someone of high standing and worthy of her. Then he wished to go and live with her for a few days before he died. And they were certain that it would all come to pass. Never had any of Sankummaman's wishes remained unfulfilled. He had always been fortunate in such matters. He was like one born blessed.

The eldest son, Govindan, was the first to pass the B.A. from that village. And because he got a first class, he had no difficulty in getting a job. He got a good position at Rs.200/- a month. The second son passed his B.L. and became an advocate in Alleppey.

And one day, through his good friend Haripad Paramu Pillai, Sankummaman received a proposal of marriage for his daughter, Bhawani. The prospective bridegroom was from near Quilon. He had a good job. His name was N. Parameswaran Pillai but they called him N. P. Pillai. He was a fine, upright man. Pillai had a sister, Yasoda, a good-looking girl, a little delicate in health. The understanding was that Sankummaman's eldest son, Govindan, would marry her. Sankummaman went visiting the party. He was satisfied with the family and the arrangement. The horoscopes of the couples also agreed. Sankummaman pledged his word.

When he returned home, something took place in the Illikkal house, the like of which had never happened before. It was really nothing. It only lasted a minute. But there it was. On that day Sankummaman lost his temper. In fact, he fainted. A decision of Sankummaman's was questioned in that house for the first time. It all lasted only a minute. A few drops of water revived Sankummaman and then all was well.

What happened was this: Sankummaman had come back from Pillai's house, excited and happy. He was describing everything to his wife when she casually said: "Govindan says he doesn't want to get married just yet."

Sankummaman jumped up in a temper: "Who said so?"

The next moment Sankummaman was unconscious. When he came to, Govindan had given his consent to the marriage.

After that there was no more trouble. Pillai's sister, Yasoda, was still a student. Her people agreed that her wedding should take place after she had finished her exam. N. P. Pillai had to go to Calcutta for some training for six months. So they decided that Bhawani's marriage should take place without delay. And so Bhawani and Pillai were married. It was a gay and auspicious wedding.

Pillai returned home from Calcutta after his training period. And Yasoda's examinations were over. But that month was a bad month. An inauspicious one for weddings. And then unexpectedly Govindan got typhoid. So another three months passed. By then the monsoon had set in. Thus the wedding of Govindan and Yasoda was put off again and again. Once or twice Pillai showed his disappointment at this. On such occasions Sankummaman would say: "He is my son. I shall see that it takes place."

Bhawani was now pregnant.

The next thing that one heard was a shocking piece of news. Govindan got involved in a love affair in Trivandrum. The girl became pregnant. Govindan had to marry her. It was a civil marriage. Not only that. It transpired that Govindan had never had any intentions of marrying Yasoda. She was a consumptive.

After that, Pillai never went back to Illikkal. Nor had he seen Bhawani again.

Bhawani gave birth to a boy. He was named Krishnan Kutti. Pillai did not see his son. He never even inquired whether his wife was in need of anything all this time. Soon afterwards, the company for which Pillai worked, sent him to England and Germany for two years' training. He did well and the company promoted him. Yes, now Pillai was drawing Rs.2,250/- a month.

Poor Sankummaman's dreams were shattered. He saw his favorite daughter's future darken. Sankummaman's face lost its lustre. Soon it was lined with wrinkles. He aged rapidly. He lost heart. There was no laughter in that home now. The house was silent and in low spirits. But Sankummaman had decided one thing. His daughter must never be in want. She must not suffer. No one must hurt her. He wanted the boy to be brought up to be somebody. But he realized that he was old. His days were drawing to a close. The end seemed to loom nearer and nearer. He was worried. He was afraid that he might die before young Krishnan Kutti was old enough to take care of his mother. Sankummaman wanted to live to see that day.

Sankummaman tried his best to see if he could not make amends and straighten out matters. But Pillai was adamant.

Days passed. For some time after his marriage, Govindan and his father, Sankummaman, did not see each other. The old father had sworn he wouldn't see his son any more. But the mother was anxious to see her son's son. That was only natural. No matter what womb had given him life, the boy was her son's. She longed for the boy. Bhawani, too, was keen to see the boy. Sankummaman could not deny Bhawani anything. And so one day, Govindan brought his wife and son to Illikkal. The son was a bright child. The wife, too, was a decent girl, thought Govindan's mother. Sankummaman himself felt something like that.

Without realizing it, Sankummaman said: "That is fate. He must have been indebted to her in his previous life. Now he is repaying that debt."

Thus that misunderstanding came to an end. Sankummaman made his peace with his son.

Time passed. Govindan now had three children. His problems and responsibilities increased. He couldn't make both ends meet within his salary. He couldn't save a thing.

One day Govindan's wife had an idea. "If there is anything due to you from your family it will be a consolation to know what it will amount to." Govindan agreed that that was so. But what right had he to ask that of his father? Everything in that house belonged to his father and to his father alone. Did he have the right to ask? He would accept gladly whatever was offered or given to him. That was all.

Govindan's wife said: "It is not necessary that we should ask for, or be given, anything. Let everything remain with your father and mother as long as they live. But they might like to decide what should be our inheritance."

Govindan Nair who had not thought too seriously about all this, said: "What is there to decide about it? We shall inherit a third of whatever there is."

Govindan's wife flared up: "That is what you think. You just wait and you will see who is getting what! The whole lot will go to your sister and her boy. Your father will put it in writing!"

She watched the expression on her husband's face and

continued: "Though he smiles and is pleasant to me, your father doesn't like me. He won't leave anything to us because he knows I shall also benefit by it."

Govindan Nair did not agree on this point. But he could not dismiss his wife's argument as completely off the mark.

He discussed this matter with his younger brother, the advocate. If his father was inclined to leave anything for them, he should indicate it clearly. That was the advocate's opinion too. He also felt that Sankummaman might leave everything to Bhawani.

The brothers decided that they should do something about Bhawani as well. Paramu Pillai who had arranged her marriage was sent for. They wanted him to go and meet Bhawani's husband. On his return they would decide as to the partition and the inheritance.

After having fixed all that, Govindan took leave for some days and arrived in Illikkal with his family. The advocate, too, came there. Everyone waited for the arrival of Paramu Pillai who had gone to see Bhawani's husband.

Paramu Pillai arrived a couple of days later. Sankummaman saw him coming. He rushed to the gate. He called out to him: "What happened, Paramu Pillai? Any hope of my son-in-law's heart softening?"

Paramu Pillai did not look too hopeful. He said: "I have only just traveled a thousand plus a thousand, two thousand miles. Let me sit down and I shall tell you."

Sankummaman felt faint. He stroked his chest and repeated: "Narayana, Narayana." He had no one else to appeal to.

At the door of the house stood Bhawani Amma, waiting anxiously. Krishnan Kutti was hanging onto her sari. Bhawani Amma sighed—a long sigh—and dried her eyes with the *palla* of her sari. And then she went inside; her son behind her. She heard Sankummaman again saying: "Narayana Narayana," his heart full of anguish.

At the portico of the house were Govindan and his brother.

Paramu Pillai was resting after his long journey. Hanging about the door and the window were Govindan's wife and the advocate's wife, itching to hear the news. Sankummaman's wife sat on a bench. Sankummaman was hanging round in the courtyard stroking his chest and repeating, "Narayana Narayana."

Paramu Pillai finished his cup of coffee and said: "I couldn't even see the man for two days. He is a big man over there. One can't just rush in and see him. I had to have some introduction and some recommendations to see him. The R.D.C. Company—well, it is worth seeing."

Paramu Pillai looked as if he was going on with his description of the company for ever. Govindan was getting impatient. He asked: "And what did the big man of that big company say?"

For a while Paramu Pillai was silent as if wondering how to cut short the whole business. Then he said: "He said his mother was not in favor of continuing with this relationship."

Krishnan Kutti came out into the portico. He took his position by his grandmother.

Paramu Pillai continued: "He argues that his party is not the one to be blamed for all this. His sister is still unmarried, in tears the whole time. She has become a perpetual sorrow in their life. Pillai married Bhawani on the understanding that Yasoda would also get a husband."

Govindan cut in: "They were trying to inflict a consumptive on someone. That is why she is still in this state. Who will marry a pack of bones?"

One could hear Sankummaman's heart-rending, "Narayana Narayana." He raised his voice, as if it were meant to reach Narayana in heaven. Govindan's wife withdrew from the door.

Sankummaman's wife said: "The poor man's heart is breaking."

Govindan was silent.

The advocate asked: "If that old woman—Pillai's mother —were to die, would he behave decently?"

It was a difficult question. Pillai didn't say he would receive his wife and son after his mother died. But Paramu Pillai did sense something. He made that clear: "Pillai did say that his mother was the obstacle. We should read our own meaning into that. Perhaps I don't have the right to say as much."

The advocate said: "Even if my brother had married that consumptive, he would have behaved in the same way. Let that be. He need not receive his wife till after his mother is dead. But what about the child? Did that beast say anything about that?"

Paramu Pillai laughed and said: "Look at my misfortune. Pillai talks about you in the same vein. Yes, beast and all. I must hear all that—and all this too. He looked me in the face and told me I was a liar and a schemer."

The advocate answered: "That is why I said we can think of Bhawani's problem later. They tried to ruin my brother's life by inflicting a consumptive on him. Let that be. What do they say about the child?"

On that point, Paramu Pillai had no doubts. And he had to say something: "They are ready to bring up the boy if you let them. His mother will do that. He told me that his mother was insisting on the child being taken to them."

Sankummaman who was in the garden could again be heard calling out to Lord Narayana, his only support.

For a little while no one spoke.

Then Sankummaman's wife asked: "Let me ask you something, Paramu Pillai. Did he seem to be fond of Bhawani?"

Paramu Pillai couldn't say for certain. Paramu Pillai had described to him Bhawani's sorrow in some detail. But it didn't seem to touch his heart.

Paramu Pillai said: "He didn't say anything bad about

Bhawani. Everyone else spoke ill of her. From that one should gauge that he harbored no ill feelings for her."

The mother said with some relief: "That is some consolation."

The advocate asked: "What consolation is that, mother?"

The mother said: "At least he does not blame poor Bhawani. He could have made up all sorts of things. If he starts saying things, what can one do?"

The advocate said: "Heartless beast. He ought to be in hell."

A faint ray of hope had entered the mother's heart and its gentle, dim light was slowly spreading round. She said: "How can God reject Bhawani's tears and your father's prayers? Some day there will be a change of heart on his part."

The advocate had no trust in that. He turned to his brother: "Why shouldn't we file a case against him for maintenance allowances for Bhawani and her child? He draws a salary of over Rs.2,000/- a month. She should get a minimum of seven hundred a month."

Govindan Nair agreed: "We can teach him a lesson that way."

From inside the house came the answer. It was Bhawani's voice: "I don't want that money. And I shan't be a party to such a case."

Bhawani's tone was clear and firm. She wouldn't go to court in any circumstances. The brothers were stunned into silence. The mother felt that they might lose their temper.

It was an explosive situation. A spark might let it off any moment. The mother said to Paramu Pillai: "Have your bath and some food. You can tell us the rest afterwards."

Paramu Pillai went for his bath. And Govindan went inside the house.

Govindan's wife asked: "Did you notice your sister's behavior? The tone of her speech? One wouldn't think she was talking to her elder brothers. No humility, no restraint, no character. I might have tricked my man into marrying me.

Admitted. And so I am a bad woman. But I would never speak to my brothers in this haughty manner."

She watched her husband's face, and continued: "To say that she didn't want Rs.700/- a month! The insolence of it. It is because she is certain of inheriting the whole property that she spoke like that. Why don't you say something? Have you lost your tongue as a result of listening to your sister?"

She wouldn't stop. She continued: "Do you know the answer to this kind of conceit? I shall tell you. We should straightaway demand our share. When her inheritance is reduced to a third, her conceit won't be there."

All this was taking place in one room. In the same house there was another room which was like a world of its own. A silent suffering woman was there, living on her tears. No one had seen her laugh. Laughter had been wiped off her face forever. That room and that world belonged to two people—a mother and her son. They had installed a deity in that little private world. But that god was not responding to the prayers of her heart. Yet she does not blame anyone.

His head on his mother's lap, Krishnan Kutti lay on his back. He asked her: "Mother, may I ask you something?"

"What is it that you want, son?"

"Will you agree?"

"Whatever is within your poor mother's power is yours."

After a minute's silence he asked: "May I go to stay with my father's mother?"

The tears rolled down Bhawani's cheeks.

"Why do you cry, mother?"

With his little hands, he wiped her tears. Her voice shaking, Bhawani said: "In that case, your mother will die."

Without a second's hesitance came his answer: "I am not going anywhere, mother. I shall always stay with you."

The mother drew him to her and kissed him.

Bhawani gave Krishnan Kutti a bath, combed his hair, dressed him in his best shirt and shorts. She kissed him, a kiss wet with tears, blessed him, and was getting ready to send him away with a prayer in her heart. Where? To his father.

Bhawani had come to know that her husband bears her no ill will. Paramu Pillai had said she need not think of re-union with him, as long as his mother lived. Now the mother was dead. Now Bhawani had hopes for her future.

She was sending God's own little envoy to her husband. The father hadn't ever seen his son. He is his flesh and blood. Perhaps his eyes would fill with tears when he saw his son. He would forget everything and clasp him to his heart. All these obstacles are man-made—problems created by man in the course of living. Nature takes no notice of such things. It is the law of nature that the father should love his son. All these days that love had had no chance of showing itself because they hadn't seen each other. When they meet today everything will change. It is even possible Krishnan Kutti would return home with his father. He must come, he has to come. So Bhawani daydreamed. The attachment of father and son. That was her hope and her security. Her husband would come home, with tears in his eyes, and would stretch out his hands to her, and hold her close to his breast. That is the lasting peace she was dreaming of.

Sankummaman took his grandson by the arm and, with Narayana on his lips, set out of the house. That old man had complete faith in Narayana. He was certain that when he saw his young son, the father's resentment would vanish.

And what was going on in Krishnan Kutti's little head? He was certainly not thinking of the bonds of paternal love. He wasn't thinking of his father's reunion with his mother either. He was going to see his father. So far he had only seen his photograph. His father would fondle him just as his uncle fondled his cousins. He was longing for his father's affection. This was what was in his thoughts. Krishnan Kutti had watched from far his uncle holding his cousin and

asking him this and that, and laughing at his childish answers and finally kissing him. Then his aunt, too, would be
near them. Today his father would hold him close like that.
His father would ask him about this and that. And he would
answer without any shyness. His father would kiss him.
How lovely it would have been if his mother, too, were with
them. When he returns he will tell Ramu that he has seen
his father.

It was from the newspapers that Sankummaman had
come to know of the death of Pillai's mother. And he had
heard that Pillai had come home in connection with that.
Govindan and the advocate were against Sankummaman
going to see Pillai. But Sankummaman was going with his
little grandson in his arms because he believed that Lord
Narayana had at last answered his prayers.

Sankummaman had been to Pillai's house only twice. This
was the third time he was going there. From far, Sankummaman pointed out the house to Krishnan Kutti. It was a
large, nice, tiled house.

Someone in a shirt and dhoti, with a cigarette in his
mouth, was in the portico. Was it his father, wondered
Krishnan Kutti. His picture wasn't like that.

The man saw Sankummaman and Krishnan Kutti entering the house. He showed no signs of recognition. There was
no change whatsoever on his face. From deep down in his
heart Sankummaman called out to Lord Narayana.

He stood in the courtyard holding onto Krishnan Kutti not
knowing what to do. No one said a word. There was no other
familiar face about. So they waited uneasily for a while.

At a distance some people were looking at them and mur-
muring softly. From the northern side two or three ladies
peeped at them. Sankummaman thought they were talking
of the boy. He turned to them and said: "Yes, this is the
boy."

Pillai might have heard it. He was walking up and down

the verandah. But he showed no discomfiture. He kept smoking cigarette after cigarette.

One of the men came towards them and took Krishnan Kutti affectionately by the hand.

"Come on, son. Let Pachussar take you and give you a kiss. Pachussar brought up your father."

Krishnan Kutti did not let go of his grandfather's hand.

An old woman came to them. She too called him. But the boy wouldn't go.

Pachussar wondered whether Pillai had recognized the boy. He took the liberty of addressing him: "Here—here is the boy."

Pachussar looked as if he had more to say.

Pillai said curtly: "So?"

Sankummaman again called out to his only refuge— "Narayana." Sankummaman asked: "What wrong has the boy done?"

Pillai answered: "I am not thinking of that."

Sankummaman asked appealingly: "This boy is of your flesh and blood. Don't you feel anything for him?"

Pillai took a little time to answer: "Love and hate are born through close contacts. They do not blossom by themselves."

Sankummaman could not understand that. Pillai continued: "Let me be frank. You need not be under any misunderstanding. You people are crooked and selfish and deceitful. I don't want to have anything to do with you."

Sankummaman begged: "Don't speak like that. What wrong has my poor daughter done? What deceit? What snare did she set?"

Pillai did not have a straight answer for that. But he seemed a little perturbed and said: "Well, go and look into that room. Look at my sister. You have been telling the world she is a consumptive. She hasn't died yet. Go and see her. Then talk to me about your daughter. As long as my mother lived there was someone to look after her. Who is there now? She hasn't got up since her mother's death.

Hasn't even had a drop of water. She has taken a vow to starve herself to death. There is nothing left for her to live for. Let her die. Go and see."

After a while, Pillai asked: "Why don't you go and see for yourself? You haven't the courage to do that. I know you will not have the courage."

Sankummaman had nothing to say. Pillai's complaint was true. It was Sankummaman's turn to speak.

A few moments passed. Krishnan Kutti who was holding fast to Sankummaman said: "Let us go, father. Let us go home."

Sankummaman had to tell Pillai something else. He wanted to know one more thing from Pillai. Sankummaman said: "Son, listen to me, please. I want to bring up this boy and make someone of him. I am sure you, too, will want that. I won't live to see that day. His mother is a very simple girl. She knows nothing. She cannot manage that. The boy has no one but his mother and me. And you, of course. So you should take charge of him. You must bring him up, educate him, and make something of him."

It was the last wish of Sankummaman. He had no hope now that his daughter would be united with her husband. Nor that he could spend a few days with them. Sankummaman waited for an answer.

Pillai shook his head and said. "No. The time and the chance for all that is now past. If I had him some time ago, I might have brought him up. My mother was anxious to bring him up. I could have entrusted him to my mother. But I cannot take on that responsibility now. How can I bring him up?"

After a moment Pillai continued: "I shall settle the money for his expenses and his education. Whatever figure you mention. But the responsibility I cannot take on."

Sankummaman's weary old face went red. His pride came up. With a firmness he had not shown till then, he said: "No. That is not necessary. I have earned enough to bring him up and to educate him. I don't need a *pie* of yours for that."

Sankummaman got up. Then he said to Krishnan Kutti: "Fold your hands and bow to your father."

Krishnan Kutti hesitated. Sankummaman repeated his words firmly. Krishnan Kutti fixed his eyes on his father and bowed with folded hands.

Sankummaman asked: "May we take our leave now?"

Pillai said nothing.

Word had gone round that Pillai's son had come to visit his father. The servants of the household, the neighbors had all gathered there by now. They watched the old man and the child leave. The women could hardly suppress their tears. Nor could Pachussar hold back his.

When Bhawani saw Sankummaman and her son return, everything was clear to her. But there was something in the old man's face which showed a new determination and a new calm. He was no longer calling out to Lord Narayana. He had now sifted the chaff from the grain.

Everything was settled. There was nothing more to expect.

As soon as he entered the house he said to his daughter: "Bhawani, you must bring him up well. Educate him. Educate him to the limit, as far as he can go. I shall provide for it, whatever the cost." Then he turned to his grandson: "Will you study hard and grow up to be a big man one day?"

Straight came the reply: "I will, father."

Sankummaman's wife pressed him to tell her everything that took place at Pillai's house. But Sankummaman wouldn't say a thing.

Krishnan Kutti, who was standing by his mother, also seemed to have changed a little.

Bhawani Amma asked him: "Did your father call you to him?"

"No, mother. He didn't say a word to me. What kind of a father is this?"

Bhawani restrained him: "Don't talk like that, son."

Krishnan Kutti took no notice of that.

"I don't like him. I shall tell Ramu that I haven't got a father."

Bhawani's eyes filled. The son consoled her.

"Don't cry, mother. I shall never leave you. We shall always be together. You mustn't cry."

Several years passed. At the Ernakulam railway station the Cochin Express for Madras was due any moment. A gentleman in Western clothes, getting on in age, was standing by some luggage labeled: N. P. Pillai, R.D.C. Co. Ltd., Bangalore. Presently a porter brought a suitcase and a holdall and placed them by the gentleman's luggage. That suitcase, too, had the name of its owner inscribed on it: Illikkal Krishnan Kutti—Thakazhi village. The gentleman's gaze fell on the suitcase and the name on it.

The train came in, in a rush. The platform was crowded. In the hustle and bustle Pillai saw the youth whose suitcase bore the inscription: Illikkal Krishnan Kutti. Krishnan Kutti's eyes fell on the luggage labeled: N. P. Pillai and his eyes turned to the face of Pillai. They both realized who the other was.

Pillai got into a first-class compartment; Krishnan Kutti into a second-class compartment. Pillai was going to Madras to attend a conference. Krishnan Kutti was going to Madras to be interviewed for a job. The train rushed on to take them both to Madras in time for their respective appointments.

At Coimbatore station, Krishnan Kutti got off the train and strolled along the platform to take a look at that first-class compartment. Pillai was sleeping. At the Arkonam junction, Pillai got off the train and took a look at the second-class carriage in which Krishnan Kutti was traveling. But Krishnan Kutti was engrossed in the morning paper.

The train was running late by over an hour. It looked as if it was going to be late by another half-hour. Pillai was getting worried. He might just reach the Central Station when the conference was due to begin. Krishnan Kutti, too, was worried whether he would be in time for his interview. It wouldn't do if he arrived before the Board straight from his railway journey.

The train arrived at the Central Station exactly an hour and a half late. Hardly had the train stopped when Krishnan Kutti jumped out with his suitcase and holdall. From his compartment Pillai saw him rushing—rushing as if he had a date with destiny.

Outside the station Krishnan Kutti had to wait in line for a taxi. As he waited, he saw Pillai moving off in a limousine —for his conference. Presently his taxi came. He jumped into it and was off—for his interview.

Translated by Narayana Menon

KHUSHWANT SINGH

Khushwant Singh, novelist, short story writer, historian, and translator, was born in 1915, at Hadali in the Punjab. His father, Sir Sobha Singh, was one of the builders of the city of New Delhi. Khushwant Singh was educated in Delhi, obtained his L.L.B. at London University and Bar-at-Law from Inner Temple, and was briefly employed as public relations officer at the High Commission of India in London. He has lectured on Sikhism at Princeton University.

Khushwant Singh's first collection of short stories, Mark of Vishnu, *appeared in London in 1950 and was an immediate success. His other books include two novels,* Train to Pakistan *(1955) and* I Shall Not Hear the Nightingale *(1958). He has also written a* History of the Sikhs.

He admires Cyril Connolly, Aldous Huxley, and the Urdu poets Ghalib and Iqbal.

His stories are vigorous, lively, down to earth, and free from clichés. Whether he writes about a Punjabi peasant, a judge of the High Court, or a family servant, he is relentlessly honest and never dull. His view of the future of Indian writing is equally uncompromising: "The present generation of writers are so immodest with so little to be immodest about, that I do not expect them to produce anything worthwhile."

Khushwant Singh writes in English. He lives in New Delhi.

Karma

KHUSHWANT SINGH

Sir Mohan Lal looked at himself in the mirror of a first-class waiting room at the railway station. The mirror was obviously made in India. The red oxide at its back had come off at several places and long lines of translucent glass cut across its surface. Sir Mohan smiled at the mirror with an air of pity and patronage.

"You are so very much like everything else in this country, inefficient, dirty, indifferent," he murmured.

The mirror smiled back at Sir Mohan.

"You are a bit of all right, old chap," it said. "Distinguished, efficient—even handsome. That neatly trimmed moustache—the suit from Saville Row with the carnation in the buttonhole—the aroma of eau de cologne, talcum powder, and scented soap all about you! Yes, old fellow, you are a bit of all right."

Sir Mohan threw out his chest, smoothed his Balliol tie for the umpteenth time and waved a goodbye to the mirror.

He glanced at his watch. There was still time for a quick one.

"Koi Hai?"

A bearer in white livery appeared through a wire gauze door.

"Ek Chota," ordered Sir Mohan, and sank into a large cane chair to drink and ruminate.

Outside the waiting room Sir Mohan Lal's luggage lay piled along the wall. On a small grey steel trunk Lachmi, Lady Mohan Lal, sat chewing a betel leaf and fanning herself with a newspaper. She was short and fat and in her middle forties. She wore a dirty white sari with a red border. On one side of her nose glistened a diamond nose ring, and she had several gold bangles on her arms. She had been talking to the bearer until Sir Mohan had summoned him inside. As soon as he had gone, she hailed a passing railway coolie.

"Where does the zenana stop?"

"Right at the end of the platform."

The coolie flattened his turban to make a cushion, hoisted the steel trunk on his head, and moved down the platform. Lady Lal picked up her brass tiffin carrier and ambled along behind him. On the way she stopped by a hawker's stall to replenish her silver betel leaf case, and then joined the coolie. She sat down on her steel trunk (which the coolie had put down) and started talking to him.

"Are the trains very crowded on these lines?"

"These days all trains are crowded, but you'll find room in the zenana."

"Then I might as well get over the bother of eating."

Lady Lal opened the brass carrier and took out a bundle of cramped *chapatties* and some mango pickle. While she ate, the coolie sat opposite her on his haunches, drawing lines in the gravel with his finger.

"Are you traveling alone, sister?"

"No, I am with my master, brother. He is in the waiting room. He travels first class. He is a vizier and a barrister, and meets so many officers and Englishmen in the trains— and I am only a native woman. I can't understand English and don't know their ways, so I keep to my zenana inter-class."

Lachmi chatted away merrily. She was fond of a little gossip and had no one to talk to at home. Her husband never had any time to spare for her. She lived in the upper story of the house and he on the ground floor. He did not like her poor illiterate relatives hanging about his bungalow, so they never came. He came up to her once in a while at night and stayed for a few minutes. He just ordered her about in anglicized Hindustani, and she obeyed passively. These nocturnal visits had, however, borne no fruit.

The signal came down and the clanging of the bell announced the approaching train. Lady Lal hurriedly finished off her meal. She got up, still licking the stone of the pickled mango. She emitted a long, loud belch as she went to the public tap to rinse her mouth and wash her hands. After washing she dried her mouth and hands with the loose end of her sari, and walked back to her steel trunk, belching and thanking the gods for the favor of a filling meal.

The train steamed in. Lachmi found herself facing an almost empty inter-class zenana compartment next to the guard's van, at the tail end of the train. The rest of the train was packed. She heaved her squat, bulky frame through the door and found a seat by the window. She produced a two-anna bit from a knot in her sari and dismissed the coolie. She then opened her betel case and made herself two betel leaves charged with a red and white paste, minced betelnuts and cardamoms. These she thrust into her mouth till her cheeks bulged on both sides. Then she rested her chin on her hands and sat gazing idly at the jostling crowd on the platform.

The arrival of the train did not disturb Sir Mohan Lal's sangfroid. He continued to sip his Scotch and ordered the bearer to tell him when he had moved the luggage to a first-class compartment. Excitement, bustle, and hurry were exhibitions of bad breeding, and Sir Mohan was eminently well bred. He wanted everything "tickety-boo" and orderly. In his five years abroad, Sir Mohan had acquired the manners and attitudes of the upper classes. He rarely spoke Hindustani. When he did, it was like an Englishman's—only the very necessary words and properly anglicized. But he fancied his English, finished and refined at no less a place than the University of Oxford. He was fond of conversation, and like a cultured Englishman he could talk on almost any subject—books, politics, people. How frequently had he heard English people say that he spoke like an Englishman!

Sir Mohan wondered if he would be traveling alone. It was a Cantonment and some English officers might be on the train. His heart warmed at the prospect of an impressive conversation. He never showed any sign of eagerness to talk to the English as most Indians did. Nor was he loud, aggressive, and opinionated like them. He went about his business with an expressionless matter-of-factness. He would retire to his corner by the window and get out a copy of *The Times*. He would fold it in a way in which the name of the paper was visible to others while he did the crossword puzzle. *The Times* always attracted attention. Someone would like to borrow it when he put it aside with a gesture signifying "I've finished with it." Perhaps someone would recognize his Balliol tie which he always wore while traveling. That would open a vista leading to a fairyland of Oxford colleges, masters, dons, tutors, boat races, and rugger matches. If both *The Times* and the tie failed, Sir Mohan would "Koi Hai" his bearer to get the Scotch out. Whisky never failed with Englishmen. Then followed Sir Mohan's handsome gold cigarette case filled with English cigarettes. English cigarettes in India? How on earth did he get them? Sure he didn't mind? And Sir Mohan's understanding smile—of course he didn't. But could he use the Englishman as a medium to commune with his dear old England? Those five years of grey bags and gowns, of sports blazers and mixed doubles, of dinners at the Inns of Court and nights with Piccadilly prostitutes. Five years of a crowded glorious life. Worth far more than the forty-five in India with his dirty, vulgar countrymen, with sordid details of the road to success, of nocturnal visits to the upper story and all-too-brief sexual acts with obese old Lachmi, smelling of sweat and raw onions.

Sir Mohan's thoughts were disturbed by the bearer announcing the installation of the Sahib's luggage in a first-class coupe next to the engine. Sir Mohan walked to his coupe with a studied gait. He was dismayed. The compartment was empty. With a sigh he sat down in a corner and opened the copy of *The Times* he had read several times before.

Sir Mohan looked out of the window down the crowded platform. His face lit up as he saw two English soldiers trudging along, looking in all the compartments for room. They had their haversacks slung behind their backs and walked unsteadily. Sir Mohan decided to welcome them, even though they were entitled to travel only second class. He would speak to the guard.

One of the soldiers came up to the last compartment and stuck his face through the window. He surveyed the compartment and noticed the unoccupied berth.

" 'Ere, Bill," he shouted, "one 'ere."

His companion came up, also looked in, and looked at Sir Mohan.

"Get the nigger out," he muttered to his companion.

They opened the door, and turned to the half-smiling, half-protesting Sir Mohan.

"Reserved!" yelled Bill.

"Janta—Reserved. Army—Fauj," exclaimed Jim, pointing to his khaki shirt.

"Ek dum jao—get out!"

"I say, I say, surely," protested Sir Mohan in his Oxford accent.

The soldiers paused. It almost sounded like English, but they knew better than to trust their inebriated ears. The engine whistled and the guard waved his green flag.

They picked up Sir Mohan's suitcase and flung it onto the platform. Then followed his Thermos-flask, suitcase, bedding, and *The Times*. Sir Mohan was livid with rage.

"Preposterous, preposterous," he shouted, hoarse with anger. "I'll have you arrested—guard, guard!"

Bill and Jim paused again. It did sound like English, but it was too much of the King's for them.

"Keep yer ruddy mouth shut!" And Jim struck Sir Mohan flat on the face.

The engine gave another short whistle and the train began to move. The soldiers caught Sir Mohan by the arms and flung him out of the train. He reeled backwards, tripped on his bedding, and landed on the suitcase.

"Toodle-oo!"

Sir Mohan's feet were glued to the earth and he lost his speech. He stared at the lighted windows of the train going past him in quickening tempo. The tail end of the train appeared with a red light and the guard standing in the open doorway with the flags in his hands.

In the inter-class zenana compartment was Lachmi, fair and fat, on whose nose the diamond nose ring glistened against the station lights. Her mouth was bloated with betel saliva which she had been storing up to spit as soon as the train had cleared the station. As the train sped past the lighted part of the platform, Lady Lal spat and sent a jet of red dribble flying across like a dart.

The Rape

DALIP SINGH lay on his *charpoy* * staring at the star-studded sky. It was hot and still. He was naked save for his loin cloth. Even so, beads of perspiration rolled off from all parts of his body. The heat rose from the mud walls which had been baking in the sun all day. He had sprinkled water on the roof of the house, but that only produced a clammy vapor smelling of earth and cow dung. He had drunk as much water as his stomach would hold, still his throat was parched. Then there were the mosquitoes and their monotonous droning. Some came too close to his ears and were caught and mashed between his palm and the fingers. One or two got into his ears and he rammed them against the greasy walls with his index finger. Some got entangled in his beard and were squashed to silence in their snares. Some managed to gorge themselves on his blood, leaving him to scratch and curse.

Across the narrow alley separating his house from his uncle's, Dalip Singh could see a row of *charpoys* on the roof. At one end slept his uncle, Banta Singh, with his arms and legs parted as if crucified. His belly rose and fell as he snored. He had had *bhang* in the afternoon and slept with utter abandon. At the other end of the row several women sat fanning themselves and talking softly.

Dalip Singh lay awake staring at the sky. For him there was no peace, no sleep. Yet, on the other roof slept his uncle, his father's brother and murderer. His womenfolk found time to sit and gossip into the late hours of the night while

* A cot.—Ed.

his own mother scrubbed the pots and pans with ash and gathered cow dung for fuel. Banta Singh had servants to look after his cattle and plow his land while he drank *bhang* and slept. His black-eyed daughter Bindo went about doing nothing but showing off her Japanese silks. But for Dalip Singh it was work and more work.

The *keekar* trees stirred. A soft, cool breeze blew across the rooftops. It drove the mosquitoes away and dried the sweat. It made Dalip feel cool and placid, and he was heavy with sleep. On Banta Singh's roof the women stopped fanning themselves. Bindo stood up beside her *charpoy,* threw her head back and filled her lungs with the cool fresh air. Dalip watched her stroll up and down. She could see the people of the village sleeping on the roofs and in the court-yards. No one stirred. Bindo stopped and stood beside her *charpoy.* She picked up her shirt from the two corners which fell just above her knees and held it across her face with both hands, baring herself from the waist to her neck, letting the cool breeze envelop her flat belly and her youthful bust. Then someone said something in an angry whisper and Bindo let down her shirt. She dropped on her *charpoy* and was lost in the confused outlines of her pillow.

Dalip Singh was wide awake and his heart beat wildly. The loathsome figure of Banta Singh vanished from his mind. He shut his eyes and tried to recreate Bindo as he saw her in the starlight. He desired her and in his dreams he possessed her. Bindo was always willing—even begging. Dalip condescending, even indifferent. Banta Singh spited and humbled. Dalip Singh's eyes were shut but they opened into another world where Bindo lived and loved, naked, unashamed and beautiful.

Several hours later Dalip's mother came and shook him by the shoulder. It was time to go out plowing while it was cool. The sky was black and the stars brighter. He picked up his shirt which lay folded under his pillow and put it on. He looked across to the adjoining roof. Bindo lay fast asleep.

Dalip Singh yoked his bullocks to the plow and let them lead him to the fields. He went through the dark, deserted lanes of the village to the starlit fields. He was tired, and the image of Bindo still confused his mind.

The eastern horizon turned grey. From the mango grove the koil's piercing cries issued in a series of loud outbursts. The crows began to caw softly in the *keekar* trees.

Dalip Singh was plowing but his mind was not in it. He just held the plow and walked slowly behind. The furrows were neither straight nor deep. The morning light made him feel ashamed. He decided to pull himself together and shake off his daydreaming. He dug the sharp point of his plow deep into the earth and thrust his goading stick violently into the hind parts of the bullocks. The beasts were jerked into movement, snorting and lashing their tails. The plow tore through the earth and large clods of earth fell on either side under Dalip's feet. Dalip felt master of his bullocks and the plow. He pressed the plow deeper with savage determination and watched its steel point concupiscently nosing its way through the rich brown earth.

The sun came up very bright and hot. Dalip gave up the plowing and led his bullocks to a well under the *peepul* tree and unyoked them. He drew several buckets of water. He bathed himself and splashed water over his bullocks, and followed them home dripping all the way.

His mother was waiting for him. She brought him freshly baked bread and spinach, with a little butter on it. She also brought a large copper cup full of buttermilk. Dalip fell to the food eagerly, while his mother sat by him fanning away the flies. He finished the bread and spinach and washed it down with buttermilk. He laid himself on a *charpoy* and was soon fast asleep. His mother still sat by him fanning him tenderly.

Dalip slept right through the morning and afternoon. He got up in the evening and went round to his fields to clear the water courses. He walked along the water channel which separated his land from his uncle's. Banta Singh's fields were being irrigated by his tenants. Since he had killed his brother, Banta Singh never came to his land in the evening.

Dalip Singh busied himself clearing the water channels in his fields. When he had finished doing that he came to the water course and washed himself. He sat down on the grassy bank with his feet in the running water and waited for his mother.

The sun went down across a vast stretch of flat land, and the evening star shone, close to a crescent moon. From the village he could hear the shouts of women at the well, of children at play—all mixed up with the barking of dogs and the bedlam of sparrows noisily settling down for the night. Batches of women came out into the fields and scattered behind the bushes to relieve themselves. They assembled again and washed in rows along the water course.

Dalip Singh's mother came with the wooden token from the canal timekeeper, showing that Dalip's turn to water his field had started. Then she went back to look after the cattle. Banta Singh's tenants had already left. Dalip Singh blocked the water exit to Banta Singh's land and cut it open to his fields. After doing this he stretched himself on the cool grassy bank and watched the water rippling over the plowed earth, shimmering like quicksilver under the light of the new moon. He lay on his back looking at the sky and listening to the noises from the village. He could hear women talking somewhere in Banta Singh's fields. Then the world relapsed into a moonlit silence.

Dalip Singh's thoughts were disturbed by the sound of splashing of water close to him. He turned round and saw a woman on the opposite bank sitting on her haunches washing herself. With one hand she splashed the water between her thighs, with the other she cleaned herself. She scraped a handful of mud from the ground, rubbed it on her hands and dipped them in the running water. She rinsed her mouth and threw handfuls of water over her face. Then she stood up leaving her baggy trousers lying at her feet. She picked up her shirt from the front and bent down to wipe her face with it.

It was Bindo. Dalip Singh was possessed with a maddening desire. He jumped across the water course and ran towards her. The girl had her face buried in her shirt. Before she could turn round, Dalip Singh's arms closed round her under the armpits and across her breasts. As she turned round he smothered her face with passionate kisses and stifled her frightened cry by gluing his mouth to hers. He bore her down on the soft grass. Bindo fought like a wildcat. She caught Dalip's beard in both her hands and savagely dug her nails into his cheeks. She bit his nose till it bled. But she was soon exhausted. She gave up the struggle and lay perfectly still. Her eyes were shut and tears trickled down on either side, washing the black antimony onto her ears. She looked beautiful in the pale moonlight. Dalip was full of remorse. He had never intended hurting her. He caressed her forehead with his large rough hands and let his fingers run through her hair. He bent down and tenderly rubbed his nose against hers. Bindo opened her large black eyes and stared at him blankly. There was no hate in them, nor any love. It was just a blank stare. Dalip Singh kissed her eyes and nose gently. Bindo just looked at him with a vacant expression, and more tears welled in her eyes.

Bindo's companions were shouting for her. She did not answer. One of them came nearer and shouted for help. Dalip Singh got up quickly and jumped across the water course and was lost in the darkness.

II

The entire male population of the village of Singhpura turned up to hear the case of *Crown* v. *Dalip Singh*. The courtroom, the verandah, and the courtyard were packed with villagers. At one end of the verandah was Dalip Singh in handcuffs between two policemen. His mother sat fanning him with her face covered in a shawl. She was weeping and blowing her nose. At the other end, Bindo, her mother and several other women were huddled together in a circle. Bindo also wept and blew her nose. Towering above this group were Banta Singh and his friends leaning on their bamboo poles, in constant and whispered consultation. Other villagers whiled away their time buying sweets from hawkers, or having their ears cleaned by itinerant "ear specialists." Some were gathered round vendors of aphrodisiacs nudging each other and laughing.

Banta Singh had hired a lawyer to help the government prosecutor. The lawyer collected the prosecution witnesses in a corner and made them go over their evidence. He warned them of the questions likely to be put to them by the defense counsel. He introduced the court orderly and the clerk to Banta Singh and made him tip them. He got a wad of notes from his client to pay the government prosecutor. The machinery of justice was fully oiled. Dalip Singh had no counsel nor defense witnesses.

The orderly opened the courtroom door and called the case in a singsong manner. He let in Banta Singh and his friends. Dalip Singh was marched in by the policemen but the orderly kept his mother out. She had not paid him. When order was restored in the courtroom, the clerk proceeded with reading the charge.

Dalip Singh pleaded not guilty. Mr. Kumar, the magistrate, asked the prosecuting subinspector to produce Bindo. Bindo shuffled into the witness-box with her face still covered in her shawl and blowing her nose. The inspector asked her about her father's enmity with Dalip Singh. He produced her clothes stained with blood and semen. That closed the case for the prosecution. The evidence of Bindo corroborated by the exhibits was clear and irrefutable.

The prisoner was asked if he had any questions to put. Dalip Singh folded his handcuffed hands.

"I am innocent, possessor of pearls."

Mr. Kumar was impatient.

"Have you heard the evidence? If you have no questions for the girl, I will pass orders."

"Thou of the pearls, I have no lawyer. I have no friends in the village to give evidence for me. I am poor. Show mercy. I am innocent."

The magistrate was angry. He turned to the clerk. "Cross-examination—nil."

"But," spluttered Dalip Singh, "before you send me to jail, emperor, ask her if she was not willing. I went to her because she wanted me. I am innocent."

Mr. Kumar turned to the clerk again.

"Cross-examination by accused.—Did you go to the accused of your own free will? Answer . . ."

Mr. Kumar addressed Bindo: "Answer, did you go to the accused of your own free will?"

Bindo blew her nose and wept. The magistrate and the crowd waited in impatient irritating silence.

"Did you or did you not? Answer. I have other work to do."

Through the many folds of the shawl muffling her face Bindo answered.

"Yes."

PALAGUMMI PADMARAJU

Palagummi Padmaraju was born in 1915, in a small village in the state of Andhra, in southern India. His family was Brahmin, and his father was headmaster of a high school in a nearby town. He took his M.Sc. in chemistry from the Benares Hindu University.

Padmaraju began writing when he was twenty years old. He writes in Telegu. His works include three volumes of short stories published between 1945 and 1953, a novel, The Human Zoo (1964), *and three plays,* Tears of Blood, Ramadu the Vagabond, *and* The Evil and Its Retribution. *One of his stories, "The Cyclone," won second prize in the World Short Story Competition conducted by the* New York Herald Tribune *in 1952.*

His influences were apparently even more varied than is usual among Indian writers. He lists Bret Harte and de Maupassant as the earliest. "Later Maugham, Chekhov, and Turgenev and still later Huxley and Hemingway." He greatly admires Raja Rao and feels that in The Serpent and the Rope *the author "succeeded in pushing the frontiers of this [English] language, and made it a superb vehicle for expressing thought and feeling in an essentially Indian manner."*

Padmaraju now lives in Madras. He writes film scripts as well as fiction.

On The Boat

PALAGUMMI PADMARAJU

AFTER sundown the world was enveloped in a melancholy haze. The boat glided softly on the still river.

The water lapped against the sides of the boat in soft ripples. No life stirred, as far as the eye could see, and the dead world hummed soundlessly. That hum was inaudible but the body felt it and it filled the mind with its reverberations. A feeling of life coming to an end, of peace inexorable and devoid of all hope, crept over one's consciousness. The vague, mysterious figures of distant trees moved along with the boat motionlessly. The trees, which were nearer, moved backwards, like devils with disheveled hair. The boat did not move. The canal bank moved backwards.

My eyes looked deep into the still waters, penetrating the darkness. The stars relaxed on the bed of water swinging dreamily on the slow ripples, and slept with eyes wide open.

No stir in the air. The rope by which the boatmen pulled the boat sagged and tautened rhythmically and the bells on the guide stick in the hand of the leader tinkled at each step. At one end of the boat, there was the red glare of a fire in the oven, alternately glowing into a flame and subsiding. With a small bucket, a boy baled out the water percolating into the boat through small leaks. Sacks filled with paddy, jaggery, tamarind, and what not were stacked in the boat.

I lay down on the top of the boat staring at the sky. From inside the boat, tobacco smoke, mingled with soft, inaudible voices, spread in all directions. In the small room where the clerk sat, there was a tiny oil lamp, blinking in the darkness. The boat moved on.

A voice hailed us from the distance, "Please bring the boat to this bank—this bank!" As the boat drew near the bank, two figures jumped on the footboard. The boat tilted slightly to that side.

"Please do not mind us. We'll sit here on the top," said a woman's voice.

The man at the rudder asked her, "Where were you all these days, Rangi? I have not seen you for a long time."

"My man took me to many places—Vijayanagaram, Visakhapatnam and we climbed together the Hill of Appanna."

"Where are you going now?"

"Mandapaka. How are you, brother? Do you still have the same clerk?"

"Yes."

The male figure fell down in a heap and his lighted cheroot slipped from his mouth. The woman put it out.

"Sit down properly," she said.

"Shut up, you bitch. Do you think I am drunk? I'll break your ribs if you disturb me."

He rolled over from one side to the other. The woman covered him with the sheet of cloth which had slipped to one side when he rolled over. She lighted a cheroot herself. When the match caught the flame, I saw her face for a brief moment. The dark face glowed red.

There was a hint of bass in her voice. When she talked, you felt she was artlessly confiding to you her innermost secrets. She was not beautiful; her hair was disheveled. And yet there was an air of dignity about her. The black blouse she was wearing gave the impression that she was not wearing any. In the darkness her eyes sparkled as if they were very much alive. When she lighted the match, she noticed me lying nearby.

"There is someone sleeping here," she said trying to wake up the man.

"Lie down, you slut. I'll break your neck if you disturb me again."

With an effort he moved away from me.

The clerk stood on the footboard with the oil lamp in his hand. He asked, "Who is that fellow, Rangi?"

"He is my man, Paddalu. Please do not charge us, sir, for the journey."

"Is it Paddalu? Get him out! He is a rogue and a thief. Have you no sense? He's dead drunk and you have brought him on to this boat!"

"Who says I am drunk?" complained Paddalu.

"You fools. Throw the fellow out. Why did you allow him to step on the boat? He is dead drunk," the clerk shouted to the boatmen.

"I'm not dead drunk. I merely quenched a little of my thirst," protested Paddalu.

"Why don't you keep mum?" admonished the woman.

"Please, sir, I beg of you. May God bless you, sir. We'll get down at Mandapaka," she pleaded.

The man joined in the pleading, "I'm not drunk, sir. Please be kind and allow us to go to Mandapaka."

"If you make any row I'll have you thrown into the canal. Be careful." The clerk went back to his room. Paddalu sat up. He was not really drunk.

"He will have me thrown into the canal—the son of a bitch!" he said in a low voice.

"Keep quiet. If he heard what you said, then we're finished."

"Let him look around the boat tomorrow morning. He puts on airs, the son of a bitch."

"S..s..s. Someone is sleeping there."

Paddalu lighted a cheroot. He had a very thick moustache. His face was oval. His spine curved like a bow drawn by a string. He was lean and sinewy and there was an air of nonchalance about him.

The boat was gliding along softly again. The boatmen were washing the utensils after food, talking among themselves.

It was not cool, but I covered myself with a sheet. I felt a little afraid to leave my body exposed helplessly to the darkness. The breeze was sharp—the boat glided softly on the water like the touch of a woman. The night was wrapped with tenderness—as in the caress of an unseen woman. I felt lost in that embrace and many memories of my past and of tales tinged with melancholy about woman tending man and bringing him happiness flitted across my consciousness.

At a little distance from me, two cheroots were glowing red in the darkness. It appeared as though life was sitting there heavily, smoking, and thinking about itself.

"Which is the next village on our way?" asked Paddalu.

"Kaldari," said Rangi.

"We have a long distance to go."

"Don't do it today. You ought to be careful. Not today. We will try some other time when it is safer. Will you not listen to me?" pleaded Rangi.

"You are afraid—you slut," said Paddalu. He tickled her side with a dig of his finger.

"Oh!" she said and looked skyward as if she wished the feeling this gave her would last forever.

Gradually I fell asleep. The boat moved downstream as if also in sleep. The two figures not far from me were talking in whispers to each other for some time. Though I was sleeping, a part of me was awake. I knew that the boat was moving, that the water was lapping its sides, that the trees on the banks were moving backwards. Inside the boat everyone was asleep, Rangi moved from my side to the rudder and sat beside the man who was handling it.

"How are you, brother?" she asked.

"How are you?" asked the man at the rudder.

"Oh! what wonders we have seen, my man and I! We went to a cinema. We saw a ship. What a ship it was! Brother, it was as big as our village. I do not know where its rudder was." She told him of a hundred things and her voice caressed me in my sleep.

"Oh girl! I am feeling sleepy," said the man at the rudder.

"I'll hold it, you lie down there," said Rangi.

The boat moved on silently—slowly. Without disturbing the silence, Rangi raised her voice into a song:

> Where is he! Oh where is he, my man!
> I put the food in the plate and
> Sit there awaiting his return.
> Like a shadow the night deepens,
> But no sleep comes to my eyes—Where is he? my man?
> The cold wind stings me like a scorpion
> And my nerves contract and ache,
> Unless you press me with your warm body
> I may die. . . . Where is he?—my man!

Rangi's voice had music in it. It seemed as though all living creatures heard the song in their sleep. Age-old tales of love reverberated sadly and mysteriously in that song. It spread like a sheet of water and the world was afloat in it like a small boat. Human life, with its love and longing, seemed heavy, inevitable, and strange.

A little distance from me, Paddalu sat with his head covered with a sheet. But a gulf seemed to separate him from Rangi.

After some time Paddalu went inside the boat. I shook off sleep and lay looking at the stars. Rangi was singing:

> You thought there was a girl in the lane behind the hut
> And sneaked there silently.
> But who is the girl, my dear man?
> Is she not I in my bloom . . .

Rangi's song traveled through the worlds; then returned and touched me somewhere in my heart. I felt drowsy. In my sleep, the elemental longing of man and woman for one another danced before me like rustic lovers playing hide and seek. A dream world, entirely new to me, spread before me in my sleep. Rangi and Paddalu moved about in a myriad of forms. The song slipped away from my consciousness, and the doors of my mind were gradually closed even to dreams.

Some confusion in the boat woke me and I sat up. The boat was tied to a peg on the bank. The boatmen were moving about hurriedly in the boat and on the bank, with lanterns. On the bank two men stood on either side of Rangi holding her by her arms. One of them was the clerk. He had a piece of rope folded in one of his hands. It looked as if Rangi was going to receive a thrashing. I jumped onto the bank and asked them what was wrong.

The clerk's face flushed with anger. He said, "The rogue has run away with some of our things. This daughter of a bitch must have got the boat to a bank while everybody was asleep. She was holding the rudder, the slut." There was a note of despair and helplessness in his tone.

"What were the goods that were stolen?" I asked.

"Two baskets of jaggery and three bags of tamarind. That was why I said I would not allow them on the boat. I will have to make up the loss." Then he asked Rangi, "Where did he unload the goods?"

"Near Kaldari, my good sir!"

"You liar! All of us were awake at Kaldari."

"Then it must have been at Nidadavolu."

"No, she will never tell us. We will hand her over to the police at Attili. Get on the boat."

"Kind sir, please allow me to go."

"Get on the boat," he ordered pushing her towards the boat.

Two boatmen dragged her into the boat.

"Sleepy beggars! Careless idiots! Have you no sense of responsibility? Why should you put the rudder in her hands?" The clerk was very much put out. He went back to his room.

Rangi resumed her former seat. One boatman sat beside

her to guard her. The boat moved again. I lighted a cheroot.

"Kind sir, spare me one too," she asked me in a tone which suggested intimacy. I gave her a cheroot and a box of matches. She lighted it.

"Dear brother! What can you gain by handing me over to the police?"

"The clerk will not let you go," said the boatman.

"Is Paddalu your husband?" I asked her.

"He is my man," she replied.

The boatman said, "He seduced her when she was a young girl. He did not marry her. Now he has another girl. Where is she, Rangi?"

"In Kovvur. Now, she is in her bloom. When she has endured as many blows as I have, she will look worse than me. The dirty bitch!"

"Then why do you have anything to do with him?" I asked.

"He is mine, sir!" she replied, as if that explained everything.

"But he has another woman."

"What can he do without me? It does not matter how many women a man has. I tell you sir, he is a king among men. There is not another like him."

The boatman said, "Sir, you cannot imagine what this fellow really is, without knowing him. She was just bubbling with life and youth when she got entangled with him. One night, he locked her up in her hut and set fire to it. She was almost burnt to death. It was only her good fortune that saved her."

"I felt like strangling him with my bare hands if I could only get at him. A red hot bamboo fell across my back from the roof of the hut." She lifted her blouse a little and even in that darkness I could see a white scar on her back.

"Why are you still with him after all this cruelty?" I asked.

"I cannot help it, sir. When he is with me, I simply cling to him. He can talk so well and your sense of pity wells up like a spring. This evening we started from Kovvur. On the way, he begged me on his knees to help him in this affair. He said he was completely broke. We reached the Nidada-volu channel by a shortcut across the fields. . . ."

"Where did he land the goods?"

"How should I know?"

"Oh! she will never tell the truth, the rogue!" said the boat-man laughing.

There was a sudden impulse of curiosity in me to have a close look at her face. But in that darkness, she remained hazy and inscrutable.

The boat crawled slowly on the smooth sheet of water. As midnight passed, the breeze developed a colder sting. There was a slight rustle of leaves on the trees. I did not sleep again that night. Rangi's guard tried ineffectually to fight his over-powering desire to sleep and finally yielded to it. But Rangi sat there listlessly smoking her cheroot, reconciled to her position.

"You were not married at all?" I asked her.

"No. I was very young when Paddalu took me away."

"Which is your native village?"

"Indrapalem. . . . Then I did not know he was a drunk-ard. . . . Now, of course, I have caught it from him. There is nothing wrong if one drinks. But sometimes when he is drunk, he is wild."

"You could have left him and gone back to your parents."

"That is what I feel like, when he becomes wild. But then there is no one else like him. You do not know him. When he is not drunk he is as meek as a lamb. He might take a hun-dred women. But he comes back to me. What can he do without me?"

The woman's attitude struck me as strange, and I could not divine what held those two together. Rangi said again: "No job suited either of us. So we had to take to thieving. When my mother was alive she used to scold me for making a fool of myself. One night, he brought that girl to my hut."

"Which girl?"

"The one he is now living with. He put her on my bed and lay down beside her. Before my very eyes! Both of them were drunk. The slut! I pounced upon her and scratched her violently. He intervened and beat me out of my breath. About midnight he went away with her somewhere. He returned again. I called him names and refused to admit him into the house. He collapsed on the doorstep and began to weep like a child. I was touched. I sat beside him. He took me into his lap and asked me to give him my necklace. 'What for?' I asked him. He said it was for the other girl. I was beside myself with anger and heaped on him torments of abuse. He told me, weeping, that he could not live without that girl. My anger knew no bounds. I pushed him out and bolted the door inside. He pulled at it for a while and went away. I lay with my eyes wide open and could not sleep for a long time. But after I fell asleep, the house caught fire. He had locked the hut on the outside and set fire to it. I tried the door desperately and at that time of the night my shouts for help did not reach my neighbors. My body was being fried alive. I fell unconscious. My neighbors must have rescued me in that state. The police arrested him the next day. But I told them categorically that he could not have been the author of the crime. That evening he came to me and wept for hours. Sometimes, when he is drunk he weeps like that. But when he is not drunk, he is such a jolly fellow. I gave him that necklace."

"Why do you still assist him in these crimes?"

"What am I to do when he comes and begs me as if his whole life depends on it?"

"Did he really take you to all those places, Vijayanagaram, Visakhapatnam and what not?"

"No. I wanted to gain the confidence of the boatmen. On two former occasions, this very boat was robbed."

"What will you do, if the police arrest you?"

"Why should I do anything? What can they do? I have no stolen goods in my possession. Who knows who was responsible for the robbery? They might beat me. But ultimately they will have to set me free."

"Supposing Paddalu is caught with these goods?"

"No, he would have disposed of them by now. I remained in the boat to give him enough time to effect his escape."

She heaved a sigh and then said, sotto voce, "All this goes to that damned bitch. He will not leave her till her freshness fades away. I have to suffer all this for the sake of that slut."

There was not a trace of emotion in her voice, nor was there any reproach. She accepted him as he was and was prepared to do anything for him. It was not sacrifice, not devotion, not even love. It was simply the heart of a woman, with a strange complex of feelings, tinged with love as well as with jealousy. There was only one outward expression of this medley of feelings and that was the longing she felt for her man. Every fiber of that heart thirsted for that man. But she had no demands to make of him, ethical or moral. She did not mind if he was not true to her, even if he was cruel to her. She loved him as he was, with all his vagaries and pettinesses and with his wild and untamed spirit. What did she derive from such a life with the dice so loaded against her? What was her compensation? Was not such a life very unhappy and burdensome? But then what was happiness except the lack of a consciousness of unhappiness? Was I happy judging by that standard?

The wind rose gradually. The boat moved faster. There were signs of the world waking up slowly from its rejuvenating slumber. Here and there peasants could be seen going to their fields. The morning star had not yet risen. Rangi drew her knees closer, folded her arms around them, and sat looking into the fading night.

"He is my man. Wherever he goes, he is bound to return to me," she said slowly, not particularly addressing me. These words summarized the one hope, the one strength, the one faith that kept her irrevocably linked with life. Her whole life revolved around that one point. There was pity, fear, and above all reverence in my heart for that woman. I wondered, how confusing, grotesque, terrifying, even insane, were the affairs of the human heart!

I sat looking at her till the day broke. Before I got off the boat, I put a rupee in her hand without being observed, and then went away without waiting to see her reaction. I never met her again.

Translated by the author

SANTHA RAMA RAU

Santha Rama Rau was born in 1923 in Madras, South India. Her father, Sir Benegal Rama Rau, was, among other diplomatic posts, Indian Ambassador to the United States. She was educated at St. Paul's School, London, and at Wellesley College, in Massachusetts.

She has been writing since her school days: "I never decided to become 'a writer.' Just found that some of my writing was publishable."

She has traveled widely, and her books include: Home to India (*1944*), East of Home (*1950*), This is India (*1954*), View to the Southeast (*1957*), Remember the House (*1956*), My Russian Journey (*1959*), Gifts of Passage (*1961*), *and* A Passage to India, *a play based on E. M. Forster's novel, which was produced on Broadway in 1962.*

Santha Rama Rau lives in New York City.

Who Cares?

SANTHA RAMA RAU

THE only thing, really, that Anand and I had in common was that both of us had been to college in America. Not that we saw much of each other during those four years abroad —he was studying business management or some such thing in Boston and I was taking the usual liberal arts course at Wellesley, and on the rare occasions we met, we hadn't much to say—but when we got back to Bombay, the sense of dislocation we shared was a bond. In our parents' generation that whole malaise was covered by the comprehensive phrase "England-returned," which held good even if you had been studying in Munich or Edinburgh, both popular with Indian students in those days. The term was used as a qualification (for jobs and marriages) and as an explanation of the familiar problems of readjustment. Even after the war, in a particular kind of newspaper, you could find, in the personal columns, advertisements like this: "Wanted: young, fair, educated girl, high caste essential, for England-returned boy. Send photograph." The point is that she would have to prove herself—or rather, her family would have to demonstrate her desirability—but "England-returned" would tell her just about everything she needed to know about the boy: that his family was rich enough to send him abroad for his education, that his chances for a government job or a good job in business were better than most, that his wife could probably expect an unorthodox household in which she might be asked to serve meat at meals, entertain foreigners, speak English, and even have liquor on the premises. She would also know that it would be a "good" (desirable, that is) marriage.

"England-returned," like that other much-quoted phrase, "Failed B.A.," was the kind of Indianism that used to amuse the British very much when it turned up on a job application. To Indians, naturally, it had a serious and precise meaning. Even "Failed B.A.," after all, meant to us not that a young man had flunked one examination, but that he had been through all the years of school and college that led to a degree—an important consideration in a country where illiteracy is the norm and education a luxury.

In the course of a generation that became increasingly sensitive to ridicule, those useful phrases had fallen out of fashion, and by the time Anand and I returned to Bombay we had to find our own descriptions for our uneasy state. We usually picked rather fancy ones, about how our ideas were too advanced for Bombay, or how enterprise could never flourish in India within the deadly grip of the family system, or we made ill-digested psychological comments on the effects of acceptance as a way of life. What we meant, of course, was that we were suffering from the England-returned blues. Mine was a milder case than Anand's, partly because my parents were "liberal"—not orthodox Hindus, that is—and, after fifteen years of wandering about the world in the diplomatic service, were prepared to accept with equanimity and even a certain doubtful approval the idea of my getting a job on a magazine in Bombay. Partly, things were easier for me because I had been through the worst of my readjustments six years before, when I had returned from ten years in English boarding schools.

Anand's England-returned misery was more virulent, because his family was orthodox, his mother spoke no English and distrusted foreign ways, he had been educated entirely in Bombay until he had gone to America for postgraduate courses, and worst of all, his father, an impressively successful contractor in Bombay, insisted that Anand, as the only

son, enter the family business and work under the super-
vision not only of the father but of various uncles.

Our families lived on the same street, not more than half
a dozen houses from each other, but led very different lives.
Among the members of our generation, however, the differences were fading, and Anand and I belonged to the same
set, although we had never particularly liked each other. It
was a moment of boredom, of feeling at a loose end, and a
fragmentary reminder that both of us had been in America
that brought Anand and me together in Bombay.

It was during the monsoon, I remember, and the rain had
pelted down all morning. About noon it cleared up, and I
decided to spend my lunch hour shopping instead of having
something sent up to eat at my desk. I started down the
street toward Flora Fountain, the hideous monument that is
the center of downtown Bombay, and had gone about half-
way when I realized I had guessed wrong about the weather.
The rain began again, ominously gentle at first, then quickly
changing into a typical monsoon downpour. I ducked into
the first doorway I saw, and ran slap into Anand, a rather
short, slender young man, dressed with a certain nattiness.
It was the building in which his father's firm had its offices,
and Anand stood there staring glumly at the streaming
street and scurrying pedestrians. We greeted each other with
reserve. Neither was in the mood for a cheery exchange of
news. We continued to gaze at the rain, at the tangle of
traffic, the wet and shiny cars moving slowly through the
dirty water on the road.

At last, with an obvious effort and without much interest,
Anand said, "And what are you up to these days?"

"I *was* going to go shopping," I said coolly, "but I don't see
how I can, in this."

"Damn rain," he muttered. I could hardly hear him over
the sound of the water rushing along the gutters.

I said, "Mm," and, as a return of politeness, added, "And
you? What are you doing?"

"Heaven knows," he said, with a world of depression in his voice. "Working, I suppose." After another long pause, he said, "Well, look, since you can't shop and I can't get to the garage for my car, suppose we nip around the corner for a bite of lunch."

"Okay," I said, not knowing quite how to refuse.

Anand looked full at me for the first time and began to smile. " 'Okay,' " he repeated. "Haven't heard *that* in some time."

We raced recklessly down the street, splashing through puddles and dodging people's umbrellas, until we arrived, soaked and laughing, at the nearest restaurant. It was no more than a snack bar, really, with a counter and stools on one side of the small room and a few tables on the other. We stood between them, breathless, mopping our faces ineffectually with handkerchiefs and slicking back wet hair, still laughing with the silly exhilaration such moments produce. We decided to sit at a table, because Anand said the hard little cakes with pink icing, neatly piled on the counter, looked too unappetizing to be faced all through lunch.

Our explosive entrance had made the other customers turn to stare; but as we settled down at our table, the four or five young men at the counter—clerks, probably, from nearby offices, self-effacing and pathetically tidy in their white drill trousers and white shirts (the inescapable look of Indian clerks)—turned their attention back to their cups of milky coffee and their curry puffs. The Sikhs at the next table, brightly turbaned and expansive of manner, resumed their cheerful conversation. The two Anglo-Indian typists in flowered dresses returned to their whispers and giggles and soda pop.

When the waiter brought us the menu, we discovered that the restaurant was called the Laxmi and Gold Medal Café. This sent Anand into a fresh spasm of laughter, and while we waited for our sandwiches and coffee, he entertained himself by inventing equally unlikely combinations for restaurant names—the Venus and Sun Yat-sen Coffee Shoppe, the Cadillac and Red Devil Ice-Cream Parlor, and so on— not very clever, but by that time we were in a good mood and prepared to be amused by almost anything.

At some point, I remember, one of us said, "Well, how do you *really* feel about Bombay?" and the other replied, "Let's face it. Bombay *is* utter hell," and we were launched on the first of our interminable conversations about ourselves, our surroundings, our families, our gloomy predictions for the future. We had a lovely time.

Before we left, Anand had taken down the number of my office telephone, and only a couple of days later he called to invite me to lunch again. "I'll make up for the horrors of the Laxmi and Gold Medal," he said. "We'll go to the Taj, which is at least air-conditioned, even if it isn't the Pavillon."

He had reserved a table by the windows in the dining room of the Taj Mahal Hotel, where we could sit and look out over the gray, forbidding water of the harbor and watch the massed monsoon clouds above the scattered islands. Cool against the steamy rain outside, we drank a bottle of wine, ate the local *pâté de foie gras,* and felt sorry for ourselves.

Anand said, "I can't think why my father bothered to send me to America, since he doesn't seem interested in anything I learned there."

"Oh, I know, I know," I said, longing to talk about my own concerns.

"Can you believe it, the whole business is run *exactly* the way it was fifty years ago?"

"Of course I can. I mean, take the magazine—"

"I mean, everything done by vague verbal arrangements. Nothing properly filed and accounted for. And such enormous reliance on pull, and influence, and knowing someone in the government who will arrange licenses and import permits and whatever."

"For a consideration, naturally?"

"Or for old friendship or past favors exchanged or—"

"Well, it's a miracle to me that we ever get an issue of the magazine out, considering that none of the typesetters speaks English, and they have to make up the forms in a language they don't know, mirrorwise and by hand."

"Oh, it's all hopelessly behind the times."

"You can see that what we really need is an enormous staff of proofreaders and only a *tiny* editorial—"

"But at least you don't have to deal with the family as well. The *amount* of deadwood in the form of aged great-uncles, dim-witted second cousins, who *have* to be employed!"

"Can't you suggest they be pensioned off?"

"Don't think I haven't. My father just smiles and says I'll settle down soon. Oh, what's the use?"

Our discussions nearly always ended with one or the other of us saying, with exaggerated weariness, "Well, so it goes. Back to the salt mines now, I suppose?" I never added that I enjoyed my job.

That day we didn't realize until we were on the point of leaving the Taj how many people were lunching in the big dining room whom we knew or who knew one or the other of our families. On our way out, we smiled and nodded to a number of people and stopped at several tables to exchange greetings. With rising irritation, both of us were aware of the speculative glances, the carefully unexpressed curiosity behind the pleasant formalities of speech. Anand and I sauntered in silence down the wide, shallow staircase of the hotel. I think he was trying to seem unconcerned.

It was only when we reached the road that he exploded into angry speech. "Damn them," he said. "The prying old cats! What business is it of theirs, anyway?"

"It was the wine," I suggested. "Even people who have been abroad a lot don't drink wine at lunchtime."

"So? What's it to them?"

"Well, Dissolute Foreign Ways, and besides—"

"And besides, they have nothing to do but gossip."

"That, of course, but besides, you're what they call a catch, so it's only natural that they wonder."

Anand frowned as we crossed the road to where his car was parked against the sea wall. He opened the door for me and then climbed in behind the steering wheel. He didn't start the car for a moment or two, but sat with his hands on the wheel and his head turned away from me, looking at the threatening light of the early afternoon, which would darken into rain any minute. I thought he was about to tell me something—about a disappointment or a love affair—but instead, he clenched his fingers suddenly and said, "Well, the devil with them. Let them talk, if they have nothing better to do."

"Yes. Anyway, who cares?" I said, hoping it didn't sound as though *I* did.

He smiled at me. "That's the spirit. We'll show them."

We lunched at the Taj several times after that, but on each occasion a bit more defiantly, a bit more conscious of the appraising looks, always knowing we were the only "unattacheds" lunching together. The others were businessmen, or married couples doing duty entertaining, which, for some reason, they couldn't do at home, or ladies in groups, or foreigners.

As we stood inside the doors of the dining room, Anand would pause for a second, and then grip my elbow and say something like, "Well, come along. Let's strike a blow for freedom," or, "Throw away the blindfold. I'll face the firing squad like a man." He didn't deceive me—or, I suppose, anyone else.

Bombay is a big city—something over two million people —but in its life it is more like a conglomeration of villages. In our set, for instance, everyone knew everyone else at least by sight. At any of the hotels or restaurants we normally went to we were certain to meet a friend, a relative, an acquaintance. We all went to the same sort of party, belonged to the same clubs. People knew even each other's cars, and a quick glance at a row of parked cars would tell you that Mrs. Something was shopping for jewelry for her daughter's wedding, or that Mr. Something-else was attending a Willingdon Club committee meeting. So, of course, everyone knew that Anand and I lunched together a couple of times a week, and certainly our families must have been told we had been seen together.

My parents never mentioned the matter to me, though there was a certain wariness in their manner whenever Anand's name came up in conversation. (It's a sad moment, really, when parents first become a bit frightened of their child.) Privately, they must have put up with a good deal of questioning and comment from friends and relatives. Even to me people would sometimes say, "Can you come to a party on Saturday? Anand will be there." If Anand's mother ever lectured him on getting talked about, he evidently didn't think it worth repeating. Of them all, I daresay she was the most troubled, being orthodox, wanting a good, conservative marriage for her only son, being bewildered by what must have appeared to her—it seems astonishing in retrospect—sophistication.

Occasionally Anand would take me home to tea after our offices had closed. I think he did this out of an unadmitted consideration for his mother, to set her mind at rest about the company he was keeping, to show her that I was not a Fast Girl even if I did work on a magazine. I don't know how much I reassured her, with my short hair and lipstick, no *tika* in the middle of my forehead. But she always greeted me politely, bringing her hands together in a *namaskar,* and gave me canny looks when she thought I wasn't noticing. We couldn't even speak to each other, since we came from different communities and she spoke only Gujerati, while my language was Hindi. She would always wait with us in the drawing room until one of the servants brought the tea; then she would lift her comfortable figure out of her chair, nod to me, and leave us alone. We were always conscious of

her presence in the next room beyond the curtained archway, and every now and then we would hear her teacup clink
on the saucer. Our conversation, even if she didn't understand it, was bound to be pretty stilted.

Perhaps it was this silent pressure, perhaps it was only a
sort of restlessness that made Anand and me leave the usual
haunts of our set and look for more obscure restaurants for
our lunch dates. Liberal as we considered ourselves, we still
couldn't help being affected by the knowing curiosity. There's
no point in denying it (predictably, I always *did* deny it to
Anand); I was concerned about public opinion. I suppose I
was beginning to lose my England-returned brashness and
intractability. I was not, however, prepared to stop meeting
Anand for lunch. I liked him and waited with some impatience for his telephone calls, the rather pleasant voice saying things like "Hello? Is this the career girl?" (This was
one of Anand's favorite phrases of defiance—a career girl
was still something of a peculiarity in Bombay in those days.
If you came from a respectable family that could support
you, you weren't supposed to work for money. Social work
would have been all right, but not something as shady as
journalism.) Sometimes he would say, "This is underground
agent 507. Are you a fellow resistance fighter?" or, "Am I
speaking to Miss Emancipation?"

In any case, I would laugh and say, "Yes," and he would
suggest that we try some Chinese food, or eat dry curried
chicken at a certain Irani shop, or, if it was one of the
steamy, rainless days near the end of the monsoon, go to
Chowpatty beach and eat odds and ends of the delicious,
highly spiced mixtures the vendors there concoct. By tacit
agreement, he no longer picked me up at the office. Instead,
we either met at the corner taxi rank (leaving Anand's car
parked in the alley behind his office building) or arrived
separately at our rendezvous.

Once, when we were driving to Colaba, the southernmost
point of the island, Anand suddenly leaned forward and

asked the taxi driver to stop. On an otherwise uninspired-looking street, lined with dingy middle-class houses, he had seen a sign that said "Joe's Place." Anand was entranced, and certainly the sign did look exotic among the bungalows and hibiscus. Joe's Place—named by some homesick American soldier, who had found his way there during the war—quickly became our favorite restaurant. We felt it was our discovery, for one thing, and then it had a Goan cook, which meant that, unlike some of the other Indian restaurants, you could order beef. Most Hindus will not eat beef, cook it, or allow it on the premises; it is, as a result, the cheapest meat in Bombay. We ate a lot of beef at Joe's Place, and I often thought that Anand, at home in the evening, probably got rather a kick out of imagining how horrified his mother would be if she knew he had a rare steak inside him.

The proprietor, whom Anand insisted on calling Joe, even though he was a fat and jolly Indian, soon got used to seeing us almost every other day. We couldn't imagine how he made any money, since there never seemed to be anyone there besides Anand and me. Joe waited on table, so there weren't even waiters. Anand said that it was probably a front for black-market activities and that you could expect anything of a man who ran a Joe's Place in Bombay. More likely, the real, prosaic reason was that most of Joe's business was in cooking meals to send out.

We came to feel so much at home at Joe's that we bought him a checkered tablecloth, to lend the place a bit of class, and he would spread it ceremoniously over the corner table, invariably pointing out that it had been laundered since our last meal. We kept a bottle of gin at Joe's and taught him to make fresh-lime gimlets with it, so that we could have a cocktail before lunch. He hadn't a license to sell liquor, so he always shook our cocktails in an opaque bottle labeled Stone Ginger, in case anyone came in. He probably watered the gin; but we didn't much care, because it was the idea that pleased us.

We would sit at our table between the windows, glancing out occasionally at the patch of straggly garden, the jasmine bush, the desultory traffic, and talk. How we talked! On and on and on. Sometimes it was "In the States, did you ever—" or "Do you remember—" kind of talk. Sometimes it was about incidents at home or in our offices. We talked a lot about Them—a flexible term, including any relatives or friends we considered old-fashioned, interfering, lacking in understanding. We often discussed Their iniquities, and many of our conversations began, "Do you know what They've gone and done *now*?" All through the sticky postmonsoon months, into the cooler, brilliant days of early winter, we talked. It seems a miracle to me now that we could have found so much to say about the details of our reasonably pedestrian lives.

If we'd been a bit older or more observant, we would certainly have known that this state of affairs couldn't last much longer. I was dimly aware that every day of life in Bombay relaxed our antagonism a tiny bit and blurred the outlines of our American years. However, I never guessed what Anand's family's counterattack to his England-returned discontent would be. Anand's mother was a direct, uncomplicated woman, and in her view there was one obvious and effective way to cure the whole disease without waiting for the slower methods of time.

It was at Joe's Place that Anand announced the arrival of Janaki. I had got there early, I remember, and was sitting at our table when Anand came in. He always had a certain tension in his walk, but that day it seemed more pronounced. He held his narrow shoulders stiffly and carried an air of trouble, so I asked him at once whether anything was the matter.

"Matter?" he asked sharply, as though it were an archaic word. "Why should anything be the matter?"

"Well, I don't know. You just look funny."

"Well, I don't feel funny," he said, deliberately misunderstanding.

Joe brought him his gimlet and inquired rather despairingly if we wanted steak *again.*

Anand waved a hand at him impatiently and said, "Later. We'll decide later." Then he looked at me in silence, with a portentous frown. At last he said, "Do you *know* what They've gone and done *now?* They've invited a cousin—a *distant* cousin—to stay."

This didn't seem to me any great disaster. Cousins, invited or not, were eternally coming to visit. Any relatives had the right to turn up whenever it was convenient for them and stay as long as they liked. His announcement came as an anticlimax; but since he did seem so distressed, I asked carefully, "And I suppose you'll be expected to fit him into the firm in some capacity?"

"Her," Anand said. "It's a girl."

"A *girl?* Is *she* going to work in the business?" This was really cataclysmic news.

"Oh, of *course* not. Can't you see what They're up to?"

"Well, no, I can't."

"Don't you *see?*" he said, looking helpless before such stupidity. "They're trying to arrange a marriage for me."

I could think of nothing to say except an unconvincing "Surely not."

He went on without paying any attention. "I dare say They think They're being subtle. Throwing us together, you know, so that my incomprehensible, *foreign*—" he emphasized the word bitterly—"preference for making up my own mind about these things will not be offended. We are to grow imperceptibly fond of each other. Oh, I see the whole plot."

"You must be imagining it all."

"She arrived last night. They didn't even tell me she was coming."

"But people are forever dropping in."

"I know. But she was *invited*. She told me so."

"Poor Anand." I was sorry for him, and angry on his be-half. There had never been any romantic exchanges be-tween Anand and me, so the girl didn't represent any personal threat; but I honestly thought that a matter of prin-ciple was involved and that one should stand by the prin-ciple. We had so often agreed that the system of arranged marriages was the ultimate insult to one's rights as a human being, the final, insupportable interference of domineering families. I tried to think of something comforting to say, but could only produce, feebly, "Well, all you have to do is sit it out."

"And watch her doing little chores around the house? Making herself quietly indispensable?" He added with a sour smile, "As the years roll by. Do you suppose we will grow old gracefully together?"

"Oh, don't be such a fool," I said, laughing. "She'll have to go, sooner or later."

"But will I live that long?" He seemed to be cheering up.

"It's rather unfair to the poor thing," I said, thinking for the first time of the girl. "I mean, if they've got her hopes up."

"Now, don't start sympathizing with *her*. The only way to finish the thing once and for all—to make my position clear —is to marry someone else immediately. I suppose you wouldn't consider marrying me, would you?"

"Heavens, no," I said, startled. "I don't think you need to be as drastic as that."

"Well, perhaps not. We'll see."

At last I thought to ask, "What's she called?"

"Janaki."

"Pretty name."

"It makes me vomit."

I could hardly wait for our next lunch date, and when we met a couple of days later at Joe's Place I started questioning

Anand eagerly. "Well, how are things? How are you making out with Janaki?"

Anand seemed remote, a bit bored with the subject. "Joe!" he called. "More ice, for Pete's sake. Gimlets aren't supposed to be *mulled*." He tapped his fingers on the table in a familiar, nervous movement. "He'll never learn," he said resignedly. Then, after a pause, "Janaki? Oh, she's all right, I suppose. A minor pest."

"Is she being *terribly* sweet to you?"

"Oh, you know. I will say this for her, she manages to be pretty unobtrusive."

"Oh." I was obscurely disappointed.

"It's just knowing she's always *there* that's so infuriating."

"It would drive me crazy."

In a voice that was suddenly cross, he said, "She's so *womanly*."

"Hovers about, you mean?"

"Not that, so much, but I can see her *hoping* I'll eat a good dinner or have had a good day at the office, or some damn thing."

"It sounds rather flattering."

"I dare say that's the strategy. It's pathetic, really, how little They know me if They think she's the sort of girl I'd want to marry."

"What sort of girl *would* you want to marry?"

"Heaven knows," Anand said in a hopeless voice. "Someone quite different, anyway. I knew one once."

"Was there a girl in America?" I asked with interest.

"Isn't there always a girl in America? A sort of tradition. In our fathers' time, it used to be the daughter of the landlady somewhere in Earl's Court. Usually blonde, always accommodating."

"And yours?"

"Accommodating. But several cuts above the landlady's daughter. She was a senior in college. And she had quite a

nice family, if you can stand families, rather timid, but determined to believe that a Good Home Environment was a girl's
best protection. I don't think they would have raised many
objections if we'd got married."

"Why didn't you marry her, then?"

"Oh, I don't know. Do those things work? I really don't
know."

"I expect your parents would have raised the devil."

"Before—if I'd told them. Not after. By then the particular alchemy that turns a girl into a daughter-in-law would
have done its work. That was really the trouble. I couldn't
see her being an Indian daughter-in-law living in a Bombay
family—and what a mess that would have made. Hurt feelings and recriminations and disappointment all around. I'm
not sentimental about her," he said earnestly, as if it were an
important point. "I mean, I know she wasn't particularly
good-looking or anything, but I had a separate identity in her
mind. I wasn't just somebody's son, or someone to marry, or
someone with good business connections."

"And all that is what you are to Janaki?"

"I suppose so. What else could I be?"

As we left Joe's Place after lunch, he said, "I think you'd
better come to tea to meet her. Would you like to?"

"I was hoping you'd ask me."

"Okay, then. Tomorrow?"

Full of excitement, the next day, I met Anand after work
and drove home with him. "Is your mother going to be cross
about your asking me?"

"Why should she be cross? You've been to tea with us
before."

"But that was different."

"I can't see why," he said, refusing to accept the situation.

"Oh, don't be so dense," I said, thinking, Poor girl, it's
going to be very frustrating for her if he insists on treating
her as a casual cousin come for a holiday. "Does your mother
tactfully leave you alone with her for tea?"

"Never. The two of them chatter about domestic details. It's really very boring."

To me it was far from boring. For one thing, Anand's mother was far more cordial to me than she had been on previous visits, and I wondered whether she could already be so sure of the success of her plan that I was no longer a danger. And then there was the suspense of waiting to see what Janaki would be like.

She came in with the servant who carried the tea tray, holding back the curtain of the dining-room archway so that he could manage more easily. A plump, graceful girl with a very pretty face and a tentative, vulnerable smile, which she seemed ready to cancel at once if you weren't going to smile with her. I saw, instantly, that she was any mother-in-law's ideal—quiet, obedient, helpful. Her hair was drawn back into the conventional knot at the nape of her neck; she had a *tika* on her forehead, wore no makeup except for the faintest touch of lipstick, and even that, I decided, was probably a new experiment for her, a concession to Anand's Westernized tastes.

She spoke mostly to Anand's mother, in Gujerati, and I noticed that she had already assumed some of the duties of a hostess. She poured the tea and asked, in clear, lilting English, whether I took milk and sugar, handed around the plates of Indian savories and sweets.

After the first mouthful, I remarked formally, "This is delicious."

Anand's mother caught the tone, even if she didn't understand the words, and said something in Gujerati to Anand.

He translated, without much interest, "Janaki made them."

Janaki, in embarrassment, wiped her mouth on her napkin with the thorough gesture that someone unused to wearing lipstick makes, and then gazed in surprise and alarm at the pink smear on the linen. She saw me watching and gave me one of her diffident smiles.

I quickly said the first thing that came into my head, "How clever you are. I wish I could cook."

"It is very easy to learn," she replied.

"There never seems to be any time for it."

Entirely without sarcasm or envy she said, "That is true for someone like you who leads such a busy and interesting life."

I felt ashamed of myself, for no reason I could quite put my finger on.

We continued to talk banalities, and Janaki kept up her end admirably, managing to seem interested in the most ordinary comments and still keeping a watchful eye out to see that cups and plates were filled. The conversation gradually fell entirely to Janaki and me, because Anand retreated into a sulky silence. I remember thinking that one couldn't really blame him. It must have been maddening to have to face this sweet and vapid politeness every day after work. At last he jumped up, said abruptly that he had some papers to go through, and left the room. I left soon after.

Janaki saw me to the front door and, with an unexpected spontaneity, put her hand on my arm. "Please come to tea again," she said. "I mean, if you are not too occupied. I should so much like it. I have no friends in Bombay."

"I'd be delighted, and you must come to tea with me."

"Oh, no, thank you very much. Perhaps later on, but I must learn the ways of this house first. You see that, don't you?"

I walked home, wondering at her mixture of nervousness and confidence, at the fact that she already felt certain she had a permanent place in that house.

At our next lunch date, it was Anand who asked the eager questions. "Well? What did you think of her?"

And I replied noncommittally, "She seemed very pleasant."

"Quite the little housewife, do you mean?"

"No. Sweet and anxious to please, I meant."

"You sound like my mother. She says, 'A good-natured girl. You should count yourself fortunate.' I suppose she asked you to be her friend?"

"How did you know?"

"She's not as stupid as she looks. She said the same to me. 'Will you not allow us to be friendly, Anand?' " He attempted a saccharin, unconvincing falsetto. He frowned. "The thin end of the wedge, don't you see? It would be funny if it weren't so sad."

"Well, at least she's very good-looking," I said defensively.

"She's too fat."

"I think it rather suits her."

"A strong point in her favor, my mother says, to make up for my puniness." Anand was sensitive about his height. He said, in a touchy voice, daring one to sympathize with him, "Eugenically very sound. Strong, healthy girl like Janaki married to a weakling like me, and we have a chance of strong, healthy children that take after her. The children, you see, are the whole point of this stratagem. I'm an only son and must produce some. My mother has a rather simple approach to these things."

"You must admit," I said rather uncomfortably, "that she'd make a very good mother."

"Not a doubt in the world. She's a natural for the part of the Great Earth Mother. But I rather resent being viewed in such an agricultural light."

In the weeks that followed, Janaki dominated our conversation at lunchtime, and I had tea with them quite frequently. Sometimes, if Anand was kept late at his office or had to attend a board meeting, Janaki and I would have tea alone, and she would ask hundreds of questions about America, trying, I thought, to build up a picture of Anand's life there and the background that seemed to influence him so much. She claimed to be uniformly enthusiastic about everything American, and for me it was rather fun, because it made me feel so superior in experience. Once she asked me to teach her to dance, and I was unexpectedly disconcerted. There was something very refreshing about her lack of Westernization, and I didn't want to see her lose it.

"I will if you really want me to, but—"

"Anand likes dancing, doesn't he?"

"Yes, but wouldn't it be better if he taught you himself, after you—I mean, when he—what I mean is, a little later on?"

"You think that would be best?" She meant, of course, "The best way of handling Anand."

"Yes, I do," I said, meaning, "You don't want to seem too eager."

"Very well." She nodded, accepting my opinion as final. On this level of unspoken frankness we understood each other perfectly.

She would question me, sometimes openly and sometimes indirectly, about Anand's tastes and preferences. We had a long session, I remember, about her looks. Should she wear makeup? Should she cut her hair? What about her clothes? I told her she was fine the way she was, but she insisted, "Has he *never* said anything? He must have made *some* remark?"

"Well," I said reluctantly, "he did once mention that he thought you were just a fraction on the chubby side."

Without a trace of rancor, Janaki said, "I will quickly become thin."

"Heavens! Don't take the remark so seriously."

"It is nothing," Janaki assured me. "One need only avoid rice and *ghi*." She did, too. I noticed the difference in a couple of weeks.

When Anand was there, the atmosphere was much more strained. From the frigid politeness of his early days with Janaki, his manner gradually changed to irritation, which expressed itself in angry silence and later in a kind of under-

cover teasing sometimes laced with malice. For instance, he
would greet her with something like, "What have you been
up to today? Hemstitching the sheets? Crocheting for the
hope chest?" and Janaki would look puzzled and smile, as
though she had missed the point of a clever joke. Actually,
she was a beautiful needlewoman and did a good deal of
exquisitely neat embroidery on all kinds of things—antima-
cassars, doilies, face towels—infallibly choosing hideous designs of women, in enormous crinolines, watering the flowers
in an English garden, or bunches of roses with ribbons
streaming from them. Once Janaki answered Anand's in-
quiry quite seriously with an account of her day, the household jobs she had done, the women who had called on his
mother in the morning and had been served coffee, and even
produced the embroidery she had been working on.

"Wonderfully appropriate for India, don't you think?"
Anand remarked to me with rather labored irony.

"I think it's lovely," I said unconvincingly.

Janaki seemed unruffled. "Men do not appreciate embroidery," she said quietly.

Anand leaned back in his chair, stared at the ceiling, and
gave an exaggerated sigh.

One couldn't help disliking him in this role of tormentor.
The fact was, of course, that, in Anand's phrase, I was
getting imperceptibly fonder of Janaki as his impatience
with her grew more overt. There was, to me, both gallantry
and an appealing innocence in her undaunted conviction
that everything would turn out all right. What I didn't recognize was the solid realism behind her attitude. I started to
suspect the calculation in her nature one day when Anand
had been particularly difficult. He had insisted on talking
about books she hadn't read and, with apparent courtesy,
addressing remarks to her he knew she couldn't answer.

Janaki said nothing for a long time and then admitted,
with a becoming lack of pretension, "I'm afraid I read only

the stories in the *Illustrated Weekly*. But, Anand, if you would bring me some books you think good, I would read them."

"I'll see if I can find the time," he replied in a surly voice.

When Janaki showed me to the door that evening, I said in considerable exasperation, "Why do you put up with it? He needn't be so disagreeable when he talks to you."

"It is natural that there should be difficulties at first. After his life in America, there are bound to be resentments here."

"Well, I think you are altogether too forbearing. I wouldn't stand it for a second." Privately, I had begun to think she must, after all, be stupid.

Then Janaki said, "What would you do?"

"Leave, of course. Go back." And at that moment I realized what she meant. Go back to what? To another betrothal arranged by her elders? Learning to please some other man? Here, at least, she liked her future mother-in-law.

"And besides," she said, "I know that really he is kind."

In the end, Janaki turned out to be the wisest of us all, and I have often thought how lucky it was that she didn't follow my advice then. Not that Anand capitulated all at once, or that one extraordinary morning he suddenly saw her with new eyes, or anything like that. He remained irritable and carping; but gradually he became enmeshed in that most satisfactory of roles, a reluctant Pygmalion.

I noticed it first one day when he finished his lunch rather hurriedly and said, as we were going back to our offices, "That girl's conversation is driving me nuts. I think I really had better buy her some books. As long as I'm stuck with her company," he added awkwardly.

We parted at the bookshop, and in later conversations I learned that Janaki was doing her homework with diligence and pleasure.

From then on things moved fairly rapidly. I began to anticipate Anand's frequent suggestions that we spend part of the lunch hour shopping—usually rather ungraciously

expressed: "We've got to get that girl into some less provin-
cial-looking saris." "That girl listens to nothing but film
music. I really must get her some decent classical stuff.
What do you suggest as a beginning? Kesarbai? Subba-
luxmi?"

"No Western music?" I asked pointedly.

"She wouldn't understand it," Anand replied.

All the same, at home he continued to be offhand or over-
bearing with her. She remained calm and accepting, a willing pupil who knew that her stupidity was a great trial to
her teacher. Still, there wasn't a doubt in my mind about the
change of attitude going on in Anand. I wanted a lived-
happily-ever-after conclusion for Janaki; but mostly I was
certain that the Pygmalion story could have only one ending,
whatever the minor variations might be.

Anand's parents were evidently equally confident of the
outcome, for one day at tea he announced, with an exuberance no amount of careful casualness could disguise, that
his father was going to send him to New York on a business
trip. He was pleased, he insisted, largely because it meant
that at last he was to be trusted with some real responsibility.

I said, "And it will be such wonderful fun to be back in
America."

"Oh, yes. That, too, naturally. But I don't know how much
time I'll have for the bright lights and parties." He had
moved so smoothly into the correct businessman's viewpoint
that I wanted to laugh.

We were absorbed in discussing the details of the trip,
and besides, by then Janaki had become such an accepted—
and pleasing—part of the scenery of the house that we
assumed she was listening with her usual attention and, as
always, trying to fit in with Anand's mood.

So it came as quite a shock when she suddenly spoke in a
flat, decisive voice. "I, too, am leaving. I am going back to
my home." Dead silence for a moment. "Tomorrow," she
said.

"But *why*—" I began.

"It is my decision," she said, and wouldn't look at either of us.

Anand didn't say anything, just stood up, with all his bright, important planning gone, and walked out of the room. We waited to hear his study door slam.

Then my affection for Janaki (and, of course, curiosity) made me ask, "But why *now*, just when things are going so well?"

"It was your advice, don't you remember?"

"But things were different then."

"Yes." She nodded as though we both recognized some particular truth.

At the time I thought she believed herself defeated. I was surprised and concerned that what seemed so plain to me should remain obscure to her. "Listen," I said cautiously, "don't you see that he—that in spite of everything, he has fallen in love with you?"

I don't know quite what I had expected her response to be—a radiant smile, perhaps, or even a sense of triumph. I hadn't expected her to glare at me as though I were an enemy and say, "Oh, love. I don't want him to *love* me. I want him to marry me."

"It's different for him," I said, as persuasively as I could. "For him it is important."

She looked at me shrewdly, making up her mind about something. "You are sure?" she asked.

"Absolutely sure."

Her voice was hard and impatient. "Love, what books you read, whether you like music, your 'taste'—whatever that may mean. As if all that has anything to do with marriage."

"Well," I said ineffectually.

How can one make the idea of romantic love attractive to someone who wants only a home, a husband, and children? Even if nothing could be done about that, I thought I knew the reason for her sudden despair. The renewing of

Anand's American experiences must have seemed to her an overwhelming menace. I tried to reassure her, reminded her that Anand would be gone only a matter of weeks, that he would miss her, that America would look quite different to him now, that he had changed a lot in the past year—more than a year, actually.

But she wouldn't listen, and she kept repeating, "I must pack my things and leave the house tomorrow."

I thought, Poor Janaki. I can see that the tedious business of starting all over again on the unraveling of Anand's England-returned tangles might well seem to be too much to face. It didn't occur to me that I might equally have thought, Clever Janaki, the only one of us who knows exactly what she wants. Leave the house? She would have slit her throat first.

When I think of it, I can't help wondering at the extent of my naïveté then. The fact is that women—or perhaps I mean just the women of a certain kind of world, Janaki's world—have inherited, through bitter centuries, a ruthless sense of self-preservation. It still seems to me ghastly that they should need it; but it would be silly to deny that, in most places on earth, they still do. That cool, subtle determination to find her security and hang on to it, that all's-fair attitude—not in love, which she discounted, but in war, for it *was* war, the gaining or losing of a kingdom—was really no more than the world deserved from Janaki. As in war, victory, conquest, success, call it what you will, was the only virtue. And, of course, the really absurd thing was that nobody would have been more appalled than Janaki if you had called her a feminist.

As it was, I heard with anxiety Anand on the phone the next day, saying, "Let's lunch. I want to talk to you. Joe's Place? One o'clock?"

I was certain that Janaki had gone home, with only the indignities of a few new clothes and a lot of tiresome talk to remember.

As soon as I saw him, I knew I was wrong. He had the conventionally sheepish look that makes the announcing of good news quite pointless. He said, "An eventful evening, wasn't it?"

"Yes, it was, rather."

Then there was a long pause while he looked embarrassed and I could think of no way to help him out. At last he said, all in a rush, "Look, this is going to seem ridiculous. I mean —well, Janaki and I are going to be married."

"You couldn't do a more sensible thing," I said, much relieved.

He looked startled. "Sensible? Perhaps it seems that way to you. Actually, we're in love with each other."

"With *each other*?" I echoed incredulously, and regretted it immediately.

"I knew it would seem peculiar to you. I daresay you've thought I hated her all this time." He smiled at me in a rather superior way. "I thought so myself for a while. And Janaki, as you well imagine, had every reason to think so. And I must say it certainly took a lot of courage on her part. I mean, when you think—"

"You'd better start at the beginning," I said, suddenly feeling depressed.

"Okay. I heard you leave yesterday, and then I heard Janaki come into the hall—you know that timid way she has of walking—and stand outside my study door. I was in quite a state; but I daresay that I wouldn't have done anything about anything if she hadn't—I mean, if someone hadn't taken the initiative."

"Yes," I said, knowing what was coming but unable to shake off my gloom. "She came to explain why she was going home."

"She said—you see, she isn't the passive, orthodox girl you think—she told me that quite against her plans or anything she's expected, she'd—I know this will seem silly—but she'd fallen in love with me."

"I see. And that accounted for her behavior. Trying all the time to please you, I mean."

"Well, yes. Then I realized that—"

"All your resentment and bad manners were just that—" I wanted to hurry him through the story.

"Well, yes."

"Well, yes," I repeated, and couldn't look at him. We were silent for a while. "Well, congratulations," I said uneasily.

"It's funny, isn't it," he said in a confident voice, "that Their plans should have worked out—but so differently. I don't suppose. They'll ever understand."

"It wouldn't be worth trying to explain."

"Heavens, no. Look, I'm taking Janaki out to lunch to-morrow. Will you join us?"

"Oh, no, surely—"

"She asked particularly that you come. She likes you very much, you know, and besides, she doesn't feel quite com-fortable going out without a chaperon."

"In *that* case—" I said, with a nastiness lost on Anand. And all the time I was thinking, Have we all been made use of? A sympathetic mother-in-law, a man you can flatter, a gullible friend from whom you can learn background and fighting conditions, with whom you can check tactics and their effects. Now that she has won, she must have nothing but contempt for all of us. But simultaneously I was wonder-ing, Is she, after all, really in love? It was a state she didn't know how to cope with, and she could hope only to use the weapon she knew, an ability to please or try to please. Why should she, or how could she, tell me all that herself—a realm of which she was so unsure, which was so far out of her experience?

Now that I have met so many Janakis of the world, I think I know which explanation was right.

"So we'll meet," Anand was saying, "at the Taj, if that's all right with you?"

He had reserved a table by the windows. Janaki was a bit

late, to be sure—she explained breathlessly—that we would be there before her, because it would have been agony to sit alone.

We ordered from the Indian menu, and Anand said, with only a fleeting, questioning glance at me, "No wine, I think. There really isn't any wine at all that goes with Indian food, is there?"

ABOUT THE EDITOR

K. Natwar-Singh *was born on May 16, 1931. He was educated at St. Stephen's College, Delhi University, where he obtained First Class Honors in History and was president of the Students' Union and university tennis champion. Later he attended Cambridge University in England. After qualifying for the Indian Foreign Service in 1953, he was, after a period of service in the Ministry of External Affairs in New Delhi, posted to the Indian Embassy in Peking. He has traveled widely in Africa, Asia, and Europe. He has also visited Australia and several countries in South America. From August, 1961, to April, 1966, he lived in New York, where he was adviser to the Permanent Mission of India to the United Nations. His assignments included representing his country on the Trusteeship Committee of the General Assembly, of which he was elected Rapporteur in 1965, and the Executive Board of UNICEF. Since April, 1966 he has been Deputy Secretary, Ministry of External Affairs, New Delhi.*

K. Natwar-Singh is the editor of E. M. Forster: A Tribute, *published in 1964, and of* The Legacy of Nehru: A Memorial Tribute, *published in 1965. He reviews books for the* All India Radio, New Delhi, The Illustrated Weekly of India, Bombay, The Saturday Review, *and* The New York Times Book Review.